THE WEDDING MURDERS

SARAH LINLEY

ONE MORE CHAPTER

One More Chapter
a division of HarperCollins*Publishers* Ltd
1 London Bridge Street
London SE1 9GF
www.harpercollins.co.uk
HarperCollins*Publishers*
1st Floor, Watermarque Building, Ringsend Road
Dublin 4, Ireland

This paperback edition 2022
1
First published in Great Britain in ebook format
by HarperCollins*Publishers* 2022

A catalogue record of this book is available from the British Library

ISBN: 978-0-00-849583-1

Printed and bound in the UK using 100% Renewable Electricity
by CPI Group (UK) Ltd

For Adam, my favourite human

Prologue

Darkness engulfs her as soon as she steps out of the clearing. She tries to get her bearings, but nothing looks familiar. She needs help. Fast.

She pulls out her phone, her hands still slippery with blood, but it's run out of battery. *Damn it.* She starts to run through the woodland, praying she's going the right way.

Branches tear at her face as roots twist around her ankles. She stumbles and nearly falls. She looks behind her, but she can't see more than a metre. Her heart is pounding and tears are streaming down her face, blurring her vision.

In the night, the trees have taken on a fairy-tale quality, a warning to little girls not to stray from the path. Moonlight stabs through the canopy, creating pools of light. An owl screeches, the sound piercing the silence like someone being tortured. The undergrowth rustles with unseen creatures.

She needs to get back to the wedding.

She pictures the guests, dancing and drinking, raising

their glasses to the bride and groom, oblivious to any danger. To the killer in their midst.

Chapter One

Libby

Friday afternoon

'I would ask your honour to take pity on my client. He is an old man in poor health, and a custodial sentence would be extremely hard on him.'

The defendant sitting in the dock was flanked by two security guards. He had given a good impression throughout the proceedings of being a decent, upstanding citizen, falsely accused. He looked composed, his chin upright and his eyes staring defiantly at the judge, but Libby could see sweat glistening on his forehead. In the public gallery, his wife, impeccably dressed, watched the proceedings with hawklike scrutiny.

The businessman had already been found guilty; now it was time for the sentencing. Libby looked down at her phone. The defence lawyer was making a meal out of the mitigation. They all knew he was going to prison – it was just a case of how long for. A notification flashed up on her screen. She was live tweeting the case and needed to concentrate but she opened the text anyway.

Running late. Really sorry. x

Shit! Her sister had promised faithfully to pick her son up from school. She knew how important this case was.

How late?

Hairdresser says maybe 20 mins?

It was three o'clock now. If Emma went straight from the hairdresser's, she would probably get there on time, but Libby knew that Emma's twenty minutes could easily turn into forty.

Libby had been working on this case for weeks. She had started at the local newspaper three months ago and there was tough competition between the recruits. Only one of them would be taken on after their probation period and this story put her as the front-runner. She was lucky to have been given such a big story to cover and it was a sign her boss, Aiden, trusted her. She couldn't abandon her post halfway through the sentencing.

The thought of Patrick left alone in the playground while all the other kids got picked up by their responsible parents gnawed at Libby's stomach. If she could only leave the room, she could call the school. They wouldn't be happy about it, but at least she'd know Patrick would be safe.

Too late. The judge had started his final remarks. It was clear from his opening comments that he was going to have no mercy on the chief executive who had got away with sexually assaulting his female staff for years. Libby checked her watch. With a bit of luck – and if the judge kept it short – she might make it on time.

'These were despicable crimes, and you have shown little remorse. I therefore have no hesitation…'

Libby's fingers were trembling as they hovered over her phone waiting to share the news.

'…in sentencing you to a total of three years' imprisonment.'

The defendant's wife let out a melodramatic gasp of horror as her husband seemed to visibly deflate in front of her. She'd probably thought he was going to get community service. With that sentence, he would also be put on the Sex Offenders Register indefinitely. Libby felt a mix of anticipation and excitement. This was what she'd been waiting all afternoon for. She tapped in the sentence, double checked the tweet, and posted it. She quickly checked the other news sites to make sure she had been the first to break the story and pocketed her phone.

Finally, the judge stood up and dismissed the court. Libby pushed past the other reporters out into the concourse, ringing Emma as she did so. No answer. She was probably still sitting in the hairdresser's chair, chatting about their holiday plans. She left her a message saying she would do the pick-up and ran out of the court building.

Libby checked the time again. Ten past three. She ran towards the taxi rank. Leeds city centre was already gearing up for the weekend. Crowds of office workers, still in business suits, piled into wine bars, while shoppers clutching overfilled bags and students dressed in flamboyant clothing weaved around The Headrow. The rank was busy, but she managed to grab a cab and tried to quell her impatience as they slowly edged out of Leeds city centre towards Headingley. It would have been quicker to walk.

In the back seat, Libby took out her laptop and finished her article, her fingers flying across the keyboard. She had secured an exclusive interview with one of the victims which they could publish now that the court case had concluded. The woman had wanted to waive her right to anonymity and share her story, but Libby had still had to work hard to gain her trust. It was an emotional piece outlining how much misery this man had caused the people who worked for him. It was the best thing she had ever written. She had a quick read through, checking for any glaring spelling mistakes and sent it through. A few minutes later, Aiden rang her.

'Great work, well done.'

'It is going to be the front-page tomorrow, isn't it?' Being the top story on the website was all very well but it wasn't the same as seeing your name in print. She would have to ask her sister to buy a few copies.

'Too right. Your first front-page. I hope you're going to celebrate this weekend.'

'Nah, I can't really. I've got this wedding to go to.'

'Oh yeah, the "Wedding of the Year". Well, bring me back another exclusive.'

'I'm off-duty.'

'Reporters are never off-duty.' Aiden rang off.

Libby smiled. Aiden was a good boss, fair and supportive. She really hoped this interview would be enough to land her a permanent job with the newspaper. She didn't want to leave Leeds now that Patrick had settled at school.

It was half past three. She imagined her son running out of the classroom, clutching a certificate or something he had created in art and scanning the playground for her. All the other kids would be getting picked up one by one until he was the only child left, afraid and alone. Would he try to walk home by himself? Her heart clenched at the thought. No, Patrick was sensible. Besides, the teachers wouldn't let him leave the premises.

She tried the school again and stifled a scream of frustration as the answering machine clicked in.

'It's Libby Steele, Patrick's mum. I'm running a little late.'

She could kill Emma. Libby wondered whether she'd done the right thing asking her sister to look after Patrick this weekend, but she'd had no choice. She hadn't wanted to take her seven-year-old son to a wedding where she didn't know anyone.

The invitation addressed to 'Matthew and guest' had arrived six months ago. The embossed cream card with gold lettering looked and felt expensive – some might say ostentatious – and yet Vicky and Daniel, the bride and groom, hadn't even bothered to find out her name. Libby usually worked Saturdays and she resented spending one of her rare weekends off celebrating the union of people she hadn't even met. It wasn't like they were her boyfriend's close friends; Matthew hadn't seen Daniel since their band split up in the 90s, but he'd insisted he wanted to go, for old times' sake.

When Matthew told her on their first date that he used to be a pop star, she hadn't believed him. She'd sneaked off to the toilet to google his name and had been surprised by the number of hits she got back. In their heyday they had supported some major bands and played at huge festivals, even touring the States before they split up. Libby had watched some of their music videos, laughing at Matthew with his floppy hair and intense expressions. She had to admit that it was kind of cool to date a pop star, albeit one that only people her parents' age would remember.

The taxi eventually arrived at the school, and Libby flew in to find Patrick in his classroom with his form teacher. She did not look impressed at the impromptu babysitting gig. Probably wanted to leave early and go down the pub with the other teachers.

'I'm really sorry. I did leave a message.'

Patrick looked up and beamed at her. Always happy, always content. She felt a rush of love as he showed her the picture he had drawn. Patrick in the middle holding hands with Libby and Matthew. The portraits were entirely out of proportion and Matthew looked twice the size of Libby. She wasn't sure what her boyfriend would make of his green nose either. At the side was a grey squiggle which Patrick explained was the dog they were going to get when they moved into Matthew's house.

'Come on, trouble. Say goodbye.'

Her sister was waiting for her outside the school, her hair gleaming in the spring sunshine. 'I'm so sorry, Libby.'

Patrick ran over to give his aunt a hug which was returned with equal enthusiasm.

'Are you sure you're going to be able to manage this weekend?'

Emma rolled her eyes. 'Stop worrying. We're going to have lots of fun.'

Lots of fun equated to lots of chocolate and late bedtimes, no doubt.

'And you'll ring me if anything happens?'

'Of course. Stop fussing.'

She gave Patrick a goodbye kiss. 'Be good,' she warned him, as he clung to her.

'Go!' Emma said, prising him away. 'Enjoy yourself. And I want all the goss when you get back. Leave nothing out!'

'It's going to be really boring.'

Emma waved goodbye. 'I'm sure it'll be anything but.'

Chapter Two

Huddersfield, 1992

'Where's Daniel?' Simon demanded. 'We're on in five minutes.'

Matt glanced over to Amir who shrugged and started paying undue attention to his guitar. They were getting ready in one of the back rooms of the grand Victorian hotel, surrounded by equipment, discarded sweet wrappers and empty cans of pop. Outside, dusk had turned to twilight and blue shadows spilled through the open curtains and across the swirly red carpet. Matt, who had just smoked a spliff, thought it was the prettiest thing he had ever seen.

'Gone off with some bird, I think,' Matt said.

'Are you kidding me?' Simon looked ready to explode.

'Chill out, Si. He'll be back in time.'

'Chill out? How the hell can we play a gig without our lead singer?'

Matt had no idea why Simon was so angry; it was only a

poxy wedding. By the time they split their earnings four ways, there would barely be enough to cover their expenses. Exposure, Simon insisted. It was all about exposure. You never knew who you might meet at a wedding. Every gig was an opportunity to be discovered.

Matt didn't give a damn about exposure. He was sixteen years old, had just finished his GCSEs, and it was the summer holidays. He should have been out with his mates, pulling girls, instead of wasting his Saturday nights watching people get pissed and try to dance.

They had formed the band four months ago and were starting to get regular bookings. Simon, on keyboards, was the principal songwriter and the one who organised most of the band's activities; Amir, moody and taciturn, was the guitarist with a head for finance; and Daniel, handsome and charming, was the lead singer who also played bass guitar. And then there was Matt, sitting in the background, producing the beats that held everything together.

Matt had always known that he was destined for a career in music. He thought he might end up in an orchestra, perhaps in the string section, until a particularly perceptive teacher introduced him to percussion in primary school. Even then, it was quite a stretch for the earnest sixteen-year-old, who won all the school music prizes and had a prime position in the local marching band, to imagine that one day he would be the drummer in a pop group. If Simon hadn't been so desperate, hadn't hung around outside music practice and specifically asked him to audition for the band, he would never have considered it himself. His heart was set on the Philharmonic, not Glastonbury.

Matt loved making music and enjoyed the camaraderie of the band, but his motivation for joining the group had been more prosaic. It was not only a means of making some extra cash, it was also a quick and easy route to get girls. Money and sex are pretty good motivators at any age, but they were particularly appealing to a teenager who had never been the coolest kid in the class. Being in a band automatically raised his credentials.

The bride's father came into the room, his cheeks scarlet and his voice slurred, and started talking to Simon. Matt checked his watch, feeling the familiar onset of stage fright. Three minutes until showtime. It didn't matter how big or small the gig was, the nerves were always there threatening to ruin his performance. He wished he had Daniel's confidence. There was no argument that Matt was the best musician in the group – he was expecting an A in his GCSE – but all the theory flew out of his head the minute he faced a live audience. It was one thing getting it right in front of his classmates, and a completely different story when it was a bunch of strangers that were paying for the privilege.

'The live music is about to start!' the toastmaster announced.

Matt swallowed his nerves and followed Simon and Amir into the conference room that had been transformed into a fairy grotto for the evening reception. It looked like every other wedding they had been to. He positioned himself at the drum set and watched Simon take his place at the keyboards. Amir stood hesitantly halfway up the stage. If Daniel didn't turn up, he would have to step in and sing.

A guy at the bar lifted his gaze and glared at Amir. Matt could see what looked like a National Front tattoo peering out of his loosened shirt collar and glanced over to Amir to see if he had noticed. Tensions had been running high in Huddersfield that summer. Amir adjusted his mic, deliberately not looking in the man's direction.

Simon nodded and Matt raised his sticks as Daniel burst through the door, pushed Amir to one side, and grabbed the mic. With his usual swagger, he greeted the guests, congratulated the bride and groom, and winked at Matt as they launched into the first song on the set list they had been asked to play. Amir retreated to the back of the stage and the man at the bar turned back to his beer.

The playlist was the usual blend of 70s and 80s classics. Once the guests were drunk enough, they would slip in some of their own songs. Daniel, as always, dominated the stage. He was not in the least self-conscious as he strutted up and down with the mic as if he were playing Wembley Arena instead of the Regent Hotel. Matt noticed the bride's mother sneaking into the back of the room, tucking her blouse into her skirt, her cheeks flushed. Daniel, the lucky sod, had landed himself a cougar. Still, if Matt played his cards right, she might introduce him to her friends.

Matt relaxed as they moved on to the second song in the set. The dance floor was slowly filling up with middle-aged women dancing around their handbags and young kids sliding across the floor, high on cake and Coca-Cola. The disco lights bathed them all in red, blue, and green. The guests were shrouded in the sickly sweet fumes emanating from the smoke machine and the ultraviolet light picked out white shirts and women's bra straps. The initial hit of the draw Matt had smoked earlier settled down into a contented buzz. It was always the same. He was always terrified before a performance but as soon as he hit his rhythm, the music took over and the nerves subsided.

With each gig, they were getting better and better, their performance slicker, their sound more polished. The audience were loving it. Even the staff, dressed in black and white like penguins, were tapping their feet and swinging their hips as they moved around the tables collecting empty glasses. It was times like this, when the band really gelled and their different sounds came together, that Matt couldn't imagine doing anything else for a living. Maybe Simon was right; it was only a matter of time before they were discovered.

Chapter Three

Libby

Libby let herself into Matthew's house to find him waiting for her in the hallway. A small leather weekend bag was sitting at his feet with a suit cover draped across it.

'Where've you been?' he said. 'I thought you'd be here an hour ago.'

'I had to pick Patrick up from school.'

'I thought Emma was doing it?'

'She was running late.'

'Why didn't you ring me? I could have picked him up.'

Libby bit her lip. She didn't want to admit that she hadn't even considered asking Matthew to do it. Patrick was her responsibility and although she didn't mind asking her sister for help now and again, she didn't want Matthew to see him as a burden. Her son worshipped Matthew, but she didn't know if she was ready to share parenting just yet.

'Was he OK?'

'Yeah, he was fine. Look, he drew you a picture.' Matthew looked inordinately pleased with the gift and carried it into the spacious kitchen to pin on the door of the fridge-freezer. 'I'll grab my bag and I'm ready to go.'

'It's already in the car. I had a feeling you might be late.'. She kissed him. 'Have you remembered the present?'

'Of course.'

Matthew had spent a fortune on the gift, driving around music shops to find a rare vintage record on vinyl. Libby was surprised at how much thought he'd put into it, particularly when she found out he hadn't even been invited to Daniel's first wedding. Still, men managed their friendships differently from women. She messaged her sister at least once a day whereas Matthew could go for weeks without talking to his mates and then they would pick up exactly where they left off.

'And my dress?'

'Laid out on the back seat.'

'You think of everything.'

Libby climbed into the passenger seat of Matthew's black Range Rover and tried to relax as he pulled away from the seven-bedroomed property he owned on the outskirts of Leeds. It was a world away from the tiny flat she rented in Headingley. Much of the surrounding area was taken up with a golf course and the roads were lined with sunlit trees which gave the impression of travelling through golden tunnels.

Matthew was a fast but steady driver and they soon left Leeds behind them and joined the motorway. The drive to the venue in rural North Yorkshire would take around two hours, traffic permitting. Libby could have done without going the day before the wedding, but there was a reunion planned that evening at the local pub and Matthew wanted to go. She wondered what the other band members would be like; she'd seen pictures, of course, but they had been kids back then. It would be interesting to see how much they'd changed.

Matthew was humming away now to a Mozart concerto and tapping his fingers on the steering wheel as he drove. Libby got out her phone. Her sister had sent her a video of Patrick playing with her lively cocker spaniel, Pippa. She sent back a heart emoji.

Matthew glanced over. 'Anything important?'

'No, just the usual.'

Matthew wasn't big on social media. He wasn't even on Facebook, and it was a wonder they had even met really. They had both been dragged along by friends to a terrible gig in the city. While their mates pushed their way to the front of the dance floor, they had sat at the bar critiquing the band.

'They're supposed to be the next Oasis!' he shouted over the music, showing her the flyer.

'Whoever wrote that has clearly never listened to Oasis!'

They ditched their friends and found a quiet pub. They talked about music and books. He wasn't her usual type; he was much older than her for a start, but there was something about him that she found attractive and when he asked her out for dinner, she accepted without hesitation. Matthew had made it clear from the start that he was committed to their relationship; he had even hinted at marriage, although she wasn't ready for that yet.

Libby looked down at her phone and checked the newspaper site. Her story was already online and attracting likes and comments. She moved onto Instagram and flicked through the profiles of the wedding party. Vicky, the bride, was beautiful: slim, but not too skinny, with gorgeous caramel hair that fell down her back in thick, silky waves; she had perfect brows and a spotless complexion with just the tiniest trace of laughter lines around her cupid-bow mouth. You couldn't tell her age from the carefully filtered photos she had posted online but there were pictures of her thirtieth birthday from five years ago, and she had two children from a previous marriage. Libby scrolled through pictures of her eldest son starting secondary school and her younger daughter starring as an angel in a nativity. Vicky worked in marketing and had met Daniel when he acted as a compere for a charity event that she had organised.

It was clear that Daniel's profile was cleverly managed by his PR team. Daniel was something of a minor celebrity, appearing on late-night quiz shows and reality TV spin-offs. He was the kind of presenter old ladies liked to simper over. He probably had a private account under a different name, but she hadn't found it. He was undeniably handsome but in a highly polished, clean-cut way that made him look like he'd stepped out of one of her gran's catalogues.

'Libby?'

Too late, she realised that Matthew was talking to her, and she'd missed the question.

'Sorry,' she slipped her phone back in her bag. She had

been running around so much today, she'd barely had chance to talk to him. It wouldn't hurt to give him her full attention. 'What were you saying?'

She settled back into her seat, ignoring the itch to check her phone again, as Matthew outlined his plans for the summer holidays. Matthew had travelled extensively, while he was in the band and afterwards, and loved taking her to new places. He was keen to show her his villa near Florence. Libby had been to Italy before with her parents, but they had just dragged her around art galleries and museums. She was looking forward to sampling the local wine and tucking into olives and pasta in the sunshine. Patrick would love playing in the swimming pool and learning the Italian names for things.

Despite his relaxed tone, she noticed that Matthew's fingers were turning white as he clenched the steering wheel. She wondered if he was nervous. He was usually so relaxed and confident about everything but something about this wedding had thrown him. Maybe it was the thought of seeing his old friends again and the stories they might tell about his younger days. Libby smiled. It would be good to find out what he'd been like as a teenager.

The sun coming through the windscreen was making Libby feel sleepy. The roads weren't busy, and they were making good progress. Libby had a map book on her lap, but the sat nav was doing all the work so there wasn't much for her to do. She closed her eyes and felt herself drifting off.

'Shit!'

The car swerved into the slow lane, knocking Libby's

head against the window. Disorientated, she looked behind her to see an ASDA lorry hurtling towards them. Everything seemed to be happening in slow motion as brakes screeched, horns blew and the smell of burning rubber filled the car. Libby closed her eyes, bracing herself for the inevitable impact.

Chapter Four

EXTRACT FROM SIMON GREENE'S MEMOIR, *UNTOLD STORY*, PUBLISHED POSTHUMOUSLY WITH PERMISSION FROM HIS SON, LEO.

My mind is a broken mirror. My memories fragmented.

Some things I remember with crystal clarity; others are hazy, shrouded in mist, and I'm not sure whether they even happened or whether they're a construct of a shattered mind. Other times, people tell me about things I've done, things I've said, and I have no recollection of them at all.

Blackouts are frightening, but they're also convenient. You don't have to take responsibility for things you don't remember. Instead, you let other people's stories fill the void until you convince yourself yes, that's what happened, that's the truth. I remember it now.

But the haziness, the clouded, half-remembered thoughts are the most difficult. The truth is tantalisingly close, but you cannot reach it, so you will never know what really happened,

23

what you are responsible for. You are constantly searching for answers, wondering if the truth is deeply buried somewhere in your head, if only you could find it.

Some things are not so easy to erase. Some things are indelibly printed on the psyche, scars on the soul. There are things you wish you could forget. Things that wake you up in the night, your mind racing, your heart pounding until you beg for mercy, a way out, something to take the edge off the utter misery of your existence.

My therapist tells me I need closure; that it would help to write things down. That by placing these thoughts on paper I can somehow be free. But I can never be free of what we did.

I am, by definition, an unreliable narrator; but I'm the best you've got.

Chapter Five

Huddersfield, 1992

While Matt was content with combining their gigs with studying for his A levels and preparing for university, Simon was obsessed with getting a record deal. He was never going to be satisfied with weddings, birthday parties, and selling copied CDs out of the back of his dad's van at the end of an evening. In vain, his parents and teachers tried to steer him towards 'a proper job', but Simon wouldn't listen. He wrote music all the time, constantly fidgeting and tapping his fingers to the rhythms in his head, humming melodies and scribbling lyrics on scraps of paper when he should have been concentrating in class. He was threatened with expulsion if he didn't knuckle down, but he carried on regardless. Music wasn't simply his passion; it was a compulsion.

It was Simon who spent hours producing demo tapes to send out to recording companies, Simon who was always pushing for them to get better slots and more prestigious gigs in the hope that one day they would get noticed, Simon who consumed all the music magazines trying to work out the magic formula for a hit record, but nothing ever came of it. They were just a small-town band of teenagers with ambition and a smattering of talent. It wasn't enough to stand out.

Simon had a part-time job in the record store in the town centre and spent all his wages on music. He had taken control of Matt's musical education, creating a syllabus of influential records for him to listen to: everything from Pink Floyd and David Bowie to the Stone Roses, Happy Mondays, and Nirvana. Matt spent his Saturday mornings happily flipping through vinyl and gazing at the fliers plastered on the walls, half listening to Simon's earnest conversations with the customers. On Saturday nights, they went to gigs together, arriving home in the early hours of the morning with ringing ears and new ideas.

As the boys started their first term of sixth form, Simon managed to get them a slot at the town's music festival. They were one of the warm-up acts and so far down the listing that the organisers were still setting up when they got on stage, but it landed them a write-up in the *Huddersfield Daily Examiner* and an interview on the local radio station.

Matt had never been to a studio before. The assistant greeted them in reception as if they were already stars. She led them down some corridors before stopping outside a door with a red light above it. She put her finger to her lips and pointed to the 'ON AIR' sign. As soon as it flicked to green, she pushed open the door and led them into the dark studio. A presenter wearing headphones around her neck was sitting at a production desk flicking switches. She stood up to shake their hands and Matt quickly wiped his sweaty palms on the back of his jeans.

'We'll be live in five,' she said, motioning for them to sit down opposite her. 'Can you test your mics for sound levels?'

Matt hadn't got a clue what she meant but copied the others as they spoke their names into the mic. They all looked so cool, as if they had been doing this for years. He imagined everyone at home listening to the programme – his mum had promised to record it – and could feel his heart pumping in his chest. He hoped the microphone wouldn't pick it up. His mouth was dry, and he desperately needed a glass of water but was too scared to ask for one.

'Just talk normally into the mic,' said the producer. 'And don't move around too much as it distorts the sound.'

Matt nodded. Why didn't they teach stuff like this at school? What use was algebra and chemistry when they needed practical skills like how to be interviewed live on local radio?

The presenter put her headphones back on and indicated that they were about to start. The assistant left the room and the light flicked back to red.

'And joining me now are a new and upcoming band from right here in Huddersfield...' the presenter announced.

Daniel took charge, flirting with the presenter and answering all her questions with well-rehearsed soundbites.

He sounded like he did this every day. Simon answered the more serious questions, about the band's influences and their ambitions for the future. Amir, as usual, kept his cool by maintaining a moody silence.

'So, Matt, how are your family feeling about this first step to stardom?'

The presenter looked at Matt expectantly. His mind went completely blank. He couldn't even remember the name of his kid sister.

'Er...'

The pause went on so long it was embarrassing but every time Matt tried to speak his throat closed up.

'They're really proud of us and very supportive,' Daniel stepped in. 'We couldn't have done any of this without them.'

Matt wanted the ground to swallow him whole as the interview continued. The presenter mercifully didn't ask him any more direct questions, but it was still the longest three minutes of his life. He left the radio station feeling flustered and embarrassed, swearing that he would never put himself in that position again.

'What the hell is wrong with you?' Simon turned on him. 'It was a simple enough question.'

'It was none of their business. It's got now't to do with my mum and dad.'

'It's going to get a lot tougher than that when we're famous. You don't need to tell them anything personal. Just tell them what they want to hear.'

'Leave him alone,' Daniel said. 'It was our first interview, and we did all right.'

'All right's not good enough. We need to be perfect. Don't you guys understand what's at stake here? This is our whole future.'

Matt shoved his hands in his pockets, keeping his temper at bay. It was fine for Simon and Daniel; they had tons of confidence. Amir hadn't said much in the interview either, but no one was picking on him. Maybe Simon was right; maybe he wasn't cut out for this.

Chapter Six

Libby

Libby opened her eyes and released the breath she had been holding as the gap between the front of the lorry and their car narrowed, and then widened again. It had missed them by inches. A blue BMW whizzed past.

'Shit. Are you OK?' Matthew asked.

Libby took a deep breath and readjusted her seatbelt which had locked and was cutting painfully into her neck. Her heart raced as thoughts of what could have happened flashed through her head. It was a miracle that the lorry hadn't hit them. 'I'm fine. What happened?'

'Didn't you see? That bastard pulled out behind me as I was overtaking and cut me off. Drivers like that shouldn't be allowed on the roads. He could have killed us.'

Matthew's face was puce with fury and his fingers were trembling. They were crawling in the slow lane now and there was a steady stream of traffic in the middle lane so they couldn't pull out. Libby could feel Matthew's rage radiating like heat from a fire. He was getting far too worked up for something that was probably an accident. He had seemed so stressed of late; maybe it would do him some good to see his old friends again?

He put his hand over hers. 'I couldn't bear to lose you, Libby.'

Half an hour later, they pulled into a rest area. Libby got out of the car, stretched her back, and turned around to grab her bag, expecting to see Matthew beside her but he had walked off. She watched him march along the row of vehicles until he stopped in front of a blue sports car. There was no sign of the occupants. He circled the car casually, looking like he was pricing it up, and then sauntered back, with a smug look on his face.

'What was that about?' she asked.

'Giving him a taste of his own medicine.' Matthew showed her the key hidden in his hand, grinning like a mischievous school kid.

Libby tried to hide her shock. This was a whole new side to Matthew's personality. He had always been the grown-up in their relationship – organised, protective, responsible. Where had this petulant child come from?

She followed him into the café, picked a cake from the stand, and ordered the coffees. Matthew seemed completely relaxed as they sat down, as if he hadn't vandalised someone's car a few minutes ago. Libby pretended to concentrate on her chocolate brownie, but her eye was constantly drawn to the door, expecting an irate driver to burst through it any minute shouting obscenities.

'I can't believe you did that,' she whispered.

Matthew grinned as he stirred sugar into his coffee. He really didn't seem to care.

By the time they got back to their vehicle, the car had gone. Perhaps the driver hadn't noticed the scratch? He was going to be in for a nasty shock when he got home. She supposed he deserved it; he had nearly killed them after all.

Libby settled back into her seat and opened a bag of mints as Matthew smoothly manoeuvred out of the space. As they left the motorway, the scenery changed from litter-strewn embankments to bucolic vistas. The sky was cobalt blue broken up by wisps of cloud, and bright sunshine bathed the hillside in golden light. The deeper into the countryside they went, the more the road twisted and turned, becoming narrow in places and sharply dipping before rising again to treat them to panoramic views of the surrounding landscape. They passed fields full of newborn lambs clamouring for their mother's attention and ivy-covered cottages. The road was lined with unforgiving stone walls that had withstood the ravages of many harsh winters and the verges were decorated with clusters of bright-yellow and pale-lemon daffodils. Libby looked with envy at the tiny cottages and the lonely farmsteads and wondered what it must be like to live out here in the middle of nowhere.

They were stuck behind a tractor for some time and the smell of manure infiltrated the car through the air conditioning system. Libby wrinkled her nose. Maybe the countryside wasn't so idyllic after all.

They arrived at the venue as the sun was starting to set.

Libby had already looked up the hotel online, but the pictures didn't do it justice. It was an eighteenth-century manor house with a long driveway and manicured lawns to the front. At the back there was a walled garden, an extensive area of woodland, and a scenic lake. The property had been built by a mad marquis and the website played up rumours that he had installed secret passages and hidden rooms. He was even said to haunt the property, although none of the sightings had been verified. The building had fallen into disrepair until the 1980s when a rich businessman completely renovated it and transformed it into an idyllic country retreat. It was a popular destination for weddings and corporate events and wasn't cheap.

As they pulled into the car park, a porter arrived to collect their bags and another uniformed member of staff held the front door open for them. Libby had never stayed anywhere so fancy before. She suddenly felt self-conscious in her scruffy clothes.

The reception area had a huge fireplace with a roaring fire surrounded by high-backed chairs. A collection of newspapers was spread out on the coffee table and the shelves housed volumes of leather-bound books. It was like something out of a Jane Austen novel.

'Here for the wedding, sir?'

Matthew gave their names, and the receptionist checked her computer. She handed over a gold key with a dark-green leather fob. They were in the Cavendish room, apparently. They followed the bellboy to a grand staircase which led to the second floor. The staircase was one of the most impressive features of the hotel, with an ornately decorated window behind it. The light shining through the stained glass left rainbows of light on the red carpet they were walking on. Libby ran her hands over the smooth oak banister, imagining how many people had walked up these steps. She could almost hear the portraits on the wall whispering at her to go home, telling her she didn't belong here; she wasn't part of this world.

All this money, all this privilege. It was a far cry from the house she grew up in and the flats she and her friends had rented, but somehow, they seemed more welcoming. She could never imagine anyone calling Harrington Hall their home, but she imagined they must have done once. One of the portraits was of a young girl, who looked about the same age as Patrick. Had she run through these halls, chasing after kittens, slid down the banister, and played hide and seek in the woodland? Or had she been confined to sitting primly in a parlour, learning to play the piano or embroider? And what about the servants? She pictured a young maid in service to the wealthy marquis, using the labyrinth of corridors and back staircases to move around the house unnoticed by the family. What secrets must she have been privy to?

Their room was on the second floor. It had a huge four poster bed decorated with rose petals, and towels twisted into the shape of a swan. There was a dressing table with a trifold mirror that looked like it could be an antique and a large wardrobe. The bathroom had a rolltop bath and a modern rainfall shower. Libby noted that the hotel had supplied a generous number of branded toiletries.

The bellboy faffed about, showing Matthew how to

operate the television and the safe. Libby walked over to the tall, narrow window which overlooked the back of the property, out towards the lake. The water shimmered a rose colour, reflecting the sky above. There was a small jetty and a rowing boat tied up alongside it. Below her, other guests were milling about the garden, taking pictures of the view. She caught sight of Daniel and Vicky walking back towards the house, but she was too far away to get a proper look at them.

Matthew tipped the bellboy and closed the door. He came up behind her, put his arms around her waist and nuzzled her neck. He seemed completely uninterested in the other guests.

'Come on,' he whispered. 'We've got just enough time to test the bed…'

Chapter Seven

I was in the same year as Matt at primary school. Back then, he was a timid runt of a kid who always got the crap kicked out of him in the playground. Sometimes, on a weekend, I would spot him in town with his stupid brass band, wearing his ridiculous uniform like he was part of the military or something, and I would duck my head and pretend not to see him. Things improved slightly when we got to secondary school and he ditched the Space Invader T-shirts and pudding-bowl haircut. Still, the kid had talent; you couldn't deny that. It didn't take much to persuade him to join the band.

Matt hero-worshipped Daniel, followed him everywhere, copied his hair and his clothes, went after his sloppy seconds. Pathetic. Daniel loved having a sycophant. He called Matt his 'wingman', but they were never equal. Daniel's attitude to Matt was that of a benevolent master, flattering him into doing his bidding. While the rest of us were battling teenage acne and raging hormones, Daniel was gliding through life like the celebrity he would become. He had a decent voice, but he was nothing special. People, girls especially, liked him though, and he knew how to put on a show.

Amir lived on my street; our mums were friends. I used to spend a lot of time at Amir's house while my mum was at work. You had to take your shoes off and watch your manners at Amir's house but there was plenty of food and his mother was always fussing around us, bringing us snacks and bright-orange fizzy pop. His sister was fit. I made the mistake of telling him that once and he punched me in the face and threatened to get his older brothers to beat me up if I ever laid a finger on her. It was the first, but not the last, time we ever fell out. Amir's room was filled with fantasy figures and drawings of vampires, werewolves, and demons. He had an eye for detail.

His dad had an extensive music collection: Hendrix, The Pistols, The Clash and music I had never come across before, imported from Pakistan. Amir copied them onto cassette for me as we listened, identifying different elements that we could incorporate into our own music. It never occurred to us that we were doing anything wrong, but that casual attitude towards plagiarism would come back to bite me. His dad had loads of stories about the old music scene in Huddersfield. We listened to his tale about how The Sex Pistols had played their last ever UK gig in the town in 1977 – when we were just babies. Amir treated his stories with the derision of a typical sixteen-year-old kid who thought he knew everything and believed anything from his father's era was pointless, but I was in rapture.

My own father hated music. He wanted me to study to become a doctor or a lawyer or shit like that. He told me I was being childish, that I had to grow up and get a proper job. We fell out all the time. I couldn't be arsed with school. Lessons, teachers, uniform, detentions. The kids at school were like sheep, docilely following their parents into a life of suburbia, 2.4 children and a mortgage that would keep them chained to a desk until the day they died. They had their whole lives in front of them; why were they content to waste them?

It was all so bloody pointless. You didn't need qualifications to be a pop star. But Dad insisted that it was either A levels or get a job, so I chose the easy route. He has never once, to this day, told me that he's proud of me.

Chapter Eight

Huddersfield, 1993

The band's first five minutes of fame was not enough to satisfy Simon's desire. If anything, it increased it. One Saturday afternoon, after band practice, he declared they needed a female vocalist. He had been flipping through Daniel's copy of *NME* and the page was open to an interview with Louise Wener, the lead singer of Sleeper.

'What about me?' Daniel protested.

'Dan, you can sing, mate, but you don't look like that.' Simon held up the magazine.

Daniel sulked, but Simon wouldn't change his mind. He designed some posters using the computer at the library and displayed them around town. He trawled through the classified ads, searching for singers within a five-mile radius who looked desperate enough to want to join them. Finally, he took £20 from their kitty and hired the back room of a pub to hold auditions. Matt didn't think anyone would turn up, particularly as the posters were so blatantly amateurish (Simon was most definitely a songwriter and not an artist) but to his astonishment, five girls arrived. They were all swiftly rejected on the grounds that they either couldn't sing, or they weren't fit enough. They were about to call it a day when Alex walked in.

Alex, with her mesmerising voice, a pure sound that captivated an audience and brought new meaning to Simon's lyrics. Alex, with those piercing blue eyes, that shock of peroxide-blonde hair, and that way of challenging all their misconceptions about women and music. Alex, who owned the stage as soon as she walked on it, who teased and played with an audience until they were begging for more. Alex who turned them from schoolboys into rock stars. They were all in love with her to some degree, even Amir, and he preferred boys.

From the start, it felt like she was auditioning them, not the other way around. She was two years older than them, had already left school, and was completely focussed on her music. None of them had a clue why she chose to lump her fortunes in with theirs. She was tiny, but her voice was huge with an amazing range. She was pretty, but not in a conventional way. You would walk past her in the street without looking twice, but on stage she transformed into someone you couldn't keep your eyes off.

They gelled immediately. At first, Matt thought it would be weird to have a girl in the band, particularly one he fancied, but her voice brought new energy to their songs. And she was a laugh. Pretty soon, the awkwardness disappeared and it was like she'd always been there.

Daniel wasn't happy. He thought Simon was trying to edge him out, changing the band's sound to suit Alex's voice, but even he had to concede that she was exactly what they needed if they were going to get anywhere. Within a few months of having Alex on board, they had gained a local following and were getting regular slots in bars and pubs around town. They were making decent money – enough to think about going full-time after their A levels – but it wasn't enough for Simon. He craved success like a starving man craves food.

One wet, miserable Saturday evening in late September, they were playing at one of their regular venues. The room was hot and smoky and the floor sticky with spilt drinks. There weren't many punters, and no one was dancing, but the band took every gig seriously, for the practice if nothing else. It was approaching eleven o'clock, last orders had been called, and the bouncers were turning away drunk customers trying their luck for one last pint, when a guy with a goatee beard who had been watching them all evening walked over and started chatting to Alex.

Daniel nudged Matt in the ribs as they watched the older guy trying to pick up their friend, waiting for the pre-arranged sign to come to Alex's rescue. She was always attracting weirdos in bars. However, this time she was nodding and smiling at the guy, and they saw her take his number. As soon as he left, she came bouncing towards them.

'You are never going to believe what's just happened! He's a scout. He says we show promise!'

Matt scrutinised the business card before passing it over

to Daniel who looked equally sceptical. It looked official but anyone could get these printed out. Simon grabbed it from Daniel's hand.

'I've heard of him. He works with some pretty major labels.'

Alex was grinning from ear to ear. 'I told you he was legit!'

'No way,' Amir said, studying the card, but even he couldn't see anything to suggest that the man wasn't who he said he was. He was a freelancer but worked for a number of labels, seeking out northern talent.

'Don't be such a cynic. This is our opportunity, man!'

It turned out that Simon's optimism was well-founded. He rang the scout the next day and they were invited to perform a showcase at a pub in London in a month's time. It was a venue synonymous with the discovery of new talent.

'This is our shot,' Simon told them, barely able to contain his excitement. 'We cannot blow this.'

They skipped school so they could practise every day, waiting for Matt's parents to leave for work before double backing and taking over their garage. It was only a matter of time before one of the neighbours, or the school, grassed them up but they didn't care. All that mattered was getting their songs perfect for the showcase. Simon grew increasingly agitated with them if they made a mistake and tempers flared between him and Alex. They were both devoted to their music but had artistic temperaments and Simon made it clear that he only saw her as a mouthpiece for his genius. Matt grew tired of their continual bickering as the pressure mounted. They were all stressed, but this was a time for coming together, not falling apart. He had enough tension to deal with at home.

His middle-aged middle-class parents were dead against the idea of him turning professional. They wanted him to carry on at school, finish his A levels and postpone his dreams. They took a lot of convincing that this could be his lucky break. College, university, real life, he could pick that all up afterwards. There were arguments, threats to move out. Eventually, they relented. It seemed that even they were not immune to the fever induced by imminent stardom.

Chapter Nine

Libby

Friday evening

T he inn Daniel had chosen for the reunion dinner had been standing in the centre of the Yorkshire village for centuries. The thick stone walls were covered in ivy and a sign suspended from a cast-iron holder creaked ominously in the wind. Amber light spilled from the windows onto the cobbled yard where a couple of desultory wooden picnic tables played host to smokers huddled in winter coats and fleece-lined boots.

Inside, the decor had a modern, hipster feel. Thirty types of gin were on offer behind the bar, accompanied by expensive tonics infused with botanicals, and the specials on the board boasted locally sourced produce. It didn't look like the type of place Libby imagined many locals enjoying and she guessed that it relied heavily on trade from the hotel. The pub was overheated, and Libby could already feel sweat sliding down her back. Some women knew exactly what to wear for every occasion. Libby wasn't one of them.

They had arranged to meet the other band members at the pub, as not everyone was staying at the wedding venue. Libby had seen pictures of his band taken in the 90s, but she would have been hard-pressed to recognise the men standing at the bar now. Their youthful appeal had long gone; they looked more like a group of her dad's friends. Matthew shook hands, patted backs and introduced them.

'Daniel, the condemned man.'

Daniel looked completely relaxed for a man getting married the next day. He took her hand and kissed it.

'Nice to meet you, Libby,' he said with a mischievous sparkle in his eye. He was not quite as handsome as he looked on the telly, but Libby could tell he was the type of man who could get any woman he wanted. She imagined Vicky would need to keep a very close eye on him. Even though she had met a few celebrities in her job, she felt slightly star struck in his presence.

'Amir.' Amir looked less charmed to meet her. He shook her hand with a tight grip. His fingers were thin and cold. He was wearing designer jeans with an open-necked shirt and looked like he would rather be anywhere else but here right now. He introduced his partner, Peter, a large man with exuberant ginger hair. The couple couldn't be any more different. She knew Amir was a lawyer with his own practice in York. She wondered if he still played guitar and if any of his clients knew about his rock 'n' roll past. Peter was a youth worker, working with underprivileged kids in the city. He had a friendly face and she warmed to him instantly.

'Simon.' Simon was the only one in the group who looked like an ageing rock star. He was stick thin and fidgeted constantly. His short black hair was flecked with grey and there were creases at the corners of his eyes. He looked about ten years older than the others, even though Libby knew they had all gone to school together. He had already drunk most of his pint of Guinness and his eyes kept flicking to the bar as if he was contemplating getting another one. He lifted his hand in an ironic wave.

'Vicky's really sorry that she couldn't come out and meet you all,' Daniel said. 'But you know what girls are like. They'll be drinking bottles of fizz and gossiping all evening.'

The men all laughed. Libby didn't blame Vicky for choosing a night in with her friends rather than being stuck in a pub listening to sexist banter. She wouldn't have come if she'd known she was going to be the only woman at the reunion. She sipped her gin and tonic, wishing she had stayed behind in the hotel and taken advantage of the room service. She'd only had five minutes to make a quick call to Patrick to say goodnight. It was nice to have an occasional break from childcare, but she was missing him already.

Daniel had reserved a table and they were led to it by a pretty waitress, with tied-back brown hair and impractical heels. Libby noticed Daniel checking her out as she leaned over to hand out their menus. He spoke to her like he was a regular; but she guessed that was the way he was with everyone. She was sitting next to Matthew and opposite Peter and Amir with Daniel at the head of the table. She was closest to the wall so she would have to squeeze past them all if she wanted to get out.

She perused the menu. All the descriptions sounded pretentious, and she wasn't sure what half the ingredients actually were. Normally, she would have got out her phone and googled them, but she guessed the others were used to fine dining so she would have to take a chance. She could see from the trays being sent out of the kitchen that the portions were tiny and her stomach growled in protest.

'Red or white? Or are you a rosé girl?'

Peter was looking at her expectantly. She hadn't even chosen a dish yet, let alone a drink to go with it. 'Oh, whatever everyone else is having, I don't mind.'

'Libby isn't fussy,' Matthew added.

'Clearly, mate.' Simon said. Libby couldn't tell by his tone whether he was joking and tried not to look offended. What did he mean by that? Matthew laughed off the comment, but she could see it irked him. He was not as comfortable with his old friends as he was pretending to be. She placed her hand on his leg under the table and he squeezed it. It seemed so weird seeing her usually confident boyfriend with this group of people. He seemed as out of place as she felt.

The waitress came back to take their orders. Libby ordered the chicken liver parfait as a starter and pork belly with caramelised apple for the main. She would have loved some chips with it, but they weren't on the menu.

'I'll have the same,' Peter said, winking at her.

She smiled back. She needed an ally.

Matthew started his usual rigmarole asking about ingredients in each of the dishes. He had a serious peanut allergy and even the slightest trace of them could trigger a reaction. He usually hated going out to dinner, hated relying on waiters who displayed varying degrees of awareness and concern about food allergies, hated the feeling that any night could end up in a trip to the hospital. Libby had got used to Matthew choosing which restaurant to eat at, as he knew which ones took allergens seriously.

The waitress, however, was well trained and answered Matthew's questions competently. She pointed to the dishes on the menu that were safe to eat and promised to inform the chef. He seemed satisfied and ordered the pheasant in a red wine jus.

The wine arrived and the waitress made a big deal of pouring out a little of the red for Daniel to try. He swirled the liquid around the glass, stuck his nose in to smell the aroma, sipped it through pursed lips and proclaimed it good.

'You looked like you actually knew what you were doing for a minute there, Dan.' Matthew said. He was kind of a snob about wine and often sent a bottle back if it wasn't perfect.

'Ah, well, looks can be deceiving.'

Libby sipped her wine. It tasted the same as the £5.99 stuff she bought from the supermarket, if she were being honest, but no one asked for her opinion. She caught Peter watching her and smiled again. In comparison, Amir had barely looked in her direction. The starters arrived and Libby tucked in. She was starving. Peter kept topping up her glass, but she needed to take it steady. The last thing she wanted was to get pissed in front of Matthew's mates.

The men continued to catch up, asking about old friends and significant others, and Libby switched off from their conversation to look around the pub. The walls were covered with an eclectic range of antiquated paintings. The one facing Libby featured a collection of men in hunting jackets and jodhpurs standing around horses and a pack of hounds. Brass horseshoes adorned some of the joists and she wondered if they still hunted in this area of the country despite the ban. A group of lads in the corner of the room were sipping pints and egging each other on to approach a couple of girls standing at the bar. The women were fully aware that they were the centre of attention and kept looking over and then back at their drinks and giggling, wielding their power. Finally, one of the men plucked up the courage to walk over to buy them a drink. Emboldened by their friend's success, the others quickly followed suit.

'Some bastard keyed it while we were in the service station,' she heard Amir say and Libby's attention snapped back to the conversation at the table.

'Homophobes. You can't get away from them,' Peter put his hand over Amir's reassuringly.

Libby felt her cheeks redden and she didn't dare look at Matthew. Would he admit he had caused the damage? Surely that was better than Amir thinking it was some sort of hate crime against them. But when she finally sneaked a look at Matthew, he was calm and collected, letting the conversation wash over him as if it was only of mild interest. How could he play it so cool?

'So, what do you do for a living, Libby?' Amir asked, making her jump. It took a few seconds for the question to sink in and she realised everyone was looking at her like she was a complete idiot.

'Oh, I'm a journalist.'

The table fell quiet. Announcing her profession often had that impact, but she had underestimated the effect it would have on the former band members. They were all looking at her.

'You brought a *journalist* to my wedding?' Daniel said to Matthew. 'You could have warned me, mate.'

'She's not a journalist, per se...' Matthew faltered, looking at Libby for help. She was too humiliated to assist him. 'What I mean is, it's just a local rag.'

Libby could feel tears pricking at her eyes. A few hours earlier she had been celebrating her first front-page and now Matthew was making it sound like her career was worthless. How dare he?

She took a sip of wine and forced herself to sound light-hearted. 'Don't worry guys, I'm off-duty. Your secrets are safe with me.'

Chapter Ten

Huddersfield, 1993

M att's dad offered to drive them down to London for the showcase. He had borrowed a van and drove about forty miles an hour down the motorway, increasing their agitation. They were all hyped up on nerves and adrenaline and Matt was in desperate need of a spliff to take the edge off but that was not going to happen with his dad in the vehicle. Simon kept checking his watch fretfully even though they had left plenty of time.

Matt had never been to the capital before and felt a surge of excitement and nerves as they eventually started to make their way through streets full of brightly lit bars and shops that you could only dream of up north. They got lost a few times, circling around, his dad swearing vociferously, and arrived at their destination with no time to spare.

From the outside, the venue looked like an insignificant back-street pub, the sort of boozer his granddad went to.

They had told everyone they were going to be pop stars. Was this all some sort of elaborate joke? They heaved their equipment from the back of the van as Matt's dad sorted out the parking. Inside, however, it was clear that this was a place that took music seriously. Signed album covers graced the walls and Matt tried not to feel intimidated by the names of the bands that had been discovered here. He tried to play it cool as they set up their equipment, but his nerves were jangling.

Anxiety was threatening to overwhelm him as he heard the name of their band announced and they walked out onto the small stage to thin applause. The bright lights made it difficult to see the audience, but they spotted the talent scout sitting at a table with two men in black leather jackets and flash trainers. His dad was perched on a stool by the bar. He gave them the thumbs up and Matt prayed no one had seen it. He was so embarrassing.

Matt could feel his hands shaking as he grabbed his sticks; he was terrified his nerves would screw this up for everyone. He was used to a certain amount of stage fright, but this was on a whole new level. He took a deep breath, but it felt like he had never even sat at a set of drums before. His head was swimming and he seriously thought he might pass out. He focused hard on getting the first bars of the intro right, trusting the rest would follow, and it did. As soon as the music got going, he could feel the rhythm flowing through his fingers and everything came together perfectly.

Alex was on fire; she had insisted on resting her voice for twenty-four hours before their showcase, to Simon's chagrin, but it had been a wise move. Daniel added an improvised flourish to one of their signature tunes and even Amir looked happy for a change. Matt was so lost in the music that he nearly forgot why they were there in the first place. The audience went wild for their last song – they had wisely saved the best to last – and they left on a high. The executives stayed long enough to shake their hands and then muttered something about heading to another appointment.

'You did all right, guys,' the scout said. 'I'll be in touch.'

'Was that it?' Alex demanded, as they stumbled out into the cold night air. A man in a beanie cap was taking a long piss against the wall of the pub and all the excitement and glamour of their first showcase started to fade. 'We came all this way for nothing?'

'It's not nothing,' Simon argued. 'He said he'd be in touch.'

Matt helped his dad load up the van, still buzzing from their performance. He didn't care what the scout and the executives thought. They had played like pros. His dad had never seemed prouder of him.

'They won't take us on,' Amir grumbled as they started the long drive home. 'They would have said something if they liked us.'

Simon, however, was full of confidence. 'That's not necessarily true. They've got to crunch numbers and stuff. Work out what to offer us.'

Matt could feel the elation of the showcase start to dissipate. What if Amir was right? It was his final year of A levels and he couldn't afford to miss any more school. He had probably put his entire future at risk by skipping so many classes. It was sickening to think that it might all be for nothing. The further away from London they got, the less confident he felt. He switched on his Walkman just to drown out Simon's relentless and pointless attempts to be positive. Maybe his parents had a point? Maybe it would be better to concentrate on his A levels and going to uni?

They waited for two agonising weeks, but the call didn't come. The executives obviously hadn't been impressed. There were so many other bands out there that were a hundred times more talented than them. Why would they take a chance on a group of kids? Matt threw himself into his studies, and pushed his dreams of becoming a pop star to the back of his mind. It had been a childish fantasy and now it was over.

Matt was in the school library when Simon and Amir burst in, disturbing everyone and earning them a look of disapproval from the head librarian. They rushed over to his table, hardly able to get the words out.

'They want us, man! We're in!'

A major record label had invited them to London to discuss a contract. Matt looked down at his schoolbooks, at his half-written essay about the lead-up to the Second World War and his pile of revision notes, and knew he was at a crossroads. This was an opportunity of a lifetime. It wouldn't come around again. Without a second glance, he walked out of school and towards his new life.

Chapter Eleven

Extract from Simon Greene's memoir, *Untold Story*.

I started smoking at thirteen. Back then it was cool. Everyone did it. You could smoke in the back of buses and at the cinema. You could get fags from unsupervised vending machines at the bowling alley and the local newsagent would often break a pack and sell you singles. No one ever asked for ID. We smoked Lambert and Butler because my dad smoked them, and it was the only brand we knew. Occasionally someone would buy a pack of Malboro Reds if they were feeling flush.

Weed was next, and then alcohol. It was easy to get served at our local offie. The guy there didn't give a shit but on the rare occasions when he refused to serve us, we nicked it anyway, hiding bottles of vodka in the large inner pockets of our parka coats and running to the park with our spoils. Alcohol was my first love. From the moment I sipped that sweet elixir that offered oblivion in the shape of a bottle, I was hooked. Weed was always second best to booze. Sure, it took the edge off but that was all.

Ecstasy was next – cheap and euphoric – but too much of a party drug for my tastes.

While I was in the band, I took everything I could lay my hands on. We all did. Drugs were everywhere in the music industry; it would have been strange not to indulge. I had an all-consuming need to escape reality and, in the process, messed everything up. It was a continual spiral downwards. I needed more and more hits to get that high and my life became a constant search for the next buzz. I surrounded myself with people who justified my behaviour, and I ignored those that tried to intervene. I told myself over and over again that I could quit whenever I wanted to. Heroin is a fickle mistress – she seduces you only to make you her slave.

Back then I believed that smack unlocked the part of my brain that produced the music everyone loved. You only need to listen to the lyrics to realise that half the best pop songs ever written are love songs to drugs. It was only much later that I realised how deluded I was. I wasn't like other people; I wasn't taking drugs to have fun. I was using them to block out the misery and futility of my existence.

When I moved to LA, I started seeing a shrink. It's practically compulsory over there. We talked about triggers and coping mechanisms and crutches, but back then we didn't have a clue. We were a group of teenaged boys; we didn't talk about emotional stuff. Back then, heroin was the only thing that blocked out the misery in my brain and yet, even while I was scoring, even when I rolled up my sleeve to prepare the hit, I knew it was a portal to hell.

Chapter Twelve

Libby

The conversation moved on to stock portfolios and the state of the housing market. Libby couldn't believe this boring group of middle-aged men had been the epitome of cool in the 90s. The pub started to fill up, mostly with drinkers, and the heat and noise in the room rose. Every time the door opened Libby felt a few welcome tendrils of cold air filter through the bodies before it slammed shut again.

Matthew's comment about her job still rankled. She had worked hard to get where she was – it hadn't been easy studying at university while raising Patrick. Since leaving uni and starting her job at the newspaper, she had been busy just trying to keep her head above water. There was tough competition amid the trainees, and she was determined to be the one to be taken on permanently. She didn't know what she would do without Emma's help – she was the only person she really trusted to look after Patrick. Her parents were in Oxford and her friends were more interested in going out and partying than meeting the needs of a seven-year-old boy.

Libby knew that Matthew didn't have much respect for her profession, but he had never openly expressed his derision like that before. He couldn't understand why she would work such long hours for such little pay. Libby's career was a far cry from Matthew's. He ran his own property business, chose his own hours, and usually worked from home. He didn't even really need the money; he had made his millions by the time he was thirty.

A bottle of wine was passed around the table and emptied. Daniel waved at the waitress to bring another. Libby wondered how much this meal was costing and who was picking up the tab. The food wasn't cheap, and they had already made their way through several bottles. No one seemed to care though. She supposed all the band members were loaded. They had made millions in their few years of fame and the royalties were still coming in from their one real hit, which was played from time to time on the radio and featured in several 'Best of the 90s' album compilations and playlists on Spotify. Simon, as the songwriter, would no doubt also get money from the publishing rights. It was enough for all of them to live comfortably for the rest of their lives.

She found Matthew's money bewildering. She had never gone out with someone rich before and sometimes the discrepancy in their income caused problems. He got offended when she insisted on splitting the bill or refused to let him buy things for her. Matthew wore his wealth like armour. Deep down, underneath that confident persona he presented to the world, she knew that he was quite insecure.

The meals arrived, and they all tucked in. Amir, she noticed, ate with precision, ensuring every mouthful had a small amount of each component of the dish. Peter ate with gusto and had already spilt apple puree down his shirt, while Simon picked at his meal. Daniel kept the conversation and the wine flowing.

He stood up and raised his glass. A few drinkers stared in their direction and Libby saw them whispering to each other as they recognised the star of daytime television. One or two of them took out their mobile phones to take pictures. He seemed completely unfazed by the attention; Libby guessed he was used to it. 'I just wanted to let you know how much it means to me to have you guys here to celebrate my big day. Cheers!'

They echoed the toast around the table as they chinked glasses.

'Soppy sod,' Matthew said affectionately, taking a sip of the wine.

Daniel sat down again, and Libby was about to turn back to her dinner when she realised that Simon was also getting up, holding onto the table to steady himself. He raised his glass.

'To absent friends.'

There was silence around the table. Libby, who had raised her glass expectantly, put it back down as she realised no one was joining in the toast. They were all looking at Simon who was staring back at them defiantly.

'To Alex,' he said pointedly.

Libby held her breath. Alex was the other band member, the lead singer. Matthew never spoke about her. All Libby knew was that she had committed suicide six months after the band split up. Libby had seen pictures of Alex online – she had been stunning. She often wondered if she and Matthew had been an item, but it had never felt the right time to ask.

Matthew stood up, held Simon's gaze, and raised his glass. His voice wobbled a bit as he spoke. 'To Alex.'

One by one, the others stood up as well. Libby felt obliged to join them although she felt ridiculous toasting a woman she had never met.

'To Alex,' they said in chorus, and Libby felt a shiver go down her spine, as if the former band member had just joined the party.

Chapter Thirteen

London, 1993

The label promised them the world. They didn't realise then how much they would want in return.

Amir's father, their unofficial manager, had accompanied them to London to make sure the record label didn't screw them but, from the minute they walked through the revolving doors of the luxurious offices, they knew they were out of their depth. The receptionist, who looked like a supermodel with swinging blonde hair and vertiginous heels, showed them into a meeting room which was all glass and sparkling chrome. A table had been laid out with Perrier water, pastries, fresh fruit, and coffee. Matt felt sick. They had stopped at McDonald's on the way for breakfast and he could feel the Egg McMuffin churning in his stomach.

His parents had insisted that he wore a suit for the meeting, but he realised immediately that it had been a mistake. He looked like he was attending a funeral, not signing a record deal. The executives arrived together and there was plenty of hand shaking and apologies for keeping them waiting before they took their seats around the huge glass table. The contract ran to several pages and was full of complicated language that Matt couldn't understand. Amir's father clarified some of the clauses, but the negotiations didn't last very long. Everyone sitting around the table knew that the band would happily sign away their souls for a record deal. The label made it clear they were taking a huge risk on an unknown band and they weren't prepared to make any concessions.

Discussions concluded, the band members signed their names several times on bits of paper and then sat back while the executives threw around ideas for recording schedules, producers, and tour dates. It was as if none of it had anything to do with them anymore. They were just another 'product' to be marketed and sold.

A bottle of champagne was produced even though they were all underage and Amir's father didn't drink. Matt had only tasted champagne at weddings and he didn't really like it. Afterwards the contract gathered dust in his father's filing cabinet. They simply did as they were told.

Two months later they moved to London. The five of them shared a miserable two-bedroom flat in Camden with a dodgy landlord who collected the rent in cash and refused to issue any paperwork. Alex insisted on having her own room which meant Simon and Amir shared the other and Daniel and Matt slept in the living room. Matt was woken up every morning by someone stepping over him or dropping their cornflakes on his sleeping bag. The room always smelt of stale smoke and B.O.

None of them could cook so they lived off takeaways and frozen food which took forever to heat up in the ancient cooker. Matt was the only one who ever cleaned the flat and that was only when the mess had reached such epic proportions that even cockroaches would think twice about living there. The surfaces were covered in a thin layer of grease and the kitchen window had been painted shut so the only ventilation came from the rattling old extractor fan which sounded like it was going to explode any minute. Sometimes Matt longed for the sanitary household he had grown up in, the clean laundry that appeared in his bedroom as if by magic, and the cupboards full of fresh, healthy food. He had never realised how much he had taken his parents for granted before he moved out of home for the first time.

Moving to London also meant they lost their rehearsal space and there was a limit to how much noise their landlord and the other tenants would put up with. The only studio they could afford to rent was disgusting, freezing cold, and infested with rats. An old oil heater cranked out some heat, but it wasn't enough to stave off the damp. The whole place was a health hazard. It was not what they'd envisioned from a rock star lifestyle, but they were making music and that was all that mattered.

Chapter Fourteen

Extract from Simon Greene's memoir, *Untold Story*.

I wake up on the floor of someone's kitchen surrounded by fag ends and discarded cans. There is a pile of vomit next to my head and I'm not even sure if it's mine. The room is washed in grey but there is a dim light creeping through the dirty window. I can hear the muffled grunts of people shagging in the adjoining room and the stink of stale smoke fills my nostrils. From my position on the floor, I can see crumbs and balls of dust underneath the cupboards. I prise my body out of its supine state and pull myself up to standing, my head swimming as I try to orientate myself. Where am I? How did I get here? What day is it?

I'm wearing jeans but my feet and chest are bare. I have no idea where the rest of my clothes are. I stagger out of the open back door and stand in the backyard breathing in the fresh cold air that hits my lungs. A fox, which has been rummaging in a pile of black bin bags, stops and stares at me. For a second, we contemplate each other before it turns and runs. I'm half minded to follow it. The house is on a hill and I look down upon the rooftops and the chimney stacks shrouded in mist. The silence is broken by the sound of birdsong and the clatter of bin wagons. It's all incredibly beautiful, like a painting.

The world starts to wake up. The clouds gradually lighten, the sun emerges, and a new day begins, and I think, fuck me, life is good. *And I want to write music so I ignore my throbbing head and my filthy clothes and the fact that I have no idea where the fuck I am or where the fuck I'm going, and I walk through the streets of London, tapping out a rhythm on the cast-iron railings, on the tops of litter bins, listening to the sound of the city coming to life. I drop my last pound in the tattered paper cup lying beside a young girl sleeping in a doorway and I watch the early morning commuters in their grey and black suits file into the underground like automatons and I breathe in the air and I thank God that I am alive, that I am free.*

By the time I get home my feet are bleeding, and I'm coming down hard, so I fall into bed, my head still full of beautiful, transcendental, transformative music, but when I finally wake up, it's all gone.

Chapter Fifteen

Libby

The weird feeling that came over Libby when the former band members toasted Alex started to subside as the conversation moved on. Acknowledging her absence seemed to have broken the ice between the group and they were now reminiscing about their time on tour. Daniel was telling an anecdote about a gig in Edinburgh. She was straining to hear him above the noise of the pub, but it seemed to involve copious drams of whisky and a set of stolen bagpipes.

She glanced over at Matthew. He had finished his dinner and had placed his cutlery neatly in the centre of his plate. He was leaning forward, listening attentively and laughing along with Daniel. His cheeks were slightly flushed and his eyes glistened. He looked younger, somehow, and she wondered if he missed the company of his former band members. After all, they must have been so close back then.

'You know, we're not too old to do it again,' Daniel suggested. 'There are plenty of bands from the 90s back on the circuit. Look at Take That.'

Libby wondered if he was serious. Matthew had told her that Daniel had contacted him over the years, wanting to reform the band, but he had always refused. It wasn't like he needed the money. Perhaps the wedding was Daniel's way of bringing them all together again? There was silence as the band members looked at each other. Then they burst out laughing.

'You have to be bloody joking!' Matthew said. 'I'm well past strutting my stuff on stage.'

'Yes, no offence mate, but over my dead body,' Amir said. Daniel looked crestfallen, but laughed it off, moving on to tell a particularly filthy tale about a stripper in Amsterdam. Matthew was laughing so hard he had tears in his eyes. Libby hadn't seen him this relaxed and happy for months.

'I'd be careful,' Amir warned in a quiet voice. 'Or it'll end up in Simon's book.'

'What book?' Matthew asked, putting his glass down. Libby saw the colour drain out of his face and the atmosphere suddenly thickened.

'You do know Simon's written a book about us, don't you?'

Matthew's fingers were trembling. 'What?'

He turned to Simon who leant back on his chair and put his hands behind his head in a relaxed fuck-you pose.

'He can't do that! Not without our permission, surely.'

'That's what I've told him. Don't worry, we've got an

injunction out.' Amir's voice was cold and controlled. Libby wouldn't like to come up against him in court. She took a sip of wine and reached under the table for Matthew's hand, but he pulled it away. The tension was unbearable. Everyone was looking at Simon who shrugged and finished off his glass of wine.

'That won't stop me.'

Matthew turned to Daniel. 'Did you know about this?'

'Of course I bloody didn't!' Daniel looked around him quickly to check if anyone noticed his outburst.

'We'll sue you for slander.'

Simon wasn't in the least intimidated by Daniel's threat. 'Can't sue me if it's true, mate.'

'Truth? What the hell would you know about the truth? You were wasted the whole time.' Matthew shouted, drawing attention to the table.

Simon sniggered. 'I remember plenty, mate. And I'm leaving *nothing* out.' He waved the waitress over to order another drink. 'Besides, I have proof.'

Proof of what? What was Simon talking about?

'We'll take you for every penny you've got.' Daniel's voice was cold and threatening.

Simon held up his hands in mock surrender. 'Go ahead. I've got nothing. Ask my accountant. Not that I can pay him. He says I should file for bankruptcy.'

'What?' There was a stunned silence. Libby had taken it for granted that all the band members were rich, particularly Simon. He was still a songwriter, working in LA, and had written music for some of the biggest names in the industry. How had he managed to squander all that cash?

'Listen, if money's the issue, then I'm sure we can help you out. Club together, slip you a few grand.' Matthew suggested.

'Don't let him blackmail you. It'll all go up his nose,' Daniel said contemptuously. As the only person there still involved in the celebrity world, he probably had the most to lose. It must be a constant fear – the almost inevitable fall from grace after the public put you on a pedestal. On the contrary, Libby doubted the tabloids would be that interested in Matthew these days. It had been a long time since he had last been bothered by the paparazzi.

'Well, you'd know all about that, wouldn't you?' Simon retorted.

Libby's mind was reeling from the continuous stream of revelations. Did Daniel take cocaine? She supposed a lot of celebrities did. Cocaine had never been part of her world. The strongest thing she had ever tried was weed at university and it had just made her sleepy, so she hadn't tried it again. Had Matthew taken drugs when he was in the band? Probably, although she was sure she would know if he still did them now. That said, she was starting to wonder how well she knew him at all. Why was he so angry? What did he have to hide? No one expected pop stars to behave like angels and it was almost a lifetime ago.

The camaraderie between the friends had completely dissolved and Libby found herself among a group of men who were glaring at each other like rival supporters at a football match. She was only glad there was a table between

74

them otherwise she was pretty sure Simon would have been punched by now.

The waitress arrived to clear their plates and deliver Simon's drink. She started her sales pitch, asking if they wanted to see the dessert menu, but the tension between the group was palpable and she drifted off mid-sentence, muttering something about giving them a minute. Libby wondered if Simon was telling the truth. He seemed unlikely to be able to finish a sentence, let alone complete a book. Maybe he was winding them all up?

'Anyone for pud?' Simon asked cheerily, but the mood was broken. Matthew looked like he was going to murder Simon while Amir appeared cold and determined, supremely confident in his legal stance. Daniel was looking around, checking that no one was witness to the drama that was brewing.

'I think we'll call it a night,' Matthew said, standing up.

'There's no need to be like that, mate,' Simon laughed.

Matthew threw a few notes on the table. 'Keep the change. And I'm not your mate.'

Chapter Sixteen

London, 1993

While his school friends sweated over coursework and university applications, Matt's life was a constant rotation of long hours at the studio, playing gigs, and partying hard. His parents loaned them the cash to buy a second-hand van to carry all their equipment. It was forever needing repairs and they soon became quite adept at motor mechanics. Once, the van broke down on the M6 on their way to a festival and they were left stranded on the roadside surrounded by kit and trying to hitch to Birmingham. The guy that picked them up looked like a serial killer but turned out to be a nice guy and they thanked him by signing a beer mat for him. He said he would keep it until they were rich and famous.

It wasn't long before they ditched Amir's father as their manager and recruited a smooth-talking Australian called Craig. Craig was ruthless, swore profusely, and was determined they were going to make it big. He liked making money and he liked spending it. He wore slick suits, handmade leather shoes, and a fancy gold watch. He openly scorned their living arrangements but recognised their potential and was completely focussed on making them a success. He seemed permanently attached to his portable phone, shouting colourful profanities and signing them up for every opportunity, even it was the 3am slot in a dodgy nightclub or supporting a crappy band that hadn't managed to sell out their seats.

They were all exhausted, but having an audience, no matter how small, kept them going. Matt had grown accustomed to carrying all his possessions in a duffel bag and packing for a gig with five minutes' notice. To those back at home, his life sounded glamorous but the most he ever saw of those cities were motorways and identikit guest houses with grumpy landladies who demanded a huge deposit in case of any damage. They weren't even really getting paid. Craig handled all the money, occasionally giving them cash for rent, food, and beer. Matt had no idea how much he actually earned.

Sometimes his mum and dad came to watch him perform. They seemed so out of place in the clubs and pubs that were now a regular feature of Matt's life. He often spotted them sitting at a table, sipping half-pints of lager and lime, or to his embarrassment, on the dance floor looking bewildered as everyone jumped around them. Most of the time he barely got a chance to say hello before he was being dragged to the next venue or an afterparty.

His mother worried. She sent him newspaper clippings

about the dangers of life in London and rang him every time there was an IRA attack in the capital, but Matt had never felt more alive. Everything in the city was different and exhilarating – the bars, the shops, the girls. It didn't matter to him where he lived or how much money he earned – he was young, free, and about to be famous. His mum wanted him to come home, to postpone his dreams until he was older, and they fell out about it on more than one occasion. She didn't understand; she could never understand. He wasn't a kid anymore. His life was changing exponentially, and he could feel himself spinning faster and faster away from his old life. The whole world lay before him and fame was a fingertip away. And if becoming rich and famous meant leaving his family and friends behind, then it was a sacrifice Matt was willing to make.

Chapter Seventeen

Libby

L ibby struggled to keep up as Matthew pushed his way through the drinkers and out of the front door of the pub. The cold air hit her like a slap in the face. There were no taxis outside, and Matthew was clearly in no mood to hang around, so they started walking back to the hotel. Libby had the Uber app on her phone, but she had a strong suspicion they wouldn't have the service here. She could barely get mobile phone reception. She regretted wearing heels as she chased after him.

'Wait, Matthew, please.'

He looked around, as if surprised to see her following him. 'I'm sorry, I'm walking too fast, aren't I?'

'A little bit.'

He slowed his pace, and she snaked her arm around his, taking advantage of the body heat emanating through his leather jacket. It was a cold night, and the sky was full of stars, so different from the city. She heard an owl hooting in the distance. The road was pitch black with only the occasional streetlamp casting its light onto the tarmac. It was quite a walk back to the hotel, but it was nice to have some time alone. It had been a difficult day with one thing and another and Libby was tired of all the drama. She could feel Matthew relaxing the further away from the pub they walked. The evening had ended so abruptly; she was still trying to get her head around what had happened and why Matthew was so angry.

'It's beautiful out here,' she said finally.

'Yeah, it's very peaceful.' He glanced up at the sky, as if noticing his surroundings for the first time. 'I'm sorry about that. I shouldn't have lost my temper.'

'You were provoked.'

'It's being around those guys again... Maybe we shouldn't have come.'

'Why did you? You don't seem to have much in common with them anymore.'

'I don't know really,' he admitted. 'Maybe I just thought, after all this time, I could lay some ghosts to rest. But these guys haven't changed one bit. They're still a set of selfish bastards, looking out for themselves.'

'Well, I'm sure Daniel's pleased you're here.'

'Daniel's all right but Simon's a git. Always has been. He only cares about himself.'

'Do you think Amir will be able to stop him publishing his book?'

'Probably. And who would believe him anyway? He's such a fuck-up.'

Libby bit her lip. She'd like to agree with Matthew, but she knew how quickly and easily a salacious story, no matter how false, could make its way around social media, even if the real media wouldn't touch it. She wondered what was bothering him so much. Did he have something to hide, or did he just value his privacy? She tried to imagine how it would feel if someone wanted to spill all her secrets like that. Matthew had every right to be angry. It would be a huge betrayal of trust.

She thought about all the celebrity magazines Emma bought, how they sat at her kitchen table with steaming mugs of tea, pouring over the tiniest details of famous people's lives, not really caring if the information was true or not. It was entertainment; she didn't spend much time thinking about the real person behind the façade. Or how much they might be hurting.

Libby had never felt any desire to be famous. Apart from Matthew, everyone she knew lived ordinary lives. She couldn't imagine what it must be like to live your life in the public eye, everything laid out like a smorgasbord for people to feed on. There were some obvious benefits to celebrity, not least the money, but was it worth it for the complete and utter loss of a private life? Whatever Simon had threatened to include in his book had happened more than twenty years ago; Libby had been just a kid when the band split up.

A car passed them at speed, making them jump to the side of the road. Libby wondered if it was one of the other band members, making their way back to Harrington Hall. If so, they hadn't bothered to stop and offer them a lift. She suddenly felt vulnerable, walking in the countryside at night. She had never experienced such a deep and utter darkness before. It made her feel small and insignificant. The Yorkshire Dales were undeniably beautiful, but this part of the world was so isolated. They could have been walking for miles in the wrong direction before they realised and even then, there would be no way of calling for help. She was relieved when she spotted the illuminated sign for the hotel shining like a beacon in the darkness.

They walked up the gravel drive which was lit by small solar lamps. Fairy lights in the trees sparkled like fireflies. There were more lights in the car park and at the entrance of the hotel and she felt foolish for being afraid of the dark. The doorman opened the door for them and greeted them with a small bow and a 'good evening'.

'Shall we get a night cap?' Matthew suggested.

She would have preferred to have gone straight to bed but Matthew looked like he needed a drink, so she followed him into the hotel bar. Like the rest of the building, it had an old-fashioned charm with a gleaming oak bar and an array of expensive whiskies on display. The walls were painted in heritage colours and long velvet curtains framed the tall windows. Leather armchairs were positioned around highly polished coffee tables on which coasters advertising the hotel chain had been strategically placed. The barman was wiping glasses with a white cloth and no doubt counting down the minutes until the end of his shift. They were the only customers.

After some discussion about vintages, Matthew bought a

bottle of Bordeaux and they took a table close to the window overlooking the back of the property. A marquee had been erected on the lawn and behind the tarpaulin, shadows flitted like a Chinese puppet show as the staff set up tables and chairs for the wedding reception. In the distance, the lake glimmered in the moonlight. It was such a beautiful setting and Libby imagined how different it would be if she and Matthew had come here for a romantic weekend instead.

A grandfather clock in the corner of the room chimed eleven o'clock and Libby stifled a yawn. She settled back into the comfy armchair and tried to enjoy the expensive wine and the understated elegance of the room. She was in danger of nodding off when the sound of giggling preceded three very drunk women spilling into the room. Libby turned to see them stagger to the bar and order two bottles of Prosecco to take away. Vicky was standing in the centre of the group, looking slightly less inebriated than the others, her hair up in rollers. She was wearing a bright-pink tracksuit with the words 'Bride to Be' on the back. Even dressed like that, she looked glamorous. Libby recognised the woman handing over her credit card as Natalya, Simon's ex-wife, and the other as Daniel's younger sister, Olivia.

Natalya's face dropped as she twirled around and caught sight of them. She must have known Matthew quite well in the 90s. In fact, Matthew and Daniel were both godfathers to her eldest son Leo, although Matthew had relinquished his responsibilities a long time ago. Natalya did not look pleased to see him. She handed over the bottles of Prosecco to Daniel's sister and marched over to their table.

'Natalya, don't,' she heard Vicky say, but her friend ignored her. Libby could feel another confrontation brewing. She glanced at Matthew in alarm, but he seemed cool and collected as he stood up to greet her.

'Matt? Well, isn't this a trip down memory lane?'

'Natalya, how are you?' The former model visibly recoiled as Matt kissed her on the cheek.

'Oh, you know, I'm fine. Leo's fine. Everyone's just fine. Thanks for asking.' She didn't sound like everything was fine. Quite the opposite, in fact.

'Is he with you?' Matthew looked over her shoulder as if hoping that his godson would come and rescue him.

'He's got a gig this weekend. So, who's your friend?' Libby felt herself blush as Natalya scrutinised her. Despite having three children – two with her second husband Philippe – and being well into her forties, Natalya had the toned, lithe body and glowing skin of a woman who looked after herself. Libby felt frumpy in comparison.

'This is my girlfriend, Libby.'

Natalya smiled, but it didn't reach her eyes.

'Reliving your youth, Matty?' she said.

Libby bristled but willed herself not to react. She could see that Matthew was struggling to remain civil. In her peripheral vision, she saw that Vicky was making her way over. Another confrontation was the last thing they needed tonight. They should have gone straight to bed. Why was everyone being so hostile? Weren't they all supposed to be friends?

'Hey, Matt. Hello, you must be Libby,' Vicky said in a sickly tone, overcompensating for her friend. She kissed them both on the cheeks. 'Sorry to interrupt but can we steal Natalya back? Bridesmaid duties.'

Natalya looked like she wanted to argue but her friend had a firm grip on her arm as she led her out of the room, glancing back at them with an apologetic smile.

Libby turned to Matthew. 'What was all that about?'

Matthew took a long gulp of wine. 'Search me. She's a nutcase. I don't know what Simon saw in her.'

'She's gorgeous.'

'Yeah, well, not my type. God, I'll be glad when this is all over.'

Libby was starting to feel the same way. She took another sip of wine, but she had lost her taste for it.

'Come on, let's go up,' she suggested. She'd had enough altercations for one evening.

'You go; I'll finish this drink.' Matthew indicated to his glass which was still full of wine. Normally she would have stayed with him, but she was tired, and it would be nice to have a few minutes to herself. It had been a shitty evening and she wanted to go to bed.

'Don't be too long,' she said, grabbing her bag.

As she made her way from the bar to the hallway, she could hear raised voices coming down the corridor. She stopped at the doorway and peeked around the corner to see Natalya shouting at the bride.

'I can't believe you invited him!'

'He's Daniel's friend. He wanted them here.'

'After what they did to Alex?'

'Come on, you've both had a lot to drink,' Olivia pleaded. 'Just leave it for tonight, yeah?'

'This is so typical of you, making a scene,' Vicky continued. 'You always have to be the centre of attention.'

'Me? Are you having a laugh? You know your problem, Vicky? You think the whole world revolves around you and Daniel.'

'Well, this weekend it does. It is our wedding, remember?'

'Oh God, how could anyone forget?'

Natalya stomped off, leaving Vicky and Olivia gawping after her.

'Come on,' Olivia said. 'Let's go to bed. We've all had too much to drink. She didn't mean it.'

'Oh, she meant it. She meant every word.' Vicky's face was like thunder.

The women moved on, leaving Libby feeling bewildered. What was Natalya's problem? Libby couldn't ever imagine speaking to any of her friends like that, particularly the night before their wedding. She waited until Olivia and Vicky had left the hallway before moving out of the shadows and making her way to their room. She had never felt so far away from home. She checked her watch. In less than forty-eight hours she'd be back with her son, curled up on the sofa with mugs of hot chocolate. Forty-eight hours and she would never have to see any of these vile people again. It couldn't pass quickly enough.

Chapter Eighteen

London, 1994

M att felt like he had been dropped into a parallel universe. A few months ago he had been living a boring life in suburbia, going to school and doing his homework, hanging out with his friends, trying to pull girls at the rec, and applying for university. Now he was cast adrift in this new world where the law and normal rules of behaviour simply didn't exist. Drugs and booze were in plentiful supply. And the girls... Never in Matt's wildest dreams had he imagined how many women would throw themselves at him. Most of them fancied Daniel, but that still left plenty for him. Simon had started dating a Russian model called Natalya and only had eyes for her. Amir wasn't interested, although he pretended sometimes to keep up appearances. He still hadn't come out to his parents and he didn't want any rumours circulating in the press.

So many girls, so many parties. They all started blurring

into one after a while. They partied all night and slept during the day; they ate cereal for dinner and pizza for breakfast. The afterparties didn't really get going until after three and quite frequently the band would stay up all night and turn up, still drunk, at the recording studio the next day. Alex worried that all the drinking and smoking would damage her vocal cords and often made an excuse to leave early. Matt could tell the parties weren't that much fun for her anyway. As a young, single woman touring with a group of boys, she was seen by plenty of men in the industry as fair game. She had to tread a fine balance between being molested and pissing off the men who could make or break her career. Alex was tiny and couldn't handle her booze. Matt frequently had to help her get home.

Afterparties were usually hosted by the headline act, and the prettiest girls in the audience were handpicked to join them. There was more booze, girls, and drugs available than they knew what to do with. Headliners were invariably arrogant and cruel to their support acts, belittling and excluding them from the action, but as newbies on the circuit, they were expected to 'network', an activity the rest of the band members left largely to Daniel and Simon. Amir, Alex and Matt usually found themselves in a corner, passing around a bottle of vodka and a joint, and taking the piss out of the groupies.

It seemed the higher profile the band, the worse their behaviour. It was 4am and they were at a party somewhere in Hull. They were supporting a band that had a reputation for smashing up dressing rooms, urinating over furniture and setting fire to rubbish bins. A lot of places had refused to host them, despite their popularity, due to their bad reputation.

'Jesus,' Alex said, pointing out a blonde girl who looked about thirteen. The girl, wearing a tiny miniskirt and a see-through lacy top, was sidling up to the lead singer who was notorious for sleeping with underage girls. 'That's sickening.'

'He gets away with it too,' Amir observed, necking his drink. 'They can do what they like; no one cares.'

'We should report him.'

'Yeah right. As if they would do anything.'

Matt watched as the singer shook a bottle of champagne and aimed the contents at the girl's nascent breasts before inviting several onlookers to 'drink up'. He turned away in disgust. The girl was the same age as his little sister, and some of the men were three times her age, but she was one of many. The girls didn't even realise they were being used; they just wanted the kudos of sleeping with a pop star. Jacqui had been desperate for him to invite her to stay with him in London, to lap up some of her brother's fame, but there was no way he was exposing her to animals like that.

As well as the afterparties, there were corporate events held by the label where they were expected to be charming and polite, and above all behave themselves. They were paraded like prostitutes in a brothel as bored executives eyed them up and down, calculating their potential. The conversation was all about sponsorship opportunities, advertising and sales. It was at one of these parties that Matt was offered, and accepted, his first line of coke from a girl in public relations. The people at that party took money for granted, sipping champagne like it was water, and talking loudly about holidays on the Amalfi coast.

Drugs were everywhere. There was always someone who could page a dealer if their supply ran out and lines of coke were offered around like appetisers. Matt took pills to help him stay awake and pills to help him get to sleep. It was the only way he could keep going. Craig turned a blind eye to the booze, the drugs, and the girls as long as it didn't impair their ability to make music. No one cared that Simon was rapidly developing a serious drug addiction, that Amir was homesick and miserable, that Matt and Daniel were running wild, and that Alex cried herself to sleep most nights. No one cared that they were below the legal age for half the activities they got up to or that their parents were worried sick about them. All anyone cared about was getting as much money out of them as possible before they crashed and burned.

Chapter Nineteen

I loathed the executives with their flash suits and their chunky mobile phones, their platinum credit cards and their parasitic attitudes, but I craved their power. We were the ones with all the talent, but they could make or break us. They held all the cards, and they knew it. We had no choice but to play their games. I had to sit in meetings about brand management, USPs, and launch plans. As they wanked off to marketing schedules and audience demographics, I nodded along and pretended that I cared. I shook hands, I signed documents, I smiled when I was told to. A puppet on their string. It was all about numbers to them. They didn't care about the music, and they sure as hell didn't care about us; they only cared what percentage they could cream off our earnings.

I knew we were better than all the other bands out there – that I was better – but it was all about image. Image sells music, nothing else. And that's where the others came in. Look at any

93

group and you can spot the winners and the losers. The ones that drive its success and those that are along for the ride. We needed Daniel. He could charm the pants off the executives, the journalists, the groupies. There was something indefinable that drew people to him; it didn't matter that the guy couldn't sing. If he'd tried to go solo, at best, he might have won a karaoke night at a local pub. He thought he was something special, but he was just a good-looking man-doll.

You couldn't trust Matt. He'd tell you anything for a quiet life. Affable, compliant Matt, everyone's best friend. Always bumbling along, never sticking his neck out for anything or anyone. Amir kept us grounded, but he always had his eye on a bigger prize. Alex was the only one who came anywhere close to my talent. She was the only one of them I admired. The rest were simply there to make up the numbers.

It was never about the money for me. I just wanted to make music. Music people would talk about for decades to come, music that would inspire a generation. Music to weep to, music to fuck to, music to fight to. I wanted to be Bowie, Elton, Springsteen. I didn't want my songs to go platinum; I wanted triple platinum. I didn't want to conquer the US; I wanted the whole damn world.

Success is a drug; you're always chasing the next high. You get a record deal, but you could have got more money; you headline a gig, but there's always a bigger venue; you win an award, but someone else sweeps the floor. We had our foot in the door, but it wasn't enough; it was never going to be enough.

Chapter Twenty

Libby

Saturday morning

Despite the comfy bed, Libby didn't sleep well, and she was woken early by the pipes gurgling in the overheated room. Matthew, who had been tossing and turning all night, was finally asleep and snoring gently. Normally, when she couldn't sleep, Libby would get up, make a cup of tea, and potter around her flat in the half-light, but she couldn't do that here without waking him up. The heavy duvet was pressing down on her, the stuffy room was oppressive, and her mind was reeling with everything that had gone on the day before.

Why were they all so upset about Simon's memoir? And why had Natalya been so cross with Vicky for inviting Matthew to her wedding? Was her boyfriend keeping secrets from her? It was all such a long time ago – who cared what a group of teenaged boys got up to in the 90s?

She supposed that Daniel and Amir might be concerned about their reputations. Amir was a lawyer and any allegations of misdemeanour, no matter how long ago or how minor, could irrevocably damage his career. It was no wonder he was trying to stop the publication. As a television presenter, Daniel, perhaps, would not be held to the same moral standards, but Libby knew that he would be dropped immediately with the first hint of a scandal. He was not the type of celebrity that the broadcasters would stand by. Matthew's career, based in property, was less at risk but she knew he had an interest in politics and had talked from time to time about standing for the local council. She doubted he would want his youthful indiscretions raked over in public. Was that all it was? Pride? Or was it something more serious?

After all, didn't everyone have regrets? Libby would never, ever regret keeping Patrick but sometimes she wondered what her life would have been like if she hadn't. She had been seventeen and in her last year of A levels when she fell pregnant. One mistake and her whole life had changed forever.

Libby tried to lie still, watching shadows dance along the ceiling, until she couldn't stand it any longer. She walked over to the heavy curtains and peeked outside. The landscape around her was obscured by mist but dawn had at least broken. It was going to be a beautiful day. A morning jog would clear her head.

The corridor was quiet. Trays filled with dirty plates and

empty bottles of wine had yet to be cleared away by the cleaners. A security guard was leaning back in his chair, playing *Candy Crush*, but jumped to attention as she walked past. She eschewed the elevator and took the staircase instead, feeling totally out of place in her scruffy joggers. She could hear noises from the kitchen and the smell of bacon wafting through the air as the staff prepared breakfast. The woman on the reception desk greeted her as she walked past but otherwise the place was deserted.

Libby walked out of the front door and breathed in the cold morning air which was a sharp contrast to the stuffy hotel. Dew sparkled on the lawn and the sky was a wash of blue and pink as the sun rose. It was the perfect weather for a spring wedding. She stretched and then started off gently, feeling her lungs expand as she settled into a steady pace. There was a circular route around the lake and through the woodland that would be just the right length for a short run.

As she reached the lake, she was surprised to see she was not alone. A woman was sitting in the lotus position on the edge of the jetty, looking out onto the water. Libby turned around to go the other way but before she could, the woman turned around and spotted her. With a sinking heart, Libby realised that the woman was Natalya. She was wearing yoga clothes and had a serene look on her face, as if she had just woken up from a pleasant dream. She was the last person Libby wanted to speak to, but Natalya had already spotted her and waved.

'I'm sorry, I didn't mean to disturb you,' Libby said.

'You didn't. I'd just finished. I'm Natalya.'

'I know; we met last night.'

A look of confusion crossed her face. 'Oh my God, did we? I don't remember, sorry.'

'It doesn't matter.'

She scrutinised her. 'Oh wait, I do remember you. You're Matt's girlfriend, aren't you? Lily?'

'Libby.'

Natalya bit her lip, obviously trying to remember the conversation. Libby stared at her coldly, wondering whether she had genuinely forgotten or was trying to cover up her rude behaviour. She wasn't really in the mood for pleasantries – she would have enough of that in the day to come – and she hadn't forgotten her snide remarks. Did she think that Libby was just another notch on Matthew's bedpost?

'Oh God, I made that terrible comment about your age. You must think I'm a right bitch. I'm so sorry – alcohol loosens my tongue. I don't drink much these days with having the kids.'

Despite herself, Libby felt herself warming to Natalya. She knew what she meant. Libby rarely went out these days, preferring to spend her evenings with Matthew and Patrick. The two of them had a special bond and Matthew loved spending time with her son. He was always inventing new games and spoiling him rotten with toys and treats. He was like a big kid himself sometimes.

'It's fine. Don't worry about it.'

It was hard to believe that Natalya had ever been married to Simon. Libby had read about her online. She knew she was a former model and that she and Simon had been together since the mid-90s. They had a child together – Leo – but Natalya had two younger children with her second husband, Philippe. Simon and Natalya had seemed like a golden couple at the time, totally besotted with each other, but their divorce had been acrimonious with Natalya giving candid interviews to the tabloids about how Simon's drinking and drug binges had affected her and their son. She had given him an ultimatum to get sober or to get out and he had chosen the drugs.

'Well, it was nice to meet you.'

'Wait, I'll come with you. I was going to go for a run anyway.'

Libby couldn't really refuse. Despite her age, Natalya looked fitter than her and Libby was worried she wouldn't be able to keep up, but it turned out that they were surprisingly well matched. They exchanged pleasantries about the beautiful hotel and the journey there while they ran around the perimeter of the lake. They paused to catch their breath at a gamekeeper's hut on the far side of the lake.

'So, how long have you been with Matt?'

'Eighteen months.'

'It's serious then.'

'I hope so.'

Natalya was quiet. Finally, she said: 'Listen, I know it's none of my business and you probably won't listen to me anyway, but you seem like a nice girl. Do yourself a favour and get yourself as far away from Matt as you can. He's not the man you think he is.'

Libby glared at Natalya. 'What do you mean by that?'

'He's not a nice man. None of them are. They're all screwed up. That's fame for you. God's gift to the world one minute, nobody wants to know you the next.'

'Matthew's not like Simon.'

'And you know him so well, do you?'

Libby felt her temper rising and took a deep breath to control it. How dare this woman project her own issues on to her? Just because Simon had problems, she didn't need to bring Matthew into it. Their relationship was none of her business.

'Yes, actually, I do.'

'Ask the others what he's really like. Ask Simon, if you like. I mean, he's never sober but he's not a liar. He'll tell you the truth about your precious boyfriend.'

'Listen, maybe you're trying to help, or maybe you're still drunk, but I really don't appreciate you trying to wreck my relationship.'

The other woman looked aghast. 'I wasn't! I'm trying to warn you. After what they did...'

'What are you talking about?'

'You really don't know about Alex?'

'I know that Alex died. That she took her own life.'

Natalya shook her head. 'You didn't even know her. You're just believing all that crap they put in the papers. You don't know the full story.'

'Look, I don't know what you're trying to imply but if you're trying to say Matthew had anything to do with her death...'

'Matthew had everything to do with Alex's death.

100

Honestly, this lot make me sick. They think they can get away with murder...'

Was she speaking figuratively? Or literally? Had Simon written about this in his book? No wonder Matthew was so angry. An accusation like that went beyond slander. It was completely ridiculous.

Libby felt a niggling doubt. Someone wouldn't say something like that without any evidence, would they? She thought she knew Matthew, but how well do you ever really know someone? Magazines were full of stories about the unsuspecting wives of paedophiles and murderers. Was she one of them?

No, Natalya must be lying. Matthew was one of the kindest men she had ever met. He would never hurt anyone. It was ludicrous to suggest that he was responsible for someone's death. All her family and friends liked him, even her dad, and he prided himself on being a good judge of character.

Libby heard a crunch on the path behind her. Natalya's eyes suddenly widened, and the colour drained out of her face. Libby turned to look. Was someone else there? Had they heard Natalya's accusation? The lake looked deserted, but it would be easy for someone to step into the surrounding woodland and be hidden by the trees.

'Is there someone there?' she asked but Natalya was backing away from her. 'Hey, wait, we're not done talking yet.'

But all she could see of Natalya was a flash of lilac amongst the trees as the other woman fled into the woodland.

Chapter Twenty-One

Huddersfield, 1994

Matt lay on his old single bed, in his old bedroom, staring at old posters on the wall that no longer meant anything to him. Posters of Pamela Anderson and Eva Herzigová didn't hold the same appeal now he could meet models in real life. He was counting down the days until he could return to London. They had been given a fortnight's holiday to catch up with friends and family, but the days were dragging.

He had never felt more like a stranger in his family home. He was accustomed by now to doing what he wanted, when he wanted, and he didn't appreciate the way his parents constantly admonished him for his drinking, his clothes, and his general laziness. Until now, his sister had revelled in the reflected glory of having a rock star brother, but even she was getting fed up of his demands and mood swings.

Matt was aware that he was acting like a twat but seemed powerless to control his irritation with his family. Everything about their life seemed so dull and provincial; the endless conversation about what to watch on television or whether the neighbours had put their bins out too early. He couldn't give a shit about the planning application for an extension on number 33, which was big enough already, or the ongoing situation with double parking in the street. He had watched *Emmerdale* with his mum, helped his dad in the garden, and played computer games with his little sister, but all the time a voice in his head was screaming to be released. He had tried to dampen the voice with the weed he had brought with him from London but the opportunities to partake were limited to after his parents had gone to bed and he could smoke out of the window like a schoolboy.

They had missed his eighteenth birthday. Matt had celebrated by taking the other band members out to an exclusive club where they had ordered champagne and got through a bag of coke in the toilets. They had been surrounded by gorgeous girls lining up to give the birthday boy a kiss and he had gone home with a perfect pair of Swedish twins. Now his father wanted to celebrate by taking him down to the local pub to buy him 'his first pint'. He didn't have the heart to turn him down.

'So, when's your record coming out?' the barman asked, handing over a frothy pint of bitter. Matt would have preferred vodka but that would be deemed a girl's drink in their local.

'Soon,' he said.

The truth was the label was prevaricating about a release date. The album was nearing completion and they had chosen the first single to be released but they didn't want to commit to a date until they could ensure 'optimum exposure'. There were so many bands vying for the top spot that it was going to be difficult for a debut to stand out. The album was good; they were all proud of it and there were a couple of tracks that sounded like hits, but competition was fierce and the label was risk averse. Matt secretly thought there might never be a 'right' time. He was desperate for them to get their music out there. Otherwise, what was the point?

He followed his dad to a ring-marked corner table next to a noisy slot machine. A girl in a long flowery skirt and Doc Marten boots was obsessively feeding it 50p coins. She had a streak of blonde hair down her fringe, but the rest was brown. In the old days, he might have fancied her but the last thing he wanted was to saddle himself with a home bird. Matt stared instead at the orange and brown swirly carpet that must have been there since the 70s, trying to work out if it had a pattern. He perched on a stool opposite his father and they made awkward small talk about football, but the conversation only served to illustrate how little they had in common these days.

When he had been a young boy, Matt had looked up to his father. Now he was grown-up and living his own life in London, his dad just seemed so ordinary. Had he ever harboured dreams of being rich and famous? If he had, he had never said so. No one really knew who Matt had inherited his musical talent from. The milkman, his grandfather had suggested on more than one occasion.

It wasn't long before they were getting approached by well-wishers coming to shake Matt's hand or buy him a drink, proud of the local lad done good. It was completely embarrassing. He could see his father inching his stool further and further away to make room for people as they vied for Matt's attention.

Afterwards, when his mum asked how it went, they both lied and said it was great, a chance to catch up and they were keen to do it again; but they never did.

Matt met up with some of his school friends, but they all seemed so young, slagging off their teachers and talking about exams like they were the most important thing in the world. They assumed Matt was loaded, and he didn't want to disillusion them, so he ended up buying them drinks, even though he could ill afford it. Girls who had never looked twice at him at school were suddenly all over him but that made the other lads resent him even more. In the end he called it a night, making false promises to meet up again soon, knowing that was probably the last time he would see them. He belonged to a different world now.

He stuck it out for eight days and then made an excuse to go back. His mum was upset but even she could see that he was suffocating in the town he had grown up in. As he walked from the tube station to their grotty flat, breathing in the London air – thick with traffic fumes and the scent of takeaways – he felt his shoulders lift and excitement run through his body. Away from his family and friends, from the place where he had grown up, he could be himself again.

When he reached the flat, he was surprised to find Simon in the living room, surrounded by sheets of music and paper filled with scribbled-out lyrics.

'All right?'

'All right. How was your holiday?' Simon asked.

'Yeah, you know, fine. How about you?'

'I stayed here.'

Matt raised an eyebrow but didn't ask any more questions. He clearly wasn't the only one feeling alienated from the place where he had grown up. In fact, when the others returned, they were all subdued. Only Daniel, it seemed, was oblivious to the distance they had travelled from their roots. Alex had also stayed in London. She rarely spoke about her parents. Matt knew, from her accent and the occasional references she made to her childhood, that she came from money. Her parents had sent her away to boarding school when she was eleven. She had an older brother in the RAF who she was close to, but she hadn't spoken to the rest of her family since she was sixteen.

Soon any thoughts of home were pushed to the back of Matt's mind. The band members were closer than friends, almost like a family, and they all had far more important things to focus on. The label had finally set a release date for their first single and put together an arduous promotional tour. Feedback from the focus groups had been positive and tickets to their next set of gigs were selling fast. Craig talked a lot about them 'generating buzz' which seemed to please the label executives.

They had even started to gather a fan base, including a few obsessive weirdos. One man sent Alex a padded envelope full of photographs of his dick.

'I bet he didn't get those processed at Boots,' Daniel commented, looking over her shoulder as she opened the envelope.

'Urgh, gross.' Alex said throwing the entire contents in the bin without looking at the accompanying letter. Daniel fished it out and started reading bits to her until she stormed off.

'Wait! You're missing the good part. He's offering to lick your lady parts!'

It wasn't only Alex who had their superfans. Daniel had also attracted the attention of a woman called Brenda, but she was considerably less sexually explicit in her approach. She only wanted to marry him and have his babies.

'She's old enough to be my mum!' Daniel had said in disgust when he looked at the picture that she had included. She had carefully cut out an image of Daniel from a magazine and sellotaped it onto a photograph of herself, so that they looked like a couple. Matt smiled but underneath he felt a bit jealous. It was always Daniel and Alex that got the attention. They all had their part to play in the band, but none of them wanted to feel dispensable.

The record company had high expectations for their first single. Simon fretted about it constantly. He worried that if it flopped, they wouldn't get a second chance. They had a whole album full of decent songs, but it was the debut single that counted. They were all 100% committed, driving each other to work harder, practise more, perform better. Matt had blisters on his fingers and sore arms from the hours and hours of rehearsal, but he ignored the pain and carried on. Nothing was going to stand in their way.

Chapter Twenty-Two

Libby

L ibby stood by the lakeside wondering whether to
chase after Natalya. Why had she run off like that?
Had she seen someone on the path behind them? Or was
she avoiding any more questions? Her behaviour was very
odd, and her accusations outrageous. If she really thought
that Matthew had something to do with Alex's death, then
why hadn't she gone to the police?

Libby tried to shake off the encounter as she made her
way through the walled garden and back to the hotel,
regularly turning her head to look behind her, but there was
no sign of Natalya. Matthew had called Simon's ex-wife 'a
nutcase'; perhaps she was some sort of fantasist? She
resolved to be polite if Natalya spoke to her again, but she
no longer wanted to know what she had to say about
Matthew. The woman was clearly mad. Or jealous? Maybe
she had a thing for Matthew and was trying to get Libby

out of the picture? Either way, she didn't want to deal with any more of her drama. She would ask Matthew about Alex when the time was right.

There were a few signs of activity at the hotel now. A gardener was already at work, weeding one of the flower beds which was filled with tall tulips. She said hello to him as she passed, and he grunted a reply. She could see staff in the dining area laying out silver trays full of food under the hot plates. The run and the early start had given Libby an appetite and her stomach growled at the thought of a hotel breakfast. A full English would set her up for the rest of the day. That was one of the problems with weddings; you never knew when you were going to eat.

Libby had just reached the back door of the hotel when a shot rang out, piercing the silence. She whipped her head around to see a flock of birds rising from the trees, silhouetted against the dawn sky. She stood still, anticipating another shot, but everything had gone quiet again. Her heart raced, her first thought to run back to the woodland and see what had happened, but that was madness.

She tried to calm her thoughts and think rationally. She needed to tell someone. The police. But she had left her mobile upstairs in her room. She looked back again but there was no movement from the woodland. Should she go and investigate? What if someone was hurt? No, she was only putting herself in danger. There would be a telephone in reception. She could use that to call 999.

Libby sprinted towards the front of the building, her feet sliding on the gravel and her breath catching in her throat.

The door swung open and a young man in uniform greeted her with a polite 'good morning'.

Libby blurted out what she had heard. He listened to her patiently, without looking the least alarmed, and then laughed softly. 'It'll be the gamekeeper, love. Probably chasing off a rabbit or a fox.'

Libby felt her heart rate return to normal as a hot flush crept up her face. Of course it had been the gamekeeper – who else could it have been? She was such a city girl; she had to keep reminding herself that she was in the countryside now. Guns were part of everyday life here. She should have realised.

'Oh, I'm such an idiot. I'm sorry.'

'I mean, I can get someone to double check, if you're worried.'

He was clearly being polite.

'No, don't worry. Yes, I'm sure you're right.'

She exchanged some small talk with the doorman; he had been in the job for the past four years since leaving school but was saving up to move to London. He wanted to be an actor. He was very excited that Daniel was having his wedding here and was taking his duties very seriously.

'Got to keep an eye out for the paparazzi,' he said solemnly.

Libby strongly doubted that the media would be that interested in Daniel's wedding. There had been no ban on photographs or mobile phones, which she would have expected at a celebrity wedding, and Libby assumed that Daniel would welcome the publicity if it came. It might even boost his ratings. His Instagram feed had been full of pictures of Vicky and declarations of how much he loved her in the lead-up to the wedding.

From the pictures they had posted, they looked like the perfect couple. They had both been married before and there was lots of talk about 'second chances' and finally finding the one. Vicky had a lifestyle blog full of parenting tips and organic recipes. Her children were beautifully dressed and pictured playing in the park against autumnal leaves or gazing angelically up at her as she prepared home-cooked meals.

Libby ran up the stairs to their room, thinking she might have a quick shower and then sneak back into bed with Matthew. Maybe she could persuade him to order room service and avoid any more awkward encounters over breakfast but as she opened the door, she saw he was already up, dressed, and pacing. She could see the remains of a cold cup of coffee by the bedside. He had obviously been awake for some time.

'Where have you been? I woke up and you were gone.' He sounded worried.

'Just out for a run. You were sleeping so I thought I'd let you rest. I'll grab a quick shower and we can go down.'

'I thought you might have got lost.'

'I was only down by the lake—' She stopped herself, quickly deciding against telling Matthew about her encounter with Natalya. It would only wind him up and they had had enough stress to deal with already.

'And?'

'And nothing. I heard a gunshot and jumped to all sorts of conclusions. The doorman had a right laugh about it.'

Matthew smiled. 'It was probably the gamekeeper.'

'That's what he said.' She kissed him. 'I'll be five minutes and we can go to breakfast, OK?'

The steaming hot water emanating from the rainfall shower and the luxurious toiletries made Libby want to miss the wedding and stay in the bathroom forever, but she made good on her promise to be quick. She skipped putting on make-up and drying her hair. She would do it after breakfast.

Matthew seemed unduly agitated this morning and kept walking over to the window to look outside. Was he still brooding about the argument last night? Or had he seen her talking to Natalya? The television was on, and she could see the news. Perhaps something had happened to make him more stressed than usual? She didn't really understand the financial information that accompanied the news headlines, but the stock market was a big deal to Matthew. Most of his money was tied up in investments.

As they joined the others for breakfast in the spacious dining room, Libby wished that she hadn't been so hasty getting ready. Even without any make-up, Vicky looked immaculate. She was wearing skinny jeans and a Breton top, and her hair was tied back in a loose chignon that appeared effortlessly elegant. She was sitting at a table in the centre of the room with her two children, a couple of the bridesmaids, and her mother. There was a huge platter of fruit in front of them.

She looked up, noticed them walking past, and flashed them a dazzling smile as Matthew wished them good morning. They didn't hang around to make small talk, but their table was close enough to overhear their conversation. Vicky's mother was trying to persuade her daughter to eat something.

'I don't want anything, Mum,' she snapped. 'Stop fussing. The last thing I want is to be bloated.'

They sat down and ordered coffees before heading to the buffet. Libby looked around for Natalya but, to her relief, she wasn't there. The other band members weren't at breakfast either. She knew that Amir and Peter were staying at the hotel, but perhaps they had come down earlier or ordered room service. Daniel was spending the night with his parents – they had a holiday cottage nearby – and she had no idea where Simon was staying. If he was as skint as he claimed to be, he wouldn't be able to afford a room here. Maybe he was staying at the local campsite down the road?

Libby walked along the heated counters, filling her plate with a bit of everything. It had been a long time since she'd had a decent fry-up for breakfast and there was plenty on offer. Matthew was more restrained, choosing yoghurt and fruit. He liked to watch his weight. Waitresses walked around with stainless steel flasks full of steaming tea and coffee, trays of bacon and sausages were filled and refilled, and there was a steady stream of visitors to the egg station where a harassed-looking chef was producing omelettes as fast as he could. Everyone was working at full pace and Libby had to admire their efficiency. The hotel clearly ran a tight ship.

When they returned to their table, they could hear Vicky telling the others about Daniel's hangover this morning.

'Honestly, boys!' she said, her laughter an elegant tinkle.

'They must have been up most of the night the way he sounded this morning. He'd better get to the church on time.'

Libby was surprised that Daniel had a hangover. He hadn't seemed that drunk when they left them last night. Perhaps the men had continued drinking? Libby wondered if anything had been resolved. Had they persuaded Simon not to publish his memoir after all? Had last night been a big fuss over nothing?

Chapter Twenty-Three

London, 1994

The band's debut single was released the same week the boys should have been sitting their A levels. While their former schoolmates were sweating in exam halls in Huddersfield, they were pacing around their London flat, trying to stave off their nerves. Finally, all their hard work was coming to fruition. They should have been celebrating but everyone was too nervous. Simon oscillated from ebullience to despair; Amir was more withdrawn than ever; Alex was chain smoking and suffering from insomnia; and even Daniel was a shadow of his usual chirpy self.

Matt felt a mixture of anxiety and anticipation bubbling away inside him. He told himself that it didn't matter if the single bombed, but secretly he knew how much this meant to him. He had given up everything to be a pop star and he didn't want to return to his hometown, his tail between his legs, and admit that he was a complete failure. He didn't want to go back to school, with everyone laughing at him, and resit his A levels. He didn't want to go back to living with his parents and act like an ordinary teenager again. He'd had a taste of fame and he wasn't prepared to give it all up.

But it was out of their hands now. Matt had never worked so hard on anything in his whole life. They had spent long days in the studio, analysing every riff, every line, to make it perfect. The producer had taken their sound to a new level, and the final mix was incredible. It had been a real collaboration. The artwork for the cover was stunning and suited the single perfectly. They had put their heart and soul into that track and there was a lot riding on it.

Hearing their music on the radio for the first time was the best feeling in the world. It was what they had dreamed about when they formed the band, what they had worked so hard for. Matt imagined children singing along to it on the car radio on their way to school, pictured people dancing to it at discos and clubs across the UK, even the world. His beats, finding their way into people's homes and workplaces. Into their lives. Into their history. There were some songs in life that had the power to transport you to a specific time and place as if it were only yesterday. Was their track one of them?

The label had spent a fortune on the rehearsal space, the production team, the music video, the artwork and the marketing, and they expected a return on their investment. They didn't care about the music; they were only interested in sales. If the band's first single wasn't a success, then the label might decide not to release another. They might drop the whole album. There were plenty of upcoming bands willing to take their place. Craig reminded them of this fact every time Simon stepped out of line.

They were given media training so they didn't make fools out of themselves in front of journalists and were under strict instructions about what they could and couldn't say. They were warned to be discreet about personal relationships; they had to appear to be available for the teenage girls which comprised their main audience. The label had even sent stylists around with bags of clothes to give them all a distinctive look. The cheesy photographs they had posed for started to appear in magazines and newspapers.

They attended parties and networked. They performed to industry executives and bored journalists. They did gigs no one else would touch, shook hands, kissed cheeks, and did bumps of coke in the bathroom just to keep going. They smiled when they were told to smile, played when they were told to play, acted as they were supposed to. And it had all led up to this moment. There was no going back now; their music was out there. It just needed to find its home.

On the day of the release, Matt and Alex went into HMV to look for their single. The record shop was dominated by Take That merchandise – Robbie, Gary, Mark, Jason, and Howard stared down at them from every angle like gods from Olympus. They had to hunt for a copy of their single but eventually they found it at the bottom of the 'New Releases' stand. They surreptitiously moved it upwards, so it was competing with Oasis and Blur. The picture on the front of the CD showed Alex upfront with the other band members standing behind. You could barely recognise Matt, yet it was still an alienating feeling seeing his own face staring back at him. Alex looked cool, like a young Debbie Harry. She pretended not to care about things like that, but Matt could tell she was pleased.

When they took a copy over to the cashier's desk, he expected the saleswoman to say something, but she put it through the till without a second glance. So much for their celebrity status.

'Weird, huh?' he said to Alex as they left the store, clutching copies of their own single.

'I can't believe it's actually happening!' she said, tucking her arm into his. 'We'd better enjoy this freedom while it lasts.'

'We should do something to celebrate our last day of not being famous,' he suggested.

'Like what?'

'Madame Tussauds?'

Inside the wax museum, surrounded by tourists, Matt felt far removed from the pressures of being in the band. Alex was like a giddy child, her eyes lit up and her cheeks flushed with excitement as she ran around the figures posing for pictures with her favourite celebrities. At one point, Matt reached out to hold her hand, his fingers just a few millimetres away from hers, but she pulled away.

'Look, it's Tom Cruise!'

He smiled as he dutifully took her picture next to the model of the film star. He kept a copy of that picture in the pages of a book for years to come. Later, he wished he had seized the opportunity to kiss her; it might have changed everything.

Early indications were that the single was going to do well. It had achieved a decent position in the mid-week charts, just outside the Top 40, and some positive reviews. Craig had been tight-lipped about sales, refusing to divulge numbers until they knew where they stood in the charts. Matt had overheard him shouting at someone on the phone about the lack of radio airplay. He looked tense and anxious when he came around, but then again, he always looked tense and anxious. He muttered something about last-minute sales and Matt felt reassured.

They gathered around the kitchen table waiting for Bruno Brookes to announce the Official Top 40 on Radio One. Matt knew his mum and dad would be doing the same thing back home. How many times had Matt tuned in to the programme without giving a second thought to the artists behind each song? Or the production company that had invested thousands of pounds in getting it to that point? The record sellers, the DJs, the promotional staff?

Alex paced up and down chewing her fingernails. Simon was busy working on some new lyrics and pretending not to care. Daniel and Matt took turns to swig from a bottle of Jack Daniels while Amir just sat in silence, staring at the radio, willing it to deliver the news they craved. Craig was on his phone, as usual. They listened patiently as the DJ built up to the main event. The wait was intolerable.

'And sliding down three more places, we have…' the DJ announced the single at number forty. Matt had liked that song, he respected the artistry of it, but every song went down eventually.

'And now we have a new band, hailing from the North of England…'

Matt held his breath, exchanging hopeful glances with the others, but it wasn't them. Thirty through to twenty and still no mention. Had they blown it? Had they not even made the Top 40? Matt felt sick. All that hard work, all those hours, for nothing. Craig moved away from them to make a phone call, with an inscrutable look on his face. The charts that week were dominated by big names: East 17 and Wet Wet Wet were jostling for top position, and there were plenty of other bands releasing singles in advance of the festival and summer season. Matt realised he was clutching Alex's hand, but he didn't let go.

Twenty. Nineteen. Eighteen. Seventeen. And then… the opening bars of their song. Amir on guitar and Simon on keyboards then Alex's voice, rich and deep, the sound of Matt's drums coming into the foreground increasing pace as the song took hold. Delight, bewilderment, sheer unadulterated joy passed through Matt like a bullet. They looked at each other in stunned amazement and then started jumping around, hugging, yelling. Matt didn't even hear the DJ announce their name. Their debut single had gone in at number sixteen in the charts. They had hit the big time.

Chapter Twenty-Four

Extract from Simon Greene's memoir, *Untold Story*.

The muse is a myth. Great songs aren't handed to you by some benevolent Greek goddess. You can't sit around waiting for inspiration to strike. It's about writing all the time, when you don't want to, when you'd rather be doing literally anything else. It's about putting up with the dumb shit that comes out of your head until you come up with something worth pursuing. It's writing a hundred songs and throwing them away. Then writing a hundred more. It's striking the balance between creating something fresh and exciting, and giving the industry something they can sell.

When you're starting out, there's no space for experimentation, but music, by its very nature, is primal, anarchic. The label wanted us to appeal to teenage girls and grannies, so I let them sanitise my lyrics, tame my spirit. I had to be creative to fit their expectations and not feel like a complete sell-out at the same time. I bet no one was telling Noel Gallagher or Shaun Ryder what they could or couldn't write.

When the writing flows, it's euphoric, like riding a wave. But then it dries up and there's nothing. No matter how hard you try, the well has run dry and you fear it will never come back. You fear that you are going mad. You experiment with different sounds, but it all feels derivative. You immerse yourself in other people's music, but the envy eats away at you. You take drugs to boost your creativity, but that leads to paranoia. The chorus in your head that tells you that you will never create anything worth listening to; that you got lucky with that first single. So, you take more drugs to shut up the voices and sink into that blessed numbness that makes it impossible to think, let alone create.

The drugs unlocked a secret passageway into the darkest depths of my soul, a space I couldn't reach without them, but it was a one-way ticket. That's where madness lives, waiting to consume you. You can feel its tendrils wrapping themselves around you, you can feel the inexorable pull into the darkness. You cannot resist its lure. I didn't want to visit that place, but it felt like the only way I could create anything with meaning.

Live fast, die young. That's what I thought.

The links between creativity and insanity are well documented. Writers, musicians, artists, visionaries – they all fall into its chasm. Perhaps it's a trade-off for seeing the world differently. In rehab I learned to accept these impulses, this predilection towards addiction and excess. I learned to accept the things I could not change; the pain and suffering I inflicted on those I loved the most. I learned to ask forgiveness, to be open and honest about my sins.

But, back then, I was just a messed-up kid in a messed-up industry. It was inevitable I was going to be crushed by it.

Chapter Twenty-Five

Libby

Breakfast hadn't improved Matthew's mood, so Libby suggested a walk down to the lake. The air was crisp with a hint of warmth from the sunshine which kept breaking through the clouds, casting dappled shadows on the gravelled walkway. Libby kept her eye out for any sign of the gamekeeper walking around with his shotgun, but the woodland seemed deserted, the only noise coming from rustling leaves as pheasants, resplendent with their russet feathers and stark white collars, hunted for sustenance.

They stuck to the pathway, following the same circular route she had taken with Natalya that morning. There was a cool breeze which gently kissed her face as she reached out and took Matthew's hand. He seemed distant this morning, unreachable, as if lost in his own thoughts. She wondered if he was still brooding about the argument with Simon last night. It would be a shame if it spoilt the wedding for him.

He had been looking forward to catching up with his old friends.

The lake was perfectly still, the surrounding woodland reflected in the clear water. They stood for a while by the gamekeeper's hut, watching a mallard lead her brood of ducklings out onto the lake. Matthew looked so handsome in his jeans and open-necked shirt and she realised how lucky she was. He could have any woman he wanted, but he had chosen her.

She had been seeing Matthew for eighteen months now and he had already asked her to move in with him. She knew he was looking for commitment – maybe even marriage – but she wasn't sure whether she was ready to take that step. She had found it hard to trust anyone after Ryan.

Her parents had been stricter than most; growing up, there had been no television in the house and they hadn't been allowed magazines or cosmetics as teenagers. Their home was filled with books and music, sheltered from the harsh realities of the world. But you can't keep your children protected from the world forever. Her parents had been furious when she told them about the baby. They couldn't believe their clever, academic daughter had got herself pregnant. They had pressured her to tell them who the father was, but she couldn't tell them the full story. She didn't want Ryan to have anything to do with her family. Life would have been unbearable if her sister hadn't offered her and Patrick a place to stay. She had jumped at the opportunity to leave Oxford behind and move to Leeds. Three years older than her, Emma had helped her through the challenges of parenting as she studied for her degree in journalism. It was a debt she would never be able to repay. She knew Emma loved Patrick as if he were her own son and had been heartbroken when they had finally moved into a place of their own. It was a hard-fought independence that Libby was reluctant to relinquish.

Things suddenly went dark as Matthew stepped behind her and covered her eyes.

'Shh,' he said. 'Just listen.'

All she could hear were birds twittering in the trees and the sound of Matthew's breathing.

'What am I supposed to be listening to?'

'Listen to the layers of sound.'

She stood still and obeyed his instructions. Without the benefit of sight, the sounds became more distinct, and she realised that it wasn't just birdsong she could hear, but different types of birdsong. Some pleasant, some repetitive and coarse. She could hear the leaves rustling in the breeze and in the distance, cars driving along the country road.

'It's all music,' Matthew said, removing his hands. 'I'm thinking of experimenting with it actually. Creating music that imitates nature in all its beautiful chaos.'

Libby privately thought that sounded a bit pretentious but didn't want to break his bubble. Matthew hadn't talked about music for ages. It would be nice for him to pursue his interests again.

She heard a loud noise behind them and turned around, peering into the dark woodland. A figure emerged about ten metres away from them. He was stripped to the waist, carrying a duffel bag over one shoulder. She saw him bend over and wash his torso, arms and face in the lake. His back was covered with fading tattoos. With a shock of recognition, she realised it was Simon. She looked away, embarrassed, as if she had been spying on him. What was he doing there? Had he been sleeping in the woodland? Had things really got that bad?

Matthew hadn't spotted him, so she steered him in the opposite direction. The last thing Libby needed was another altercation. She glanced over her shoulder and caught Simon's gaze. He was standing up now, his chest glistening in the sunlight, watching them retreat. Matthew didn't seem to notice her consternation as he started talking about his ideas for composing. She tried to concentrate but her mind was buzzing with what she had seen. Simon had come all the way over from Los Angeles to attend this wedding but couldn't afford to stay in a hotel. Had Daniel paid for his ticket?

By the time they reached the hotel, a small army of women was bustling in and out of the marquee. The wedding planner, a tiny woman with silver hair streaked with purple, was issuing orders like a football manager on the stands, as an enormous and elaborately decorated cake was carefully removed from the back of a baker's van and carried in. Libby spotted Vicky's mother overseeing the final touches to the table decorations. There had obviously been no expense spared for the wedding, and she felt even more strongly the contrast between Daniel and Simon's situations. Of the two of them, Simon should have been the more successful. He had built a career from his songwriting after the band split up. How could he have gone from being rich and famous to sleeping in the woods?

More guests were checking in as they walked through the reception. It was going to be a big wedding, maybe 200 guests altogether, although some people were only attending the night do and not everyone was staying at the hotel. Libby guessed the B&Bs dotted around the local area would be benefitting from the extra trade. She scanned the room to see if she could spot anyone famous. She thought she recognised a newsreader from Channel Four and a woman who looked the spitting image of Davina McCall until she turned around. She tried to engage Matthew with a bit of celebrity hunting, but he wasn't interested. He had got over the thrill of showbusiness a long time ago.

As they entered the hallway, they could hear a commotion coming from the top of the staircase.

'Well, where the hell is she?' a sharp voice shrieked.

Daniel's sister, Olivia, came running down the steps, her hair still up in rollers. 'Have either of you seen Natalya?' she asked.

Libby hesitated. She hadn't planned on telling Matthew about her conversation with Natalya this morning.

'Not since last night,' Matthew answered before she could.

'Vicky's going ballistic. She hasn't turned up for hair and make-up and no one can reach her on her mobile.'

She had to tell someone. What if something had happened to Natalya in the woodland? Her mind went back to the gunshot this morning. Had she been too quick to accept the doorman's explanation? What if Natalya had been hurt?

'I saw her this morning by the lake,' she admitted. 'But that was hours ago.'

Matthew gave her a sharp look.

'I'm sure she'll turn up,' he said. 'She's probably gone for a walk or something.' He didn't sound remotely interested in the drama that was unfolding upstairs.

'Have you tried her room?' Libby suggested. It sounded like an obvious question, but she had learned that was always a good place to start.

'Yes, but there's no answer.'

'Maybe the housekeeper will let you in? Then you can at least see if her stuff is still there.'

Olivia checked her watch. 'Good idea, thanks. I'll just quickly check the dining room. Maybe she's gone down for a late breakfast or something.'

Libby and Matthew exchanged glances as she hurried away.

'You didn't tell me you saw Natalya this morning,' he said.

'Oh, it was nothing. I saw her when I went for my run.'

'Did she say anything to you?'

'No,' Libby lied. 'She was doing yoga, so I left her in peace. It's just…'

'What?'

'The gunshot.'

'You think someone shot her?' Matthew looked incredulous.

'No, of course not. Not on purpose. But, maybe there's been an accident?'

Matthew pressed the button for the lift. 'Natalya's a drama queen. She's probably being deliberately late to get attention.'

'Maybe you're right. Do you think I should maybe tell the receptionist anyway? Ask someone to check the woodland?'

The lift door opened, and a couple of other guests walked out. Matthew checked his watch. 'We need to get ready. Leave them to it. I'm sure Natalya is absolutely fine.'

Libby followed him into the elevator. Matthew was right. She was letting her imagination run away with her. Of course nothing had happened to Natalya. She glanced down at her phone. The hotel's Wi-Fi kicked in and the screen was filling up with notifications. She took a quick glance at them. They were mostly unimportant, but she noticed nestled among them a WhatsApp message from Aiden.

Your story's gone national.

This was exciting. The nationals often scouted local newspapers for stories, and it was quite a coup for them to get picked up. She had checked the story on the website this morning and, against her better judgement, had read some of the comments underneath. Several defending the businessman, saying his victims had been 'asking for it' and that they shouldn't have put themselves in that position. Libby had warned her interviewee that this would happen, but the cruelty of the remarks still shocked her. The woman had insisted that she wanted the truth out there, no matter the consequences.

That's great!

She messaged back with a thumbs up emoji as they got out of the lift and made their way down the corridor.

You'll be getting headhunted next.

She replied:

Ha! Doubt it. Happy where I am thanks.

Good. I wouldn't want to lose you.

She felt her cheeks redden. Was he flirting with her? She was just deciding how to respond when another message pinged.

How's the wedding anyway? Spotted any celebrities?

Not yet. Will keep you posted.

Her finger hovered over the X button. She always signed off her messages to friends with a kiss; but Aiden was her boss, and she didn't want to be inappropriate. She settled for a smiley emoji instead.

'Who was that?' Matthew said as he opened their bedroom door.

A wave of guilt washed over her.

'Just work.'

'Can't they leave you alone for one weekend?' he grumbled.

Libby put the phone away, trying not to resent the fact that Matthew still hadn't congratulated her on her first front-page.

Chapter Twenty-Six

Libby

Saturday afternoon

Libby had borrowed a dress from her sister for the wedding. It wasn't a style she would have chosen for herself, but she had to admit that the blue halter-neck looked good on her. Emma had great taste in clothes and always kept them immaculate, unlike Libby who felt most comfortable in her jeans and a hoodie. Her shoulders felt exposed, so she teamed it up with the cream pashmina that her sister had lent her. The soft material smelt of the fabric conditioner she used.

Staring at herself in the mirror, trying to flatten her stomach, brought back memories of her pregnancy. At first, she had tried to hide her bump under big jumpers but, after five months, just as she turned eighteen, it became blatantly obvious. She remembered sitting her A levels with the baby squirming and pressing on her bladder. The teachers had been kind; the other kids less so. She was the one they whispered about in the toilets, the one they called a slut. Like she had got pregnant all by herself. She remembered the look of horror on Ryan's face when he saw her waiting outside the hall for A level English, the sneaking glances he gave her during the exam, the way he had almost run out of the room when the invigilator called time. He needn't have worried; she had no intention of talking to him.

Then came the terror of the birth, gripping Emma's hand, barely able to grasp the concept of breathing; the mixture of elation and exhaustion that came afterwards; and holding Patrick in her arms, his big eyes staring up at her. So tiny, so vulnerable. Worth all the judgement and the sneers. Worth all the pain.

'You look beautiful,' Matthew stepped behind her and kissed Libby's neck. She turned around and kissed him back. He responded hungrily, looking like he was going to lead her back to the bed but checked his watch.

'We'd better get going. I want to make sure we get a decent car parking space. You know what these things are like.'

She knew what Matthew was like. Libby picked her bag up. 'Ready.'

'You mean we're not going to be half an hour late?' he teased. 'Who are you, and what have you done with my girlfriend?'

Other guests were mingling now in the reception area, drinking coffee by the fire, and reading the papers. Simon, dressed in a crumpled suit, was standing in the corner of the room scowling. Some of the guests turned to stare at them as they pushed their way through, no doubt recognising Matthew. He nodded to a few people but didn't stick around for any conversation. If he saw Simon, he didn't acknowledge him.

They reached the car park and Libby could immediately tell that something was wrong. People were standing around shouting and waving their hands around. As they got closer, they could see the problem. The tyres had been slashed on several vehicles, including Matthew's, and red paint had been thrown over the bridal car.

'What the hell?' Matthew kneeled on the ground to examine the damage to his own car. The tyres were completely deflated. Libby looked around and saw at least five other cars in the same state, one of them she recognised as Amir's.

'It must have been kids,' she said.

'Kids, out here?'

It was hardly inner-city Leeds. The nearest village was several miles away, but what other possible explanation could there be? It certainly looked like it had been a deliberate attack on the wedding party.

'I'll let the hotel know. They can book some taxis.'

Other guests were arriving now, reaching their cars and finding them in the same state. Libby walked in the opposite direction to the hotel reception where she located the manager and told him what had happened. He switched instantly into crisis management mode, uttering profuse apologies and ordering the receptionist to get on the phone to the local minicab company.

'We will report this to the police, madam, don't worry.'

'Thank you.'

'Nothing like this has ever happened before, I can assure you. We have very good security.'

Libby thought about their walk back to the hotel last night. There had been someone on the gate when they got back. He had nodded them through, but would he have stopped them if he hadn't recognised them from earlier and asked to see their guest pass? How had Simon managed to camp in the woods if there was extra security? Nothing was infallible.

'You think it was one of the guests?'

'I couldn't say. Please don't let it spoil your day. We have good CCTV in the car park.'

They were interrupted by the gamekeeper, asking for the manager's attention. He took him to one side and spoke to him quietly, but the staff member was agitated, and she overheard him talking about a gun cabinet.

'I'll report it,' she heard the manager say.

It seemed like this was the manager's answer to everything. She left them to it, trying to make sense of what had happened. Had someone slashed the tyres deliberately? And if so, why? Was someone trying to stop the wedding?

Chapter Twenty-Seven

London, 1994

Their debut single climbed to number seven, a phenomenal achievement for a new band, before eventually falling back down the charts again. Suddenly, they were the hottest property in the city. They were invited to film premieres and after-shows, asked to perform at glamorous events, and besieged with offers of advertising and sponsorship deals. Everywhere they went, they were met with screaming girls and their pissed-off boyfriends.

Having a Top 10 single meant they got to appear on *Top of the Pops*, the holy grail of pop music. Matt had grown up watching the show but never in his wildest dreams did he think that he would be asked to perform on it one day. Elstree studio was awash with celebrities and TV stars and they were like over-excited kids in a sweet shop.

'Do you think it would be completely uncool to ask for his autograph?' Alex mused as Robbie Williams walked past. He looked over at her and winked. She flushed like a schoolgirl.

The stage was small; there was barely enough room for the five of them, let alone the dancers. This was one of the most important performances of their lives and they were all petrified they would screw up. Alex's hands were shaking as she adjusted her mic and she stumbled in her high platform heels as she walked on. Fortunately, they didn't broadcast that. Matt was pleased he was sitting at the back, his floppy hair providing a screen from the glare of the bright lights and the scrutiny of the cameras. They had chosen to perform live for the show, but Matt was already regretting that decision. He had been drinking steadily all day trying to stave off his nerves. They were surrounded by the audience on three sides and the fans were reaching out to try to touch them as they played. Their performance lasted just over three minutes but felt like seconds. Afterwards, Matt wished that he had been sober enough to recall it properly. His mum and dad sent him a VHS cassette which he watched over and over again until the tape broke.

Their lives were transformed overnight. They were no longer a struggling support act, desperate for attention, but a bona fide pop group with a Top 10 single. They actually started turning down offers to perform now and were assigned their own publicist. The record company booked them for festivals the length and breadth of the UK and they even managed to get a coveted slot at Leeds and Reading. They were interviewed by *Smash Hits* and Daniel was voted 'Hottest Hunk of the Week' by one of the teen magazines. Matt forgot what it was like to pay for his own drinks. He was being sucked into a whirlwind; a chaotic, crazy, exciting new world that kept threatening to overwhelm him.

The only thing that kept him grounded was his friendship with Alex, although he knew his feelings for her were not entirely platonic. Craig had made his opinions very clear about relationships between band members.

'Things just get messy,' he had told them in no uncertain terms. Matt felt like the comments had been directed at him and hadn't dared look at the others.

There wasn't any time for relationships outside of the band. There was barely any time for making music, but no-one seemed to care about that apart from Simon. The label was delighted by their early success, sending over a case of champagne and even mooting the possibility of appearing at the Brits. The money was rolling in, and everyone was buzzing.

Daniel was the first to strip off for the camera, promoting a famous brand of boxer shorts. It was unnerving to see their friend six storeys high, staring down on the streets of London. Matt had never been particularly shy about his body but realised he could do with buffing up if he wanted the same opportunities, so he gave up smoking and hit the gym. Alex was already a member, using the exercise to manage her anxiety, but to Craig's chagrin, she refused all modelling contracts and had no interest in appearing on billboards or on the covers of glossy magazines.

'They airbrush all the pictures anyway,' she said scornfully.

Living their life in the public eye was hardest on Alex. Her refusal to engage with publicity gave her a reputation in the media for being standoffish and she quickly made enemies. Her outfits were ridiculed by the tabloids and the gossip magazines, and rumours circulated about her sex life and her eating habits. Barely a week went by without one of them calling her anorexic, bulimic, or conversely, in need of a diet.

She was more sensitive to criticism than the others, and got more flack, as the lead singer and a woman. She read comments about her weight and her appearance and became increasingly depressed. She received letters telling her that she was fat and ugly and that she should kill herself.

'I never wanted to be famous,' she sobbed. 'I just want to make music. Why can't they leave me alone?'

'They're jealous,' Matt told her, giving her a cuddle. 'They want what you have.'

Alex looked around their tiny flat, the clothes and pizza boxes strewn around the floor, the candles stuck in empty vodka bottles lined up on the windowsill and laughed. 'They're welcome to it.'

'Tomorrow's fish and chip wrapping,' he said, folding up the tabloid that she had been reading and putting it in the bin. 'It'll die down soon.'

Matt couldn't have been more wrong.

Chapter Twenty-Eight

Libby

The hotel manager was true to his word and fifteen minutes later a suite of taxis arrived to take the guests to the church. He also promised to get a local garage out to assess the damage to the cars and replace the slashed tyres before they drove home the next day. Libby couldn't imagine how much all that would cost. Some of the cars were worth more than three times her annual salary.

The ceremony was being held in the same picture-postcard village where they had eaten the night before. In the daylight everything looked different. Libby climbed out of the taxi and found herself looking up at a quintessential village church with crumbling gravestones to the front. The walls around the church were covered with bright-purple rock cress and creeping phlox. A pathway of stone flags led up to a large oak door and the bells were ringing as guests arrived and greeted each other. A huge clock on the church tower declared it was twenty to two. A photographer took their picture as she and Matthew walked up the main steps.

Libby didn't go to church very often. Her parents were not religious, and she had never been encouraged to go, even as a small child. She wondered whether it had been Vicky or Daniel that had wanted a church wedding and, cynically, whether it was because it would make a pretty backdrop for their pictures.

Peter and Amir emerged from a taxi. She waved at Peter who walked over to join them. Matthew rolled his eyes at Libby.

'Afternoon,' Peter seemed cheerful. He was wearing a navy suit with an incongruous Donald Duck tie and matching socks. He had made some effort to tame his hair, but it was quickly bouncing back to its natural state. 'Nice day for it.'

Matthew murmured in agreement. Amir kept his distance, talking into a mobile phone. He looked over and nodded a greeting.

'He's trying to get a specialist out to look at his car,' Peter explained. 'Doesn't think the local guy will do a proper job. What, with the scratches yesterday and the tyres this morning, he thinks someone's got it in for us.'

'Our car was damaged too,' Libby said quickly, but they weren't listening to her. They were looking over her shoulder to the entrance of the church where a middle-aged woman was being dragged away by two burly men in suits.

'Get your hands off me!' The woman screamed.

'What the hell?' Libby asked as the trio walked past them and delivered the woman to a waiting police car.

Matthew started laughing. 'Oh my God. It's Mad Brenda!'

'Who?'

'Have I never told you about Daniel's stalker? She's been with us since the early days. She's obsessed with him. I bet it was her that slashed the cars.'

Did fans really do things like that? She guessed Matthew knew better than most. People only saw the good stuff about being a celebrity: the money, the adulation, the flashy lifestyle. They didn't see the more sinister aspects: the invasion into their privacy, the trolling, the obsessive fans. She'd hate to live her life always looking over her shoulder, never being able to completely relax.

Amir joined them, looking a bit happier. He shook Matthew's hand and kissed Libby on the cheek. 'Sorry about that.'

'Sorted?' Peter asked.

'Got it booked in for Monday. And it's covered by the insurance.'

'Excellent, well you can relax now. Matthew thinks Daniel's stalker might be behind it. You've just missed all the drama.'

'What? Mad Brenda? Is she still on the scene?'

'Apparently.'

'God, I thought she would have given up by now. She must be in her sixties! Still, it doesn't explain the scratches, does it? Unless she was following us on the motorway as well.'

Libby changed the subject quickly. 'It looks like people are moving in. Shall we?'

Inside the church, sunlight poured through the windows, but it made little difference to the temperature – the unforgiving stone kept the interior like a fridge. A group of children was racing up and down the aisle, threatening to trip over some of the more elderly members of the congregation who were being helped to their seats by the groomsmen.

They found a pew towards the back. Libby looked around the church, trying to identify the principal wedding guests. You could see a distinct difference between family members and friends. The latter, male and female, looked well-groomed and coiffed, as if they had stepped out of *Made in Chelsea*. Most of the women over forty had clearly had Botox and most of the men were flashing dazzling white teeth. Libby couldn't imagine spending so much money, not to mention time, on her appearance. There were a couple of minor celebrities that she recognised and a supermodel in a stunning red dress standing next to a man old enough to be her grandfather. They couldn't be together, surely? Then she noticed he had his hand protectively around her waist, as if he were afraid someone would steal her if he let her go and concluded they could.

The family members, on the other hand, were an eclectic mix. Vicky's family were from Bristol and their accents mixed in with Daniel's native Yorkshire. Daniel's mother and Vicky's aunty had worn the same dress and were trying to make light of the fact, posing together for pictures. Libby noted a sense of glee among the other female guests who had not made the same faux pas.

It was quite chilly in the church and Libby shifted in her

seat, trying to keep warm. She was only wearing her pashmina and wished she had brought a jacket. Peter was reading through the order of service while Amir was tapping into his phone with a concerned look on his face.

Daniel was standing at the altar with his best man, talking to the vicar. He looked handsome in a grey suit with a pale-pink waistcoat that matched the flower arrangements at the front of the church. Libby suspected that he had had little say in his outfit. His face looked relaxed but his clenched fist and tapping feet told another story. He kept glancing around to the back of the room, smiling at the guests.

The church filled up and the clock struck two with no sign of the bridal party. You could see people looking around expectantly, but it was customary for the bride to be a few minutes late. The vicar went through a few housekeeping rules and Libby noticed a mother feeding sweets to an impatient toddler to keep him quiet. It got to twenty past two and Libby could feel the tension rise in the church. Had something happened to Vicky? Then one of the groomsmen, who had been stationed at the door, walked down the aisle and spoke quietly in Daniel's ear.

There were lots of whispers around the church as people checked their mobiles and shook their heads in answer to unvoiced questions. Some of the guests looked worried but most of them were enjoying the drama. Had the bride got cold feet? Had the wedding been cancelled? Had Brenda struck again? Libby tried to read Daniel's face, but he was a good showman and was hiding his feelings. Vicky's mother, on the other hand, looked furious.

Libby stretched forward to try to overhear the conversation in front of her. A woman with heavily lacquered hair and overpowering perfume noticed her eavesdropping and leaned backwards.

'One of the bridesmaids has gone AWOL,' she said in a loud stage whisper. 'Didn't turn up for hair and make-up.'

Libby rested back in her seat with a sinking heart. She had an uncomfortable feeling that the missing bridesmaid was Natalya. Maybe the gamekeeper had accidentally shot her in the woods? What if she was lying there injured and Libby was the only one who knew where she was? She should have insisted on talking to the hotel manager. She glanced behind her; should she sneak out now and ring the hotel?

'What's going on?' Matthew whispered.

She repeated what she had heard to Matthew. 'Do you think I should say something?'

'Like what?'

'About the gunshot I heard.'

'I'm sure that's got nothing to do with it. She's probably gone back to bed. She was pretty pissed last night,' Matthew said.

'True.' But she hadn't seemed hungover this morning. And hadn't Olivia said they were going to ask the housekeeper to check her room? As soon as she got back to the hotel, she would tell someone what she suspected. She just had to hope she wasn't too late.

Chapter Twenty-Nine

EXTRACT FROM SIMON GREENE'S MEMOIR, *UNTOLD STORY*.

I never thought I would fall in love. It wasn't something I wanted in my life. I thought love would get in the way of my music. None of the girls I slept with meant anything to me. Sex was just a way of releasing energy, a biological drive, an itch I needed to scratch. But everything changed when I met Natalya. Some people don't believe in love at first sight, but I was smitten from the moment she stepped into the room. She was stunning, there was no question about that. But she was also funny, vibrant, pragmatic. She understood me in ways that no one ever had or ever will. I believed, still believe, we were soulmates, destined to meet, destined to fail.

She deserved so much better than me.

I never cheated on her, but I was never there for her. She put up with my bouts of misery, my temper, my excesses, my paranoia. She listened when I wanted to talk, kept quiet when she should have spoken. She was my rock. The only reason I kept going.

I wasn't a good husband. I only asked Natalya to marry me so that I could keep her. I hadn't considered the extra pressure of sharing a home, having a child, having to compromise. I hated her spending time with her friends, suspicious when she wasn't at home when I called. I went through her phone expecting to find evidence that she was leaving me.

They say when you have kids your whole perspective changes and I wish I could say that I cleaned up my act, that I pledged to be a good husband and father. If I did, it was bullshit. The night Natalya told me she was pregnant with Leo, I went out and got wasted. Celebrating. Wetting the baby's head. Except it wasn't like that. Not really. I was drinking, smiling, saying the right things but I was really running away, seeking oblivion, trying to drown out the thoughts that I was going to be a dad. That there was no going back.

I couldn't be a father; I could barely look after myself. By the time Leo was born, the band had already split, and I didn't think I would ever work again. I was a screwed-up, tormented, waste of space. I was full of self-pity and bitter rage. I knew that I could never be the man that Natalya or my son deserved. She should have left me there and then.

Natalya was in it for the long haul. We meant every word of our marriage vows but in the end, she had to go. I was destroying her. Leo was frightened of me, I could see it in his face. She said she would never leave me, but I gave her no choice.

I'm glad she remarried. Her husband, Philippe, is a decent guy. He treats Leo like his own. My son looks up to him in a way he can't look up to me. He's a better father to my son than I could ever be.

But he doesn't love Natalya like I did. No one could.

Chapter Thirty

Libby

The clock struck half past two. All around her, Libby could hear people gossiping about what was causing the delay. Once or twice, she heard the word *jilted* and she wondered if that was also going through Daniel's mind. She had never been to a wedding before that hadn't gone ahead. What happened under those circumstances? Would they continue with the party as planned or send the guests home? All that time and money wasted.

Finally, the vicar nodded to one of the groomsmen standing by the church door and the organist started to play. Everyone got to their feet, pointed their phones and cameras towards the huge oak door and waited for Vicky to make her appearance. All eyes should have been on the bride, but Libby didn't think she was the only one holding her breath to see if Natalya was among the entourage.

A little flower girl came in first, scattering rose petals along the carpet and drawing the attention of the congregation. She was blonde and cute, wearing a little white dress and cardigan and matching T-bar shoes. She was doing very well until halfway down the aisle she spotted her mother and ran towards her. Her mother gave her a hug and lifted her on her knee with an apologetic glance at the bride's mother. Next came Vicky's kids, the older boy scowling as he held his little sister's hand.

Vicky looked stunning in an elegant silk dress with a long train. Her hair hung loose, glossy and shiny, and her eyes sparkled with happiness. She was carrying a bouquet of pink roses. Daniel looked like he had just won the lottery. Vicky's father accompanied the bride down the aisle, and gave her a look of such tenderness that Libby felt herself welling up.

Behind Vicky came the bridesmaids. Four when there should have been five. She saw some of the guests exchange glances, eyebrows raised. The remaining bridesmaids looked around the congregation for their missing friend. Libby felt a surge of anxiety. Natalya was hardly likely to miss her friend's wedding without good reason. Something must have happened.

The vicar indicated for everyone to sit and began the service. Libby tried to concentrate on the words, but her mind was whirring. From what everyone had told her, Natalya had an appetite for drama. Perhaps she was staying away deliberately, making a scene in order to steal Vicky's thunder? Or perhaps there had been an emergency at home, and Natalya had left the wedding without telling anyone? Perhaps her mobile had run out of battery and she hadn't had a chance to call? That seemed a much more likely explanation.

The vicar reached the point in the ceremony when he asked if anyone knew of any lawful impediments to the marriage. Having read *Jane Eyre* at school, Libby half expected to see the doors burst open at this point and someone rush in to stop the wedding, but there was no such drama today. The vicar paused and then moved on. The couple exchanged their vows and Daniel kissed the bride to the applause of the congregation. They disappeared to the back of the church to sign the register and Libby used the opportunity to check her mobile phone.

Natalya's Instagram account hadn't been updated since last night when she had posted a picture of Vicky and her bridesmaids with glasses of Prosecco. It was from the start of the night and they were all looking sober and gorgeous. There had been no updates later that evening or this morning. Still, that wasn't particularly unusual. She checked Natalya's Facebook page, but it was locked down and she couldn't access it without being accepted as her friend. There were a few updates from wedding guests on Vicky's page, mostly pictures of people getting ready or travelling to the ceremony, but nothing about or from Natalya.

The organ began to play, and Vicky and Daniel emerged from the back room and walked back down the aisle. Libby followed everyone out of the church, blinking at the bright sunshine, a sharp contrast to the dark interior. She was pushed into the background as everyone gathered around the bride and groom to congratulate them and throw confetti. An older man asked her if she was 'Mary's daughter' but lost interest when he found out she wasn't. She could hear people speculating about Natalya's disappearance and wondered how Vicky felt about her friend stealing all the attention on her wedding day.

The gunshot was still niggling at the back of her mind. It had been hours now since she had left Natalya by the lakeside. If she had been shot, she could be lying there injured – she could even be dead. She had to tell someone. Quickly she searched for the number and rang Harrington Hall, asking to be put through to the manager. He sounded harassed and distracted as she outlined her fears.

'I really hope you are not insinuating that a member of my staff has shot a guest?' The manager said.

'No, of course not. I'm just worried about her, is all. She missed her best friend's wedding.'

'I checked Ms Bisset's room personally, madam, and there was nothing to indicate that she had not left of her own accord,' he reassured her. 'She may not have formally checked out, but she wouldn't be the first guest to leave the premises without doing so. I'm sure she had her reasons for missing the wedding.'

'Is her car still there?'

'I believe Ms Bisset came by train.'

'But I definitely heard a gunshot this morning. Please could you ask someone to check the woodland?'

'As you wish.' He rang off.

Libby felt a bit better. If Natalya had been injured, surely all her stuff would still be in her room. It did seem a more likely explanation that she'd left in a hurry and forgotten to check out. Obviously no one had shot her; the idea was ludicrous.

Chapter Thirty-One

London, 1995

The band couldn't put a foot wrong. Their next single also charted high, narrowly missing out on the number one slot. They started to be recognised in the street and they couldn't go anywhere without their pictures appearing in the tabloids the next day. Everyone wanted a piece of them. They got to stay in better hotels now they were getting famous, and Matt would often look out of the window and see the paparazzi hanging around outside the entrance, hoping to catch a picture of them coming in from a night out stumbling around drunk or high. Daniel courted the publicity, making sure he was always pictured with the latest It-girl hanging on his arm like an accessory, but Matt found it a nuisance.

The press even camped outside his parents' house one night, to the amusement of his mother, who brought them out cups of tea on a tray.

'I think they thought I was going to invite them in and show them your baby pictures,' she laughed over the phone.

Despite the complete lack of privacy, some of the publicity was fun. They got tonnes of free gear and most of the journalists that came to interview them were not much older than them, and up for a party. Daniel often slept with them.

'Give them something to write about,' he bragged.

It was a relief to escape London and go on tour but that meant sharing a compact sleeper bus and living and working together in such close proximity caused tempers to flare. The arguments usually erupted between Simon and Daniel. Daniel hated sharing the limelight with Alex. He accused Simon of writing songs that played up to her talents and pushed him aside. He liked to dominate the stage and would often get in Alex's way when she was performing. He threatened to leave the band on a weekly basis and dropped hints about going solo or having better offers. Amir never got involved with any of the arguments. He was the quietest of the group and tolerated the fame without enjoying it.

They were all drinking heavily and popping pills like sweets. Simon was barely sober and constantly jittery. He said he needed drugs to write, he needed them to perform, and he needed them to come down. He needed them full stop. He had graduated from the weed and Es that everyone was taking to the harder stuff, including heroin, and it was rapidly becoming a problem. Once or twice,

Craig threatened to send him to a rehab facility if he didn't sort himself out.

One night, in Newcastle, they couldn't find him anywhere and had to go on stage without him. They muddled through, but Craig was furious. Simon turned up twenty-four hours later without an apology, simply shrugging his shoulders when the manager railed at him. Then he handed over a song which, to this day, was their most successful hit.

In February they shot a music video at a disused warehouse somewhere in the Midlands. It was snowing outside, and the temperature was hovering around zero, but no one seemed to care that Alex was freezing her tits off in a tiny metallic dress that barely covered her knickers. They had painted her mouth pillar-box red and she was convinced that she looked like a slut. Matt thought she looked stunning. Daniel caught Matt looking at her and winked. Matt hadn't told Daniel how he felt about Alex, but he was pretty sure his best friend knew.

The director was making them shoot the same scene over and over again, and Alex was virtually in tears.

'We've been doing this for hours,' she said. 'Can't I just take a break?' The director ignored her. 'This outfit is ridiculous. I'm a singer, not a doll.'

Craig looked at her like she was a complete idiot.

'Talent's ten a penny, love. You've got to be the complete package these days if you want to get anywhere. You want to get to number one, don't you?'

He then listed the many female singers he worked with that would be happy to appear on camera naked if he asked them to. Matt kept quiet throughout their exchange, but he was desperate to step in. Alex had been having a rough time of it recently; there was constant pressure on her to look and behave a certain way and she was close to cracking. Craig had no time for her complaints and was losing patience with her.

It was much easier for the men. They could get away with wearing baggy jeans and T-shirts and combing some gel through their hair occasionally, but Craig wanted Alex to wear as little as possible on stage: tiny bikinis with hot pants, sheer crop tops and tight Lycra dresses. Alex compromised as much as she could, but she still felt uncomfortable with some of the outfits they put her in and was happiest when she came off stage and could get back into her baggy jeans. In a heated exchange at Christmas, Craig had told her to lose weight even though she was barely a size 10. Once or twice, she threatened to quit the band, but music was her whole life. She didn't want to do anything else.

The director was now positioning Alex around a metal pole that he wanted her to gyrate against and his hands were roaming freely all over her arse. Matt caught Alex's eye and could sense her humiliation and anger. Any minute now she was going to burst into tears or punch the director.

'Hey, man. That's not cool,' he shouted over.

'What's your problem?'

'Treat her with some respect, will ya?'

The director dropped his hands and held them up in mock surrender. 'Bunch of fucking amateurs,' he muttered under his breath.

Still, the intervention had the done the trick and the director made a big show of not touching her for the rest of the day.

No one said much in the minivan on the way home; they were all too knackered. They had spent all day filming that scene and it would probably end up getting cut in the final edit anyway. The director was some hotshot from New York; Craig said they had been lucky to secure him, but that didn't give him a licence to paw Alex like a piece of meat. Matt was worried about her. One day they would push her too far. Amir and Simon seemed oblivious to what had happened on set, but Matt could see that Daniel was still fuming. He thought Alex acted like a diva about this sort of stuff.

Back home, they ordered Chinese food, and Matt poured Alex a large glass of wine. They could afford the good stuff now. They were alone – Amir and Daniel had gone out, and Simon was in his room with Natalya.

'You didn't have to make a scene,' Alex said.

'I didn't.'

'He won't want to work with us now.'

'Then we're better off without him. He's a perv.'

'Thank you, Matt. But next time let me fight my own battles. I can handle the likes of him.'

'I know you can, but you shouldn't have to.'

She leaned over and kissed his cheek. 'It's just the way it is.'

Matt could feel the kiss burning his cheek. It had been a friendly kiss, nothing more, but he wished that he had the courage to turn it into something else. He didn't want her to think that he was like that director, only interested in her body. He had feelings for her that ran far deeper than that; he was falling in love with her. He had tried to assuage his feelings with other women, but it wasn't working. All he could think about was Alex. The frustration of not telling her how he felt was starting to get to him. He thought she might feel something in return, but they had never discussed it.

They settled down to watch a video – an old horror film, one of those B-movies with terrible special effects and lots of screaming blondes. Alex, for some unfathomable reason, loved them.

When they first heard the scream coming from the bedroom, they thought it was part of the film. Then Alex reached over, paused the video, and they listened again.

'That's Nat.'

They were getting up to investigate when Natalya flew into the room. 'Call an ambulance!'

'What's happened?' Alex asked as Matt dialled 999.

'It's Simon, he's— Oh my God, he's…'

They followed her into the room to find Simon spreadeagled on the bed, unconscious. There was a strap around his arm and a syringe beside his hand. Natalya was hysterical as Matt spoke to the emergency services. He walked up to Simon and touched his face. His skin was cold, and his lips were blue, but he was still breathing.

'Help me get him into the recovery position,' he told her, following the instructions from the call operator who had already dispatched an ambulance.

Matt stuck his fingers in Simon's mouth to check his

airway wasn't blocked and opened his eyelids to see if he could get his reaction. Alex checked his pulse and nodded. He scanned the room, considering hiding the drug paraphernalia, but the paramedics would need to know what he had taken. They would have to risk it.

'I'm going to ring Craig,' Alex said. Matt nodded. An incident like this needed 'managing' whether it hit the press or not.

The paramedics arrived while she was speaking to him and hooked Simon up to breathing apparatus. Natalya went with Simon to the hospital while Alex and Matt stood at the window watching the ambulance disappear into the night.

'I can't believe it. What if he dies?' she said in horror.

Until that point, Matt had only been thinking of the impact Simon's overdose might have on the reputation of the band and felt ashamed of himself. It had never crossed his mind that his friend wouldn't survive.

'He'll be OK,' he promised, with a certainty he didn't feel.

Chapter Thirty-Two

EXTRACT FROM SIMON GREENE'S MEMOIR, *UNTOLD STORY*.

You would think that nearly dying would be the tipping point, wouldn't you? That it would make you get your shit together. But addiction doesn't work like that. You make excuses, you blame other people, you tell yourself that everyone is over-reacting; you can give up at any time.

The truth is you don't want to. It's too bloody hard and the thought of going through life sober is terrifying. Drugs are the only thing that make you feel normal. You're not convinced you can live without them. You tell yourself you're still young, there's plenty of time.

The truth is I was weak.

The truth is I was irresponsible.

The truth is I deserved to lose Natalya and my son.

And the truth is that heroin made me the person I am today.

If you want to hear the truth, ask someone in recovery. Take away heroin and you face your darkest demons. Rehab strips away every layer of self-delusion and deceit, every white lie, every little secret. You have to peel back every ugly layer of your façade and find the real you. You never know how strong you are until you have faced up to the reality of yourself.

Rehab was my wake-up call. This was my life, my one opportunity to make amends for all the hurt I caused, and I was wasting it. When did I lose sight of that? When did injecting my veins with poison become more important than my family, my life, my music? I had been sleepwalking through life, passively accepting what happened to me. Not caring, not taking control. I had never been like that as a teenager; my ambition had fuelled me. But when I got what I always wanted, I let it slip through my fingers.

The truth is I was an idiot.

What is 'truth' anyway? Truth is just a story, one version of events. Truth isn't about facts; it's about credibility. The truth is nothing more and nothing less than what people choose to believe.

We all tell stories – about ourselves, about other people. I heard stories in group therapy that you wouldn't believe. Dramatic sagas, epic tragedies, even romance from time to time, but it was those little stories, those seemingly inconsequential cruelties that we inflict daily on those we claim to love, that stung the most.

These days we are all curators of our own story. If you don't like the truth, call it fake news. Apply a filter, delete a comment, pay someone to make it all go away.

You really want to know what happened? What led to the band splitting up? The truth that Alex couldn't live with? I will tell you the story, but only you can determine what you believe.

Chapter Thirty-Three

Libby

Libby shivered as she stood in the churchyard waiting for the official photographs to be taken. The sun had gone behind clouds which had turned slate grey and threatened rain. The grounds were showing signs of neglect; weeds flourished around the crumbling gravestones, the grass was scattered with dandelions and early daisies, and the cast-iron fencing needed a lick of paint. A faded notice appealing for bell ringers fluttered in the wind. The blossom was out in force however, making everything look pretty, and spring flowers added a splash of pink and yellow to the dark-grey stone.

She watched the photographer trying and failing to manoeuvre the guests into position and get them to look at the camera and smile in unison. Daniel and Vicky were in their element but many of the guests were trying to hide behind each other or sneak off when they were called. Shorter people were pushed reluctantly to the front as the taller people huddled at the back. Matthew was called over to pose with the other band members. Daniel casually threw his arm around Matthew's shoulder and they all postured for the photograph like they were the best of friends. Even after all this time they knew how to put on a show.

Social media had already picked up that Natalya hadn't turned up for the wedding with the hashtag #noshownatalya starting to pick up traction. Most of it was speculation, but Libby gathered that Natalya and Vicky were perhaps not the close friends they appeared to be. Vicky was keeping quiet, but she could tell some of her family members were not best pleased. She couldn't blame them – a wedding like this must have cost a fortune. No one seemed particularly worried about Natalya's disappearance however, and the general consensus on social media seemed to be that she was unreliable and flaky, unable to stand her friend being the centre of attention. Libby spotted Peter standing by himself at the gate smoking a cigarette and walked over.

'Having fun?' she asked.

'Not really. I hate weddings,' he said. 'Can't see the point in them. I mean, why do you need a piece of paper to prove you love someone?'

'So, you and Amir aren't planning to tie the knot?'

'Well, if we did, it would be a quick trip to the registry office followed by a pint, not this charade. How about you?'

Libby hadn't really given much thought to marriage. It

seemed incomprehensible to her to promise to love someone for the rest of your life. Feelings changed; people changed. How could you know at twenty-five what you would feel like at forty? Sixty? Eighty? Matthew was her first long-term relationship and although she loved him, she knew she wasn't ready to commit to him for life.

'I guess so, when the time is right,' she said, deliberately keeping it vague. She wasn't sure if she could trust Peter yet.

'Matthew seems a decent guy.'

'He is. He's great.'

'Amir always speaks highly of him. Hates Simon though.'

'He does seem a bit difficult.'

'He's only out for himself. That whole book thing. It's all about the money. He doesn't care about the impact it will have on anyone else.'

'How come you guys knew about it anyway? Last night was the first Matthew had heard of it.'

Peter bit his lip. 'Simon got in touch a while back to verify a few things.'

This was her opportunity. 'Like what?'

'Oh, you know. Stuff about their time as a band, going on tour.'

'That doesn't sound so bad. What are they all so upset about?'

Peter was about to say something when he glanced over her shoulder and clammed up. Libby turned around and saw Amir approaching them in a hurry. Peter knew something, she was sure of it. She would have to corner him again at the reception. Amir greeted her coldly and walked past them towards the row of taxis that were waiting to take them back to the hotel. Peter waved goodbye and trotted after him. She wondered how someone as laid-back as Peter could be attracted to Amir, who seemed to be in a permanently foul mood.

All the guests were starting to leave now. Libby looked around for Matthew and finally spotted him standing around the side of the church with Daniel. They looked like they were arguing. She crept a bit nearer to hear what they were saying, keeping close to the wall of the church so they wouldn't see her approach. It sounded like they were talking about Simon's book.

'No way. Not a chance.' She heard Daniel say.

'But if we go to the press ourselves, we can control the story.' Her ears pricked up at Matthew's response. It sounded like he was pleading with Daniel. 'It was a different time back then. People might understand.'

'Oh, come on, don't be so naïve. They'd crucify us.'

'Maybe we can talk to Simon, make him change his mind. He's got as much to lose as any of us. Besides, it's our word against his.'

'He says he's got proof. Bank statements. Phone records.'

'You really think Simon kept things like that from the 90s?'

'No, but the police could get them, couldn't they? We have to pay him off. All he cares about is making money. Now, if you'd agree to go back on tour—'

'How will that help? That'll make everything ten times

worse. Don't you remember what it was like? They'll be watching our every move.'

Daniel turned and spotted her eavesdropping. He plastered on a smile. 'Hey, Libby. Didn't see you there.'

Matthew recovered slightly less quickly than Daniel, looking like a naughty schoolboy caught behind the bike sheds with an illicit cigarette.

'Well, I'd better get back to my lady wife. See you at the reception.' Daniel bid a hasty retreat, walking over to where Vicky was waiting for him, surrounded by her acolytes.

The first drops of rain started to paint the pathway as Matthew grabbed Libby's hand and marched her away from the church. His face was thunderous, and he was gripping her fingers so hard that they were hurting. 'What was that about?' she said.

'Nothing. It doesn't matter.'

'You can talk to me, you know. If you want to.'

He stopped and turned to her. His face was white, worry etched into his skin. 'I know. I know you won't judge me. It's just... some things are hard to talk about.'

'Are you talking about Alex?'

A flash of something went across his face. Fear? Guilt? She couldn't tell. 'No, it's not about Alex.'

'It's OK. I understand.'

'No, you don't. How could you understand? How could anyone who wasn't there understand?' He was angry now, his voice raised. He dropped her hand. 'Come on, they'll be leaving without us and we'll be stranded.'

'I love you, Matthew. Whatever it is, it won't stop me

loving you.' Even as she said the words, Libby wondered if they were true. Could anyone make that promise?

Matthew turned to face her. He ran his fingers through his hair, looking like a condemned man. 'I will tell you, but not here, not now. As soon as we get this bloody wedding over and done with, I promise I'll tell you everything.'

Chapter Thirty-Four

London, 1995

Simon was far from OK. The hospital saved his life that night, but it wasn't enough to persuade him to stay off the drugs. He refused any help and was back on smack within hours of being discharged. It was like he was on the fast train to self-destruction, and no one could divert his course.

Worse, someone at the hospital sold the story to the press and the tabloids were full of it. The press had always been favourable to them up to this point but now they were like vultures, swooping down and picking the bones clean. Natalya went through hell, hounded by the paparazzi wherever she went. Pictures of her wearing large sunglasses, holding her hand over her face, were plastered all over the tabloids. She begged the others to intervene, to hold Simon hostage in his room if they had to, but he wouldn't listen to reason. His friends were no match for his addiction. Daniel told Matt to stay out of it.

'Simon needs this,' he said. 'Don't you understand? He's a creative person. He needs this release.'

Craig was constantly fielding phone calls from worried parents, sponsors, and venues, and there was talk of postponing the album release until the fuss had died down. He was fuming, but Simon didn't seem to give a damn. He didn't even turn up for the meeting Craig called at his office to discuss the situation.

'You guys don't know you're born,' Craig ranted. 'You would be nothing without me, nothing. I could drop you like that.' He clicked his fingers in Alex's face.

They were sitting in a conference room at the record label with views over the London skyline. Matt thought back to the day he had spent with Alex at Madame Tussauds, running around the wax figures. It seemed so long ago now. Everything had changed and not all of it for the better.

'Don't you think everyone's over-reacting a little bit?' Daniel said, leaning back on his chair and looking bored. 'It's not like he's the first rock star to take drugs. They all do. All the greats.'

Matt glared at him, willing him to shut up.

'You are pop stars. Not legends. You're not even close to being legends. You can't afford to screw up like this.'

'We haven't screwed up. Simon has.' Amir pointed out quietly.

'Yeah, so where is he?'

Craig glared at Matt like he was his babysitter. He

shrugged. Simon was a law unto himself. They had told him about the meeting, begged him to come and face the music, but he had just smirked.

'You all need to grow up and get your shit together.' Craig finished his rant and stormed out of the room, slamming the door behind him.

There was an awkward silence as his words sunk in.

'Jesus, what a drama king!' Daniel said, trying to diffuse the tension, but he was met with a cold silence.

Matt looked down at his hands and kept his thoughts to himself. Craig was right to be angry; Simon's behaviour was putting everything at risk. Would the record label really drop them? They were on the cusp of success, they had everything in front of them, and Simon was ruining it for all of them. Simon, the one who wanted this most.

'Craig's got a point,' Amir said quietly. 'We can't afford for Simon to keep screwing up like this. He's bringing us all down. We need to do something.'

They all turned and stared at him.

'What are you suggesting?' Daniel said, his voice controlled and dangerous.

'I'm just saying... there are other songwriters.'

'This is Simon's band,' Daniel said. 'He bloody well put us together in the first place.'

Matt glanced at Alex but neither of them said anything. What was she thinking? He was surprised by Daniel's loyalty to Simon; perhaps their friendship was stronger than it seemed. Matt was uncomfortable with the thought of mutiny, but Amir was right. They stood to lose a lot of money if they were dropped from the label.

'No one's dropping anyone,' Alex said firmly.

Matt nodded his head. 'I agree with Alex.'

'Well, there's a surprise,' Amir replied sourly.

Daniel fiddled with a sheaf of paper. 'So, what do we do now?'

'We need to find Simon and get him some help. Rehab or something,' Alex suggested.

'He won't go. He doesn't think he's got a problem,' Matt replied.

'It's a load of fuss over nothing.' Daniel said. 'Craig won't drop us; he can't afford to. Simon's more talented than the rest of us put together.'

This was a rare admission from Daniel who usually thought he had the monopoly on talent.

'We're a group. A team. We stick together, no matter what.' Alex said firmly.

'Even Amir? After the stunt he's just pulled?' Daniel said, glaring at Amir who returned his gaze defiantly.

Alex stood between them. 'Even Amir.'

Chapter Thirty-Five

Libby

They didn't have a chance to talk in the taxi as they were squeezed in with a couple and their two young children. The mother looked exhausted, trying to pacify her little girl who was whining that she was hungry. She fished out a banana from her huge handbag and the child mushed it between her fingers before deliberately wiping it down her white dress. The father seemed oblivious to his daughter's actions and was busy jiggling a baby up and down on his knee. The child's nappy obviously needed changing and the smell was unbearable. Matthew took Libby's hand and squeezed it in way of an apology.

'Bride or groom?' the woman asked.

'Oh… groom,' Libby answered when Matthew didn't.

'We're with the bride. Known her since university. Of course, we move in quite different circles these days!'

'You can say that again,' the husband said sourly.

'Oh, ignore him; he's only jealous,' the woman chatted. 'They look really happy, don't they?'

Libby smiled in agreement.

'I can't believe Nat didn't show up though. Poor Vic.'

Libby's ears pricked up. 'Do you know Natalya?'

'No, not really. I mean, I've met her a couple of times. I was invited to the hen night of course but I couldn't go because of the little one. I heard it got pretty wild. To be honest, I was surprised she asked Natalya to be her bridesmaid. I didn't think they were that close.'

'Good publicity boost for them,' her husband added.

The woman rolled her eyes. 'I'm sure it's nothing like that.'

'Really? You're her oldest friend and she didn't ask you.'

'She probably didn't think I would want to do it. You know how things are; people grow apart.' She looked towards Libby for support who smiled uncomfortably. 'We don't see her much these days, since...'

'Since she met Daniel and ditched all her old friends,' her husband finished.

'Well, at least we still got an invite.'

Libby was glad when the taxi arrived at Harrington Hall and they could escape the awkward conversation. A red carpet had been rolled out and waiters in smart uniforms handed out flutes of champagne as they walked into the bar. A string quartet was playing in the corner of the room and the music drifted through the hubbub of people talking and catching up. The bar area was busy as people supplemented their glasses of champagne with more substantial drinks. Matthew ordered a pint of Black Sheep Bitter and a gin and tonic for Libby.

Through the window, Libby could see Vicky and Daniel posing for pictures down by the lake. Vicky was a couple of inches taller than Daniel, but she noticed that the photographer had placed her slightly downhill, so they looked the same height. The rain had started to fall in earnest now, but the hotel staff were on hand with large golfing umbrellas sheltering the bride. Natalya had still not made an appearance. If she had been hurt or even killed in the woodland, surely someone would have found her by now?

Should she call the police about her suspicions? That was going over the top, surely. She barely knew these people and no one else seemed particularly worried about Natalya's disappearance. Maybe she was just incredibly rude? Was Libby letting her imagination run away from her? It was, after all, a big jump from a bridesmaid going missing to suspecting she had been killed.

Libby checked social media again in the vain hope of any updates but there was nothing. Emma had sent her a picture of Patrick, beaming with his face covered in chocolate ice cream. She'd give anything to be with them right now instead of here, embroiled in this awful atmosphere between Matthew and his old friends.

The idea that something had happened to Natalya down in the woods was niggling her and Libby knew she wouldn't be able to relax until she investigated. She would go down to the woodland and have a quick look around herself just to put her mind at ease. The manager hadn't seemed that concerned when she rang him earlier; she wasn't sure she could trust him to keep his promise to look for her. If Natalya was lying there injured, or worse, dead, it was surely better to find her sooner rather than later.

'I'm going to get some fresh air,' she told Matthew, who nodded in acknowledgement but was engrossed in the conversation about football. She would have a quick walk through the woodland and be back before the wedding breakfast. She was being ridiculous, she knew it, and would probably ruin her heels, but she couldn't just stand there while Natalya could be hurt.

Libby slipped past the string quartet and out of the side door into the garden area. It was a walled garden and beautifully kept. A wildflower area was attracting bees and butterflies and a pair of blue tits were squabbling over the contents of a bird feeder. Vicky and Daniel were posing for pictures under the arbour. Keeping out of sight, she walked around the garden and towards the lake. The rain had stopped but the ground was soggy, and she could feel her heels sinking into the moist grass.

'Hey, wait up!' She turned to see Peter running towards her, his suit jacket flapping in the wind.

'What are you doing here?'

'Saw you sneaking off and wondered what you were up to. Whatever it is, it's got to be more interesting than being in there.'

Libby hesitated. She still didn't know if she could trust Peter, but she would be glad of his company. She quickly summarised her fears about Natalya.

'Blimey. You really think someone might have killed her?'

'I don't know. Do you think I'm mad? I'm sure Matthew does.'

'Maybe he's the *mur-der-er*?' he said, drawing out the last word in a dramatic fashion.

'No one said anything about murder. Besides, I thought you said Matthew was a good man.'

'Well, looks can be deceiving. And it didn't stop him vandalising other people's cars, did it?'

Libby looked down at her feet, mortified. 'You knew about that? Why didn't you say anything?'

'I recognised him in the pub last night.'

'Does Amir know?'

Peter shook his head. 'He was wound up enough about the book; I thought that might send him over the edge. Sometimes, silence is the best policy.'

They walked through the woodland to where Libby had last seen Natalya. It was dark and shaded under the canopy of the trees. There was a smell of wild garlic in the air and they passed patches of delicate bluebells. The woodland path was strewn with tree roots and Libby stumbled, cursing her shoes. She imagined Natalya running down this path. How far had she gone before the shot rang out?

'Over here.' Peter was holding up a scrap of fabric with a twig, being careful not to touch it with his bare hands. The lilac fabric was ripped and saturated with a rust-red stain. 'Do you recognise it?'

'It could be Natalya's top. It looks the same colour. I'm not sure.'

Libby looked at the ground beneath them. It looked like something had been dragged further through the wood towards the edge of the lake. 'We should call the police.'

Peter appeared to be enjoying his role of amateur sleuth. He stood looking at the ground, his hand on his hips. All he needed was a deerstalker hat and a magnifying glass and he would be a regular Sherlock Holmes.

'Hmm, there's not much to go on, and there'll be hell to pay if you break up the wedding because you found a bit of rag in the woods.' He paused thoughtfully. 'Do you think they'll let us into her room?'

'The manager said he'd already looked.'

'Maybe they missed something? I mean, they were looking for Natalya, not for clues.'

'You make it sound like we're in a crime drama. This is someone's life we're talking about. She's got children.'

'I know. I'm sorry, but we don't really know her that well, do we? And it's more likely she's done a bunk, surely? God knows, I wish I could.'

Libby checked her watch. They had been gone ten minutes already. Long enough for Matthew to get worried about where she was, but she couldn't stand around and do nothing.

'OK, but if we're still worried after we check her room, then we ring the police.'

'Whatever you say, partner.'

'What should we do about the fabric?'

Peter dropped it back where he found it. 'Leave it. If something has happened, then the police will need to see it in its original position.'

'You sound like you've done this before.'

'Yeah, well, spend long enough with Amir and some of his common sense rubs off on you.'

They started retracing their steps back to the hotel, keeping their eyes out for any other evidence that Natalya had been there or come to any harm.

'You and Amir, you seem so different,' Libby said.

'How so?' There was a touch of defensiveness in Peter's voice and Libby instantly regretted raising the issue.

'I don't know, he seems so...'

'Uptight? Arrogant? Difficult?'

Libby realised that she had offended him. 'I'm sorry, I didn't mean anything.'

Peter looked serious. 'Yes, you did. You don't know him. You don't know the first thing about him or what he's been through. Do you know how difficult it was for him to come out to his family? His father threw him out of the house; they haven't spoken since. His mother has never visited our flat. You're like everyone else. You only see what's on the surface. Do you know how much pro bono work he does? He never stops. He's intelligent and kind and...' There were tears in Peter's eyes.

'I'm sorry. You're right. I don't know him.'

'Yeah, well. I'm not sure what you see in Matthew either, if I'm honest. I mean apart from his good looks and bank account.'

'I'm not with him for his money!' she protested.

'Yeah, right.'

'I'm not.' She was furious at this stranger for judging

her. What gave him the right? 'I'd love Matthew if he didn't have a penny.'

'Hmm. If you say so.'

They fumed at each other for a while. 'Well, this is getting us nowhere, is it?' he said finally.

'I'm sorry. I really didn't mean to offend you.'

'I'm sorry too. I had no right to judge you either. This wedding, all these people flaunting their wealth, it's getting to me a bit.'

'Me too. There are a lot of advantages to being ordinary.'

'Like not having to wear a tie.'

'Or high heels.' She looked down at her shoes which were, as expected, coated in mud.

'Drinking lager instead of champagne.'

'Eating burgers instead of foie gras.'

'Buying things in Primark instead of Armani.'

'Having a Fiesta instead of a Ferrari.'

'Yeah, God, who would want a Ferrari?' Peter grinned and she had the sense that she was forgiven. The argument rankled though; is that what people thought of her? That she was only with Matthew for his money? She tried to tell herself that she didn't care. She didn't know Peter, and she would probably never see him again after this weekend, but it hurt that people could make assumptions about her like that without any foundation. She supposed they were all guilty of it, to some extent or another, and resolved to be a bit more accepting in future.

Chapter Thirty-Six

Libby

Libby went to the ladies' while Peter went to charm the receptionist into handing over the key to Natalya's room. As she sat in the stall, she heard the toilets flush and a couple of women gossiping while they washed their hands.

'Vicky's certainly done very well for herself, getting her claws into Daniel. He must be worth a fair bit.'

'Not to mention good-looking. I wouldn't kick him out of bed.'

'From what I've heard, he probably wouldn't turn you down,' the other woman said in a loud stage whisper. There was a tinkle of malicious laughter and a shuffle of dresses being adjusted. Libby peeked at their footwear, trying to work out who was talking, but she didn't recognise the shoes.

'I'm surprised there aren't more photographers hanging

about. You'd think Daniel would want them to cover his wedding. He'd do anything for a headline.'

'I heard they tried to sell the rights, and no one would pay!' They laughed cattily before the door slammed behind them.

The women had gone by the time Libby came out of the cubicle. She washed her hands before checking her make-up in the mirror. Being at this wedding was like being back at school, with all the cool kids in their cliques bitching about everyone else. Ryan had been one of the cool kids. He had never showed her any attention until the night of that Year 13 house party when, fuelled by alcohol and egged on by his friends, he had asked her if she wanted a drink. Her face burned with embarrassment when she thought about how naïve she had been. She had really thought he liked her.

One of the stalls opened and Vicky stepped out. Her eyes were puffy and red, but she held her head high as she approached the basins. Libby swallowed hard. Had she heard those women talking about her? She must have done.

'Can I borrow your mascara?' Vicky asked. 'They don't make these dresses with pockets.'

'They should.' Libby said, rummaging in her make-up bag and retrieving the old unbranded mascara that she hardly ever used.

'Are you OK?' she said, handing it over.

'I'm fine. I've heard much worse, believe me.'

Libby slipped off her heels and started sponging the satin with a wet hand-towel. The mud was coming off, but it had stained the fabric. Another pair of shoes ruined. She had nothing else to change into, apart from her biker boots or muddy trainers, and Matthew would never forgive her if she turned up to the reception in those. She would have to wear the stained shoes and hope nobody noticed.

Vicky handed her back the mascara. 'How do I look?'

'Beautiful,' Libby said honestly.

Vicky shook her hair out and inspected herself in the mirror. 'Toothpaste.'

'I'm sorry... what?'

Vicky nodded at Libby's shoes. 'Toothpaste. It works wonders on stains. When you have kids like mine, you learn about how to deal with all sorts. Mud. Blood. Chewing gum. The lot. You should check out my blog.'

'Thanks, I will.' Libby hesitated, wondering whether she should bring the subject up, but not wanting to pass up on the opportunity. 'Listen, about Natalya...'

'What about her?' Vicky gave her a sharp look.

'I was wondering whether she'd been in touch.'

'No, we think she went home. We checked her room this morning and all her stuff has gone. It's typical of Natalya. She thinks the whole world revolves around her.'

'I'm sorry.'

'Don't be. And don't believe a word those women said about me and Daniel. We love each other to bits; I'd do for anything him. I've made mistakes in the past, and people love to remind me of them, but he's all I need.'

'I'm happy for you.'

'You can put that in your paper if you like,' she said as she moved towards the door. 'Of course, that won't sell nearly as many copies, will it?'

Libby started to protest that she wasn't planning on

writing anything about Vicky or Daniel, but the door had already closed behind her. Feeling aggrieved, she put the heels back on and followed her. She might try Vicky's toothpaste trick later, but she certainly wasn't planning on subscribing to her blog.

Peter was waiting for her in the reception area, dangling a key in front of him. 'Ta-da!'

'How did you manage that?'

'Oh, it was all down to my good looks and charm. And I slipped her twenty quid.'

'I think we're getting carried away. Natalya's probably gone home. I've just seen Vicky and she said they'd already checked her room.'

'Well, there's no harm in taking a quick look now we've got the key. Put our minds at rest?'

Libby checked her watch. She had been gone twenty minutes and Matthew would be wondering where she was, but curiosity got the better of her. She followed Peter up the stairs and along the corridor to Natalya's room. It was on the second floor but on the opposite side of the building to their suite, looking out towards the front of the property. A CCTV camera in the top corner of the corridor captured their movements as Peter turned the key in the door.

It was a small room, one of the singles, as Natalya's husband and children hadn't come with her to the wedding. The room smelt of stale perfume. The bed had been roughly made and there was an empty champagne flute on the bedside table. Peter opened the wardrobe as Libby headed into the en suite bathroom. There was a pile of used towels on the floor but no toiletries or personal effects.

'Nothing,' Peter called out to her.

Libby came out of the bathroom. 'Nothing in there either.'

'She must have packed and left.'

'It looks like it.'

Peter bent down to look under the bed. 'Wait, there's something here.' He pulled out a mobile phone. It was one of the latest models and very expensive.

'Do you think it's Natalya's?'

Libby looked at the phone. The display showed that she had ten unread messages and several missed calls. The last one was from Vicky at 2.03pm. Peter tried to open it, but it was locked with a PIN code.

'What do you think?'

'It would explain why she hasn't been in touch,' Peter said.

'I guess so. But what about the fabric in the woodland?'

'She could have just torn it when she was out running. It looks like Vicky's right; she's just gone home.'

Unless someone wanted them to think that. If someone had deliberately hurt Natalya, then it wouldn't have been hard to sneak up and clear the room to make it look like she had left. She would probably have had her room key with her when she went out for a run. But that ruled out the gamekeeper. Had someone at the wedding shot Natalya? Had they killed her and cleared the room to cover their tracks? Who would do such a thing?

Peter placed the phone on the table. 'Let the hotel deal with it. Come on, we're going to miss dinner with all this sleuthing.'

Libby reluctantly followed Peter out of the room, still not convinced. If Natalya had been called away, wouldn't she have left a message or something with the hotel reception? Or tried to call from a pay phone? Still, there was nothing Libby could do about it. She couldn't call the police without any evidence. And no one else seemed to suspect anything had happened.

Perhaps this was entirely in keeping with Natalya's character. Maybe she felt uncomfortable around her ex and decided she couldn't face spending the weekend with him? She tried to imagine spending an entire weekend with Ryan. Awkward wouldn't cover it. She could completely understand Natalya wanting to get as far away from Simon as possible.

Amir was waiting for them in the reception area. He glared as he watched them descend the grand staircase together. Libby felt her cheeks redden even though they had done nothing wrong.

'I've been looking all over for you,' Amir said to Peter as they reached the ground floor. 'Come on, they're calling people in.'

Peter discreetly handed over the key to the receptionist without Amir noticing. She wondered how much he was planning on telling his partner about their suspicions and why he hadn't got him involved already. Did Peter suspect Amir had something to do with Natalya's disappearance?

Amir wasn't physically very strong, but you didn't have to be to shoot someone. If someone had shot Natalya in the woods, and it was a big if, then they must have moved the body otherwise it would have been found by now. Could

Amir have moved the body on his own? She doubted it. If Amir was a killer, then he must have had an accomplice and Peter was the most likely candidate. Peter seemed friendly enough but maybe he had a vested interest in helping her? Maybe showing her the empty room was a ruse to put her off the scent? She shivered. If Peter was involved, then was she also in danger? Was he keeping her close to find out what she knew?

Chapter Thirty-Seven

London, 1995

'F or fuck's sake, are you guys trying to ruin your careers?'

Daniel picked up the tabloid newspaper that Craig had thrown at him across the table. A blonde girl with huge breasts was featured in a barely there bikini and the headline screamed:

MY NIGHT OF PASSION WITH POP STAR DAN NEARLY KILLED ME

Daniel smirked. 'Lighten up, will ya?'

'It says she needed hospital treatment afterwards.'

'Well, you know, I'm a lot to handle.' He gestured to his crotch and winked at Matt. Craig was not finding him amusing.

'It says you tried to strangle her.'

The colour drained out of Daniel's face as he grabbed the newspaper and scanned the contents. 'She's lying.'

'She's got bruises around her neck.'

'So? Now't to do with me. She probably did it to herself to get more money.' He tossed the newspaper back at Craig. 'No one believes any of that shit anyway.'

'Mud sticks. Listen, guys, I really need you to clean up your act. I can't be wasting my time dealing with your mess. Matt?'

Matt snapped to attention. He had been drifting off, amused that it was Daniel in trouble for a change. 'What have I done?'

'I want you to keep an eye on Dan. Stop him from going off with any more skanks.'

Alex looked like she was about to object to the word, but Craig silenced her with a glare. Matt rolled his eyes as Daniel sat back in his chair looking disinterested. The meeting moved onto sales figures and the next single. Matt was fuming. Why should he have to look after Daniel? Daniel would just see it as a challenge to get him into trouble too. First Simon, and now Daniel. Up to that point, they had been 'golden boys', beloved by teenage girls and their grandmas, but the media were swiftly turning against them. Now they were beginning to get a reputation and it wasn't one the record company welcomed. It was like they weren't allowed to be human, to make mistakes, to have a life. Alex gave him a sympathetic smile. She knew that keeping an eye on Daniel was easier said than done.

'We're still going out tonight though, aren't we?' Daniel asked as soon as they had left the meeting.

'Do you think we should after what Craig said?'

'Oh, sod Craig. He's like forty or something. He's forgotten what fun is.'

They were going to the opening of an exclusive club in Kensington that night. The others cried off, but Daniel insisted on going, so Matt was forced to tag along. The club was like every other in the city. Different bars offering different vibes and a VIP section in a roped-off area overlooking the dance floor. There were a few footballers there and a B-list movie star who was surrounded by sycophants. Daniel eyed up the talent lazily.

'These girls, they'll do anything, man. They're begging for it,' he slurred.

Matt followed his gaze. It was the usual scene. Women with fake boobs and fake handbags flirting with men with big wallets and big egos. Same old, same old. Daniel seemed to love it, but the novelty was wearing off for Matt. He had thought London would be glamorous, but sometimes he longed for the simplicity of his life back in Yorkshire.

'Was it true? About you hurting that girl?'

Daniel turned his attention back to Matt. 'Nah. It wasn't like that. It was just a bit of fun. She said she liked it rough.' Matt knew him well enough to know when he was lying. 'You need to get out more. Live a little. Try new things.'

'I'm fine, thanks.'

'You're a fucking monk. Saving yourself for one girl. It's stupid, man.'

Matt stayed quiet. Maybe Daniel was right. Matt had thought Alex was his soulmate, but she only seemed interested in him as a friend. Was he wasting his time waiting for her? Should he be looking around for someone else? But the thought of starting a relationship with any of these women depressed him. They weren't looking for love. Money, fame, status, perhaps, but nothing real. Everything about his new life was manufactured. He'd had his share of one-night stands, but they'd left him feeling empty. It seemed pathetic to say it out loud, but he wanted more than that. He wanted a relationship, someone to talk to, someone on his side. He wanted marriage, kids, a house in suburbia with a garden. Someone to grow old with. Was that so wrong?

'Look over there.' Daniel pointed out a group of women on the dance floor. 'Which one do you fancy? No, let me guess, the small one with peroxide hair.'

Matt turned to look too quickly. There wasn't anyone matching that description. Daniel was winding him up and he was not in the mood. 'I'm going home.'

'Oh, don't be like that. Come on, I'm sorry. I was joking. Seriously, what's your type?'

Matt looked around the VIP area and spotted an attractive girl with long dark-red hair and freckles over her nose standing at the bar. 'She looks nice.'

Daniel beckoned her over and Matt watched him whisper in her ear and hand over a £50 note. She sidled up to him, but he shifted away. He had totally misjudged the situation. He had thought she looked sweet.

'I don't need you to buy me a girl.'

Daniel waved her away, admiring her arse as she

shimmied back to the bar. 'I don't think you know what you need.'

'Come on, let's call it a night.'

'It's early,' Daniel protested. 'Stay, do some coke or something. That'll perk you up. We'll hit a dance club later, work off some steam.'

It was all so tedious. The music was too loud and the people too pretentious. Everyone looked like they were trying hard to be cool. The drinks were expensive and the conversation inane. Matt felt a million years old. 'I'm going to get a proper drink.'

He walked over to the bar, ignoring the advances of the redhead, and bought a bottle of Jack Daniels. Maybe if he got drunk enough, he could forget about Alex.

'Hey, you're that drummer from that band!' Matt looked around to see a very drunk man veering towards him. Matt handed over his money to the barman and ignored him.

'Matt somebody or other.'

He smiled and nodded an acknowledgement. Surely the whole point of a VIP area was to keep the knobheads out. He looked over to where the bouncers were standing but they seemed oblivious to the situation.

'Oh man, that lead singer of yours is hot. Can you give me her number?'

Matt ignored him.

'Can I take your picture, mate?'

'I'm just enjoying a quiet night with my friend,' Matt said firmly, accepting his change from the barman. 'Maybe another time.'

'No need to be like that.'

'I'm not being like anything,' Matt said firmly, pushing past him. 'Nice to meet you.'

He walked over to where Daniel was sitting in the booth, still eyeing up women, finishing off his champagne. Daniel eyed the bottle of bourbon.

'Jack?' he asked, with a raised eyebrow. They both knew it made Matt aggressive.

Matt sat down beside him and poured them both large measures. He looked over to the bar where the man was still standing, pointing them out to his friend. Daniel followed Matt's gaze.

'Have we got a problem?'

'Not yet. Just some tosser.' Matt downed the shot and poured another.

The man got his camera out and pointed it in their direction. Matt turned his head away. This guy wasn't giving up. Was he from the press? They didn't usually allow snappers into the VIP areas, but occasionally they managed to sneak in. They had already posed for publicity shots at the start of the night; surely, he was entitled to a drink in peace? The guy was now blatantly taking photos of them. Definitely an amateur, but even so, he might sell the picture to the tabloids. They paid good money for candid celebrity shots. Had he seen them with the hooker? He'd sent her packing, but pictures could be misconstrued. Was he next in line for a lynching? Or was he being paranoid?

'Uh-oh, he's coming over.' Daniel said, laughing. He seemed to be getting a kick out of the attention. Matt could feel his temper rise.

'Hey, I'm a big fan. Wanted to say hello.' The guy was

shaking hands with Daniel and looked like he was going to sit down next to them. Matt beckoned to the bouncers, but they didn't respond.

'Look, mate, I've already told you. We're having a quiet drink.'

'Just one picture, and I'll leave you alone.'

'No.'

The man looked affronted. Daniel glared at him, but Matt was sick of it. What gave this guy the right to disrupt their evening? He was tired of being polite. He wasn't getting the message.

'Think you're really something, don't you?' The man sneered.

Matt stood up and leaned over the man. He was only a couple of inches taller than him, but it was enough. 'Get lost, will you?'

The man turned to leave, and Matt sat down. As he walked away, he saw him take out his camera and take another picture of them. Without stopping to think, Matt jumped up, chased after him and grabbed the camera from his hand. He threw it on the floor, stamping on it.

'What the—? That cost a fortune.'

The man squared up to him. He didn't look much like a fan anymore. He may have been shorter than Matt, but he was broader and looked like he could pack a punch. If Matt hadn't been so drunk, he would have recognised he had met his match. He could see people staring at them.

'Come on then,' Matt taunted him.

Daniel was by his side now, trying to placate the man. 'We'll pay for the camera.' He dug into his pockets and retrieved a wad of notes. 'Here's £500. That should cover it.'

The bouncers were coming over now. Typical, where had they been when Matt needed them?

'Is there a problem, gentlemen?'

'This man broke my camera. And threatened me.' The man jabbed his fingers close to Matt's face.

'There's no problem,' Daniel pressed the money into the stranger's hands and smiled at the bouncers. 'We were just leaving, weren't we Matt?'

Matt's anger meant he couldn't think straight. All he could think was how much he wanted to punch the lights out of the man in front of him, but the bouncers were standing in his way now and he recognised that they were making a scene. He could envisage Craig's reaction if he didn't simmer down. He reluctantly allowed Daniel to lead him out of the club. As they sneaked out the back door, there was a flash of cameras in his face and he could hear their names being called by the snappers waiting outside. Why wouldn't they leave him alone?

Daniel dragged him towards the town car and pushed him into the back seat.

'Nothing to see here folks. Have a good night!' he gave the photographers a cheeky wave as he climbed in after him. Matt could see the lenses of several cameras being pressed against the blacked-out windows as the car smoothly accelerated away.

Chapter Thirty-Eight

Libby

L ibby followed the other guests heading to the marquee for the wedding breakfast. It had stopped raining, but the ground was still soft underfoot and the pewter clouds threatened another downpour.

Stepping inside the marquee was like entering fairyland. Tiny lights sparkled from the ceiling and each table was lit by twinkling tea lights. The flower arrangements in the centre were chic and understated but obviously expensive. The name cards were handwritten in an elegant script and pale-pink silk pouches held a cluster of sugared almonds for each guest. In the corner of the room, she spotted the tiered cake with an ornate ceremonial knife lying beside it. She found Matthew already sitting at their table which was close to the exit. It wasn't the worst placement, but it was still pretty far from the top table. As she took her seat, Libby noted that they had spelt her name wrong on her place card.

The staff had discreetly shifted the seats on the top table so that it wasn't obvious that one of the bridesmaids was missing. She was relieved to find that they hadn't been seated with any of the other band members. She needed time to think. Had one of the guests killed Natalya? And if so, why?

She glanced over at Simon's table. He was talking to a couple to the right of him and seemed totally oblivious to the trouble he was causing with his tell-all memoir. She wondered if he knew or cared that his ex-wife had gone missing. Their divorce had not been amicable, but it was a long time ago. Did he still bear a grudge towards his ex-wife? Libby suspected that Natalya's disappearance had something to do with the band's secret but maybe there were other factors at play that she wasn't aware of. Something to do with their son, perhaps. Simon would have had plenty of opportunity to kill Natalya and hide her body while they were all at breakfast. At the very least, if he had been sleeping in the woodland then surely he must have seen or heard something?

Libby looked over to where Amir and Peter were sitting. Despite Peter's feelings towards marriage, the couple looked to be enjoying themselves. She thought she caught Amir smiling for the first time since she had met him, and she finally caught a glimpse of what Peter saw in him. He could be quite attractive when he relaxed. Was this all a front? Had Amir killed Natalya? He didn't look like the type to get his hands dirty, but she knew some crooks, like the defendant yesterday, could lead the most respectable of lives without suspicion. And what about Peter? He came across as friendly, but perhaps that was a cover? The couple hadn't been at breakfast. They would have had plenty of time to kill Natalya and hide the body while everyone was in the dining room. But why? Simon, she could understand, but what had Natalya ever done to them? And why would Peter be helping her if he had something to hide?

'Thought you'd got lost,' Matthew remarked. His cheeks were flushed with alcohol, but he seemed relaxed.

'There was a queue for the loos,' she said, relieved that Matthew didn't question her further. He seemed preoccupied with looking at the menu card on the table. His name card was marked with a red sticker to mark his peanut allergy and Libby was pleased that the hotel had a system in place. It was always awkward for him eating at mass catering events. Matthew had even resorted to taking food in a Tupperware box sometimes to events where he couldn't be certain that the food was safe to eat.

She didn't tell him about their investigations. He would think she was being over-dramatic. But deep down she knew there was another reason she hadn't confided in him. She knew Matthew was hiding something about his time in the band, but how far would he go to keep his secrets? Natalya had tried to warn her and she hadn't listened. Now it was too late to find out what she had meant. Libby was surrounded by people she didn't trust, but Matthew wasn't one of them, was he?

The waiters walked around the table with bottles of wine and Libby accepted a glass of white. Matthew went for red and swirled the wine around in his glass before tasting it, screwing up his nose in disgust. She wasn't sure what he expected; no one served fine wine at a wedding, even minor celebrities.

Libby introduced herself to the couple on her right, an older couple who were Vicky's godparents and had travelled from Ireland. They seemed friendly enough and she tried to relax but her mind kept returning to Natalya. She was certain that something had happened to her, but she didn't have any evidence, apart from an empty hotel room and a scrap of fabric. Should she call the police anyway? She imagined the scene if they burst in, told everyone to stay where they were while they searched the premises. Peter was right; it would be a hell of a disruption, particularly if her suspicions proved unfounded.

She checked her phone. There was a message from her sister that made her heart stop.

Patrick's been sick. Too much ice cream, I think!

There was a little green puking emoji next to it.

Are you sure he's OK?

she quickly typed.

Yes, don't worry.

Does he have a temperature?

No, I've checked. Just keeping you updated. Honestly, hun, everything's fine. You enjoy yourself.

There wasn't much chance of that.

Matthew glared at her, but she was willing to risk his wrath for this. She waited for a few minutes for a reply, but it looked like Emma had gone offline. She would just have to take her word for it that Patrick was OK. She hated being this far away from him.

The starters came around. Duck pâté with tiny slices of

sourdough toast. Matthew slipped off his jacket and chatted to the woman on his left who started flirting outrageously with him. Matthew had a way with women, but she knew she could trust him. He had told her from the start that he was a one-woman man and had a low opinion of anyone who committed adultery. Until this weekend, she had never had any reason to doubt her relationship with Matthew. Now the cracks were starting to show.

The pâté was delicious but the portions were tiny. Libby could have eaten it all over again. At the top table, Vicky and Daniel were laughing about something, their heads close together, enjoying a private moment. In the fuss over Natalya's disappearance, she had almost forgotten the reason they were there. Daniel had loosened his tie but was still wearing his waistcoat. Their parents sat either side of them and the bridesmaids had been placed at the far ends of the long table. Two pairs of little shoes poked out from underneath the white tablecloth and she guessed some of the children had made a den in there. It was a typical, traditional English wedding. There was nothing to suggest that a murder had been committed.

The main meal was corn-fed free-range chicken in a white wine sauce with organic vegetables artfully arranged in a cube. More wine was served, and Libby started to feel a bit tipsy. She had never been a heavy drinker and she would have to slow down if she wanted to last the night. She surreptitiously checked her phone under the table and was surprised to see that it was nearly six o'clock. It would be starting to get dark soon. The other guests at her table were now taking bets on how long the speeches would be. The money was on Daniel's being the longest.

As the main meal was cleared away, lots of people took advantage of the gap before dessert to push past them towards the toilets. Simon knocked into Libby's chair, propelling her forward and causing her to spill her wine. He didn't even bother to apologise. Peter stopped to say hello as Amir sneaked out to make a phone call. She was glad he didn't mention their expedition into the woodland.

'Make way for the bride!' she heard Olivia shout.

Libby turned to see Vicky heading across the room, picking up her dress so the long train didn't get caught on the chairs. She was surprised when they stopped at their table.

'Hi Libby,' Vicky said with a smile. 'How are the shoes?'

Matthew looked at her quizzically. Libby put one foot behind the other, embarrassed that she had forgotten all about the state of her heels.

'Bearing up. Your dress is beautiful,' she said to change the subject.

'What, this old thing?' Vicky said, twirling. 'I'm sorry I've not had much chance to talk to the guests, you know how it is.'

Not really, Libby thought, but she appreciated the sentiment.

'Well, it's good to see you both again. Hopefully, we'll get chance to catch up properly later.'

The group of women disappeared towards the hotel and Libby sat back down with Matthew.

'What did she mean by that?' he asked.

'Oh nothing. I just got mud on my shoes and she gave me some advice on how to get rid of the stains.'

Fortunately, Matthew didn't question where the mud came from. She didn't fancy trying to explain her expedition into the woodland.

Vicky returned to the top table just as the waiters emerged from the kitchen, carrying plates laden with profiteroles and chocolate sauce. The guests hurried back to their tables, pushing past them in their rush for dessert.

'Nut-free,' said the waiter, placing Matthew's dish in front of them. It had been marked with a red sticker.

Libby dug in, relishing the rich chocolate and the creamy choux pastry. She dabbed her mouth with a napkin and turned to Matthew to comment on the dessert. He had gone silent, his lips puffed up like bad cosmetic surgery. His breath was rasping.

She knew instantly it was an allergic reaction.

'Oh shit.'

She scrabbled in her handbag for the EpiPen that Matthew had given her to carry. It wasn't there. Libby emptied the bag out onto the floor and searched through the contents, but it was definitely missing. She could have sworn she had packed it, despite the rush to get ready. She was always very careful to remember it.

Matthew grasped her hand, pointing to the bag but she shook her head. There was a spare one in their room, but there was no time to go and get it. Matthew was struggling to breathe and going into anaphylactic shock. He needed adrenaline fast.

Chapter Thirty-Nine

Libby

Saturday evening

'Call an ambulance!' Libby shouted as she unfastened Matthew's collar. He was trying to say something but couldn't breathe. His face was swollen and there was a look of panic in his eyes. 'Has anyone got any antihistamine?'

The antihistamine wouldn't solve the problem, but it would help slow down the reaction. Someone handed her a packet of tablets but there was no way Matthew was going to be able to swallow them. People were crowding around them now, and Libby thought she could see someone filming the incident on their mobile phone. How sick could you get? A woman in her forties pushed her way through.

'Make way, I'm a doctor.' She knelt beside him and Libby felt a wave of relief. A doctor would know what to do. She could see people staring at their table, whispering to each other. Vicky and Daniel were standing up, looking over in alarm. Everyone looked like they were torn between rushing over and giving them some space.

How could the catering staff have been so careless? They knew Matthew had a peanut allergy; they had even marked his plate. The waiter had been keen to assure him when he put the dessert in front of him that it was nut-free. Accidents did happen; no kitchen can be entirely uncontaminated with allergens, but they had made promises. Could it be a mistake? Or had the dishes been swapped?

Matthew could die. And where had the EpiPen gone? Libby was certain that she had put it in her bag. It wasn't something she would forget. The liquid antihistamine was missing too. Had someone removed them? Could this be deliberate?

It seemed to take forever before they heard sirens and two paramedics came through the entrance to the marquee, directed by the hotel manager. One took over from the doctor and the other asked Libby for details of Matthew's age, medical history and more information about his allergy. They administered adrenaline and Libby held her breath as she waited for it to take effect. All she could do was pray Matthew wouldn't die.

The paramedics manoeuvred Matthew onto a stretcher and Libby followed them out of the marquee. It was dusk and the first bright stars of the evening were just visible like tiny beacons of hope. The ambulance was parked in front of the building and the blue lights reflected in the tall windows gave it a ghostly feel. She climbed into the back of the vehicle and held Matthew's hand as the paramedics hooked him up to monitors and placed an oxygen mask over his nose and mouth. Libby prayed to a god she wasn't sure that she believed in that he would survive.

The nearest hospital was about thirty minutes' drive from the hotel, but the journey seemed to take hours. You could tell just by looking at Matthew that things were serious, but they weren't using the sirens – that had to be a good sign, didn't it? The paramedic in the back of the ambulance was calm and reassuring but Libby imagined they were like that with everyone. She wished they could go faster but the roads were narrow with tight bends and so they were forced to take it steady. Libby could see the blue lights flashing as they rushed past dark hedgerows. Matthew was awake but not making much sense. She could feel the warm blood pumping through his fingers and a flickering of faith.

Once at the hospital, Matthew was rushed through A&E and she had to answer the same questions all over again. She wondered whether she needed to call his family and let them know what had happened, but she didn't want to worry them. Matthew was breathing normally now but they wanted to monitor his heart rate and run some tests. He clutched her hand as she tried not to convey how scared she was. In the huge hospital bed, he looked smaller somehow, more vulnerable.

'I'm sorry,' he kept saying but she wasn't sure why he was apologising. It was hardly his fault that he had ended up in hospital.

Libby longed to hear Emma's reassuring voice that everything was going to be OK, but she didn't want to leave Matthew long enough to ring her. They had been taken to a small, rural hospital, but it was Saturday night, and the A&E department was noisy and busy. As they rushed through the waiting area, Libby spotted children holding floppy wrists, drunks swearing loudly about waiting times and an elderly woman looking like she'd rather be tucked up in bed. Everywhere was a flurry of activity and the nurses were run off their feet. Life, death, and everything between was taking place in this building tonight.

The room was divided into cubicles with curtains across them but several, including theirs, had been left open. Libby tried to calm her fears by watching people coming and going. Opposite them an old man was sitting up in bed, surrounded by his extended family, including a woman with a small baby. They all seemed so cheerful, and Libby wondered what their emergency had been. She suddenly felt very alone.

Finally, the doctor returned and closed the curtain behind him. Libby held her breath, mentally preparing herself for bad news. The doctor seemed impossibly young – perhaps only a couple of years older than her – and she hoped he was fully qualified. He checked the display on the machine Matthew had been hooked up to and compared it to some notes on his clipboard.

'You're going to be fine,' he said to Matthew. 'But I'd like to keep you in overnight to be on the safe side.'

Matthew looked like he was going to protest but thought better of it.

'And it was definitely a reaction to peanuts?' Libby asked.

'As far as we can tell. It's unlikely anything else would cause such a serious reaction. You should report the incident. In our experience, not all catering establishments take these things seriously.'

'Don't worry, I intend to,' Matthew said. 'Thank you.'

'We'll sort out a bed for you soon. You shouldn't be waiting long.' The doctor fussed about in the corner of the room, filling out a form and putting away some instruments.

Matthew squeezed Libby's hand. 'Go back to the party. You heard the doctor; I'm going to be fine.'

Libby checked her watch. It was five past nine. Dinner would be over, and guests would be arriving for the evening do by now. The thought of going back to the hotel without Matthew and returning to a party where she didn't know anyone, filled her with dread.

'I'm not leaving you.'

'You're going to have to, I'm afraid,' the doctor intervened. 'This man needs his rest. Leave him with us; he's in safe hands.'

'Five more minutes?'

The doctor nodded and closed the curtain behind him to give them some privacy. She stroked Matthew's hair. He looked exhausted and ready to go to sleep. Libby couldn't make sense of what had happened. The hotel had been so on top of things, had made so many reassurances, and it wasn't as if a peanut allergy was uncommon. They must deal with food intolerances every day. It seemed unlikely that they would have slipped up like that.

She couldn't shake off the feeling that this was deliberate. Could someone, knowing Matthew had a severe peanut allergy, have put something in his dessert? There had been so many people milling about during dinner, it would have been possible. The slightest dusting of peanuts would have been enough to trigger a reaction.

First Natalya and now Matthew. Was there a killer at the wedding?

Libby cast her mind back to who had been near their table but plenty of people had passed them on the way to the exit. It would have been a huge risk to sneak nuts into Matthew's dessert. The killer was clearly getting more confident, or desperate.

She was getting ahead of herself again. Who would want to hurt Matthew? She could understand if it had been Simon under threat but what harm had Natalya and Matthew ever done? Was this something to do with Alex's death?

'I don't understand how this happened. You're always so careful,' she said.

Matthew shrugged. 'You know what it's like.'

'First Natalya goes missing, and now this happens to you. I don't like this, Matthew. Something's going on and I want to know what it is.'

'You're being melodramatic. It'll be a mistake. We'll take it up with the hotel tomorrow.'

'You could have died.'

She knew she should leave Matthew alone to recover

but she wouldn't be able to sleep until she'd asked him. 'What were you arguing with Daniel about earlier?'

Matthew looked sheepish, like Patrick did when he was caught telling a fib. 'That's got nothing to do with it.'

'Humour me.'

Matthew hesitated. 'It was Simon's book. There's some stuff in it that Daniel doesn't want in the press. I suggested that we pre-empt the book, take control of the story, but he didn't agree.'

'What story?'

'Something that happened while we were in the band. I think that if it's going to hit the media anyway then it would be better coming from us. Daniel disagrees.'

'What kind of story? What are you keeping secret, Matthew?'

He hesitated, then looked her in the eye. 'You have to understand… it was a long time ago and things were different back then. We were kids really, out of our depth.'

'You can tell me anything, you know that.'

'We…' Matthew looked up, startled, as the curtain opened. Libby cursed as Amir slipped into the bay. What the hell was he doing here?

'How are you doing, Matthew?' Amir had a serious look on this face. Libby couldn't tell if it was genuine concern, or something more sinister.

Matthew paled. 'Amir? You didn't have to come.'

'I came to see if I could do anything, give you a lift back to the hotel perhaps, but the doctor says they're keeping you in overnight?'

'That's right. I'm fine but thank you. It's kind of you to come.'

'Is there anything you need me to get?'

'I'm good, thanks, but Libby could do with a lift back.'

Libby glowered at him. What was he thinking? She didn't want to go anywhere with Amir.

'There's no need, I can get a taxi.'

'You might as well. I'm going back anyway.' It would seem churlish to refuse. Libby couldn't help feeling suspicious. Why had Amir come? Was he intending to finish the job? If so, it was probably better that she kept an eye on him and steered him away from Matthew, but was she safe getting in a car with someone she suspected of murder?

'He's been lucky,' she said. 'Someone took the EpiPen out of my bag.'

Amir looked genuinely surprised. 'Really? Are you sure you didn't forget it?'

'No, I would never forget something like that.'

'You think this was deliberate?'

'I'm sure of it.'

'Why would anyone want to hurt Matthew?'

'To shut him up, perhaps?'

Amir was about to reply when the doctor came back. 'I'm going to have to insist this man gets his rest. You can come back in the morning.'

Libby leaned over and kissed Matthew. He squeezed her hand. 'I'll be OK,' he whispered. 'Go with Amir. You can trust him.'

Libby squeezed it back, wishing she shared his

conviction. Reluctantly, she bid Matthew goodnight, promising to ring him before she went to sleep. She had absolutely no desire to return to Harrington Hall, but she followed Amir through the hospital corridors towards the exit.

A drizzle of rain coated her face as they walked out into the floodlit car park and towards Amir's car. It was now dark. The sky was inky black, heavy with dark grey clouds. At the taxi rank, a line of cabs hustled for business. It wasn't too late; she could insist that she took a taxi. She didn't care if Amir were offended. At least she would be safe.

Chapter Forty

Libby

'I can take you to the train station if you like?'

'What?' Libby turned to look at Amir's profile. He was staring straight ahead, focussed on the road. The interior of his car was pristine. A small tin of mints was in one of the drinks holders and the car smelt of lemon air freshener. It had all the latest technology and tinted windows. It must have cost a fortune; no wonder he was so upset when it had been damaged twice in the space of one weekend. Unlike Matthew, Amir drove in silence, the only sound coming from the sat nav on the dashboard between them.

'You could catch a train home.'

'At this time of night? Besides, I'm not leaving Matthew.' Libby had to admit the offer was tempting. But why was Amir so keen to get rid of her?

'A hotel then, in town.' Libby suspected that all the hotel

rooms in this small market town would be taken up with evening guests. 'I'll pay, if that's an issue.'

'It's not an issue. I'm fine at Harrington Hall, thank you.'

'You're in danger.' Amir said it so quietly, she wasn't sure she had heard him correctly.

'I beg your pardon?'

'It's not safe for you up there. You've been digging around too much. Asking too many questions.'

'Are you threatening me?'

He turned his head. 'I'm warning you. Peter's told me what you've been up to. You're putting yourself at risk.' Amir's voice was calm and steady; it was the voice of a lawyer advising his client.

Libby bit her lip and looked out of the rain-streaked window. She wished she had never to come to this wedding. She'd give anything to be back home right now, tucked up with a good book and a glass of wine.

'What is it that you lot are so keen to hide?'

'Can't you see that questions like that are going to make things worse?'

'Make what worse? I haven't got a clue what's going on. Is this about Simon's book?'

'There are things in that book that people will go to extreme lengths to keep out of the public domain.'

'Including you? Do you know what happened to Natalya? And Matthew?'

'I don't know anything, but I have my suspicions.'

'Then we should call the police. Tell them everything.'

Amir slammed on the brakes and Libby felt herself thrown towards the window as he made an emergency stop. They were on a deserted but well-lit main road out of the town. Was this her opportunity to make a run for it?

'I'm telling you, Libby. Leave it be. You don't know what you're getting into.' Amir sounded desperate. Was he going to hurt her?

'I'll take my chances.' He looked like he wasn't going to move but another car drove up behind them and started flashing his lights before swinging dangerously around them. They were blocking the road. Amir reluctantly turned the key in the ignition and started making his way to Harrington Hall.

'It's your funeral,' he said.

Libby tried to relax as Amir wove around the dark country roads, his car lights on full beam. It was so dark out here and creepy. Amir's words echoed in her head. Maybe she should have taken up his offer to drive her to the train station. It would surely be safer than returning to Harrington Hall. She didn't know, or trust, anyone at the wedding, least of all the person who was driving her there.

Libby got out her phone and kept it in her hand while they drove, but if Amir was going to hurt her, it was unlikely she would be able to alert anyone in time to stop him. She kept her eyes on the sat nav, checking that he wasn't making any detours, but he seemed to be heading straight back to the hotel. She wracked her brain for a piece of small talk, anything to reduce the tension, but she couldn't think of anything.

The whole thing felt surreal, like it was happening to someone else. What was Matthew hiding from her? She thought she had met someone who was open and honest, someone she could envisage spending the rest of her life with, but maybe she had got it wrong. If Matthew couldn't trust her with his secrets, then what chance did they have? They needed to sit down and talk, get everything out in the open if they wanted their relationship to survive.

Libby was more convinced than ever that Matthew's allergic reaction was connected to Natalya's disappearance. She tried to recall where Amir, Peter, Simon, and Daniel had been before dessert was served, but everyone had been moving about. It would have been relatively simple to sprinkle Matthew's dessert with nuts as they walked past, or even to swap the stickers on the dishes. Any one of them could have done it. But why? Was it some form of retribution? Had it been a warning to keep his mouth shut or had they intended to kill him? If so, they had very nearly succeeded.

Chapter Forty-One

Europe, 1996

The fuss over Simon's overdose and Daniel's kiss-and-tell died down, and the album was eventually released, going straight in at number twelve. They had hoped for a higher slot, but they knew they were being optimistic. Take That had split up but there were plenty of bands vying to take their place. Besides, nobody could compete with the Spice Girls that year.

Sales were good enough to earn them their first international tour, travelling around Europe in a sleeper bus. Up to this point, Matt had only been abroad with his parents and the freedom was exhilarating. He got to see all the cities he had read about, although there was barely any time for sightseeing and their exposure to local culture was limited to the inside of bars and music venues and grey motorways criss-crossing the continent. It was incredibly cool, and lucrative, to be playing their music to new audiences every night and the European girls were hot.

The cash was rolling in now. Thousands and thousands of pounds which, following Amir's advice, Matt invested in buy-to-let properties. He paid off his parents' mortgage and set up a trust fund for Jacqui to go to university. A few more years and he would have enough savings to ensure he would never have to work again. He longed for a place of his own; a modest home, like the one he grew up in, with a garden and room for kids. A wife. When he fantasised about this domestic set-up, it was always with Alex, but he still hadn't mustered up the courage to tell her how he felt.

Simon had no such compunctions about Natalya. The couple had married a few weeks before the tour in an informal ceremony. Natalya had just turned eighteen and had none of her family around her, a move she later told the press she deeply regretted. But they were young, stupid, and in love.

There was no point in Matt declaring his feelings for Alex now anyway. She had started dating one of the crew and was besotted with him. He was a skinny guy with yellowing teeth and long greying hair, improbably called Phoenix, who was at least twenty years older than her. Matt didn't have a clue what she saw in him. He was constantly patronising them with his stories of being a roadie for other bands. Alex listened agog when he related his bullshit memoirs of touring with some of the greats. The guy would have to be 120 years old to have done everything he claimed. Monterey, Woodstock, Glastonbury. He had apparently been instrumental to the success of every major festival, every major band.

For three agonising months, Alex was head-over-heels in love with him. Matt couldn't move without stumbling upon them eating each other's faces. It wasn't the shagging that bothered Matt, it was the fact that Phoenix was always hanging around, interrupting their conversations, pedalling his paternal advice.

'Can't you get rid of him?' Matt moaned to Craig.

'What, get rid of Phoenix? He's the best in the business. You're lucky to have him on board.'

'So he keeps telling us. He's a knob.'

Craig patted him on the back. 'Bit of advice, son? Move on. You're young, single. You can have any girl you want.'

'That's totally not the point.'

Craig gave him a knowing smile but refused to discuss the issue again. Matt fumed. Everyone treated him like a kid. He was a star. He should have a say in who was in the crew. He thought briefly about paying the guy off but if Alex found out, she'd never speak to him again. He would have to bide his time.

Holland. France. Germany. Spain. They posed for photographs at iconic landmarks and collected tacky souvenirs to take home. They raved to Eurodance. They brought their own chef with them at Matt's insistence. He couldn't risk eating out all the time with his food allergies and the band couldn't risk his absence.

They had been on tour for four weeks when Alex pulled him to one side before a gig. She looked worried.

'I need your help,' she said. 'I need you to get me a pregnancy test.'

'What the hell?'

'Shhh! No one can find out.' Alex was right; she might be recognised if she tried to buy it herself and she couldn't trust anyone in the crew not to sell the story to the tabloids.

'You're pregnant?' he whispered.

'Not necessarily. My period's late, is all.' She bit her lip. 'I was on the pill, but I guess I must have missed a few days.'

'What about Phoenix? Why don't you ask him?'

She looked over her shoulder nervously. 'I don't want him to know.'

He did as she asked, humiliating himself in the local pharmacy as he tried to explain what he wanted. He slipped it to her in a brown paper bag when they were in the bar.

'Come with me?' she whispered.

He followed her into the ladies' toilets and hovered outside the stall, smiling nervously at the drunk women that filed in and gave him funny looks. Alex... pregnant? He couldn't get his head around the idea. He had always consoled himself with the idea that she and Phoenix were a passing fling, that she would come to her senses sooner or later, but if they had a child together, he would be in her life forever. They might even get married.

Eventually she came out, shaking her head.

'False alarm.'

'That's... good?'

Alex looked at him with a neutral expression.

'Of course,' she said, walking over to the sinks and washing her hands. She dropped the test in the bin with a dismissive gesture as she walked away from him without another word.

Matt walked back towards the booth where she was already sitting next to Phoenix, his arm draped possessively around her shoulders. They never spoke about it again.

It was a relief when the summer season came to an end and the crew disbanded. Phoenix, thank God, was hired by another band to go to Australia and Matt had to endure another month of Alex moping after him. Eventually, he stopped calling and texting and the last they heard he had hooked up with another singer.

Chapter Forty-Two

EXTRACT FROM SIMON GREENE'S MEMOIR, *UNTOLD STORY*.

Whoever said that line about hell being other people must have been in a band. We couldn't get away from each other. It was even worse on tour; you were literally breathing in the same stale air night after night in a stuffy bus.

One night, in Holland, I went outside for a fag. We had parked in a campsite en route to somewhere or other, in a beautiful place surrounded by trees. The air was still and there was the brightest moon that painted everything silver. I started to walk towards the forest, to immerse myself in nature, to escape for a few minutes, but Daniel called me back.

'You don't know what's out there,' he said.

'That's the point.'

Daniel loved company. Parties. Girls. He hated silence and emptiness, but I craved it. Being famous is like living in an aquarium. Everyone's watching you. Sometimes they love you, sometimes they hate you. They all think they know you. They don't. They only know the part of you that you choose to reveal, and we only ever reveal our best selves. Even our closest friends and family don't know everything about us.

Of course we were going to fail eventually. Our success couldn't last forever, nothing ever does, although plenty of bands last longer than we did. Four years. That's all it took to break us.

I didn't think so at the time, but looking back, I realise that some of our singles weren't that great. The lyrics, in particular, were crass, reflecting our immaturity. We were teenagers, for Christ's sake, singing about heartbreak we hadn't experienced, philosophy we had only borrowed, and giving advice when we didn't have a clue about anything. We cared too much about what people thought of us. We listened to 'experts' instead of following our instincts. The industry treated us like children; they sanitised most of my lyrics. We weren't allowed to write about sex or use profanities. We were Peter Pans in Neverland, never allowed to grow up.

Fame is a vicious circle. At the start you're a shiny new toy to play with, full of potential and enthusiasm, but then you get old, you get wise, and people start to lose interest in you. There's always someone younger and more talented waiting in the wings to take your place. A steady stream of naïve young people willing to prostitute themselves for fame. It's survival of the fittest at its most brutal.

I don't know who was to blame for the demise of the band; we all had our part to play. Was it Daniel who destroyed the band? Or Matthew? Or did it start much earlier than that? Was the writing already on the wall by the time we went to Asia? I knew about Amir's suggestion of mutiny; Craig took great delight in telling me. I didn't blame him – I was off my head for most of that time – but it still hurt that my closest friend in the band would stab me in the back. We had grown up together, practically lived in each other's houses. If he had a problem with me, he should have told me to my face, but I guess, all's fair in love and music. Was it Alex's fault? She was as devastated as I was when the band broke up. She couldn't handle it. No, her suicide was the result of our actions, not the cause. I shoulder some of the blame, I know that. They looked to me to be the leader and I let them down. I was so wrapped up in my own problems that I didn't think about how it affected them.

Perhaps it was inevitable. The world is full of bands like us. You're only as good as your last single and fans are fickle. We used to laugh at them. The women that followed Daniel around. The men that perved after Alex. I even had my own small set of fans, although they tended to be attracted to my music rather than my looks. The industry is full of fake friends and frenemies. We quickly learned that you couldn't trust anyone.

Chapter Forty-Three

Libby

It was nine-thirty by the time they reached Harrington Hall. As they pulled up outside the entrance of the manor house, Libby saw guests in evening dress milling about, laughing and smoking. It all looked so elegant and convivial, not a place where a killer was at large. Amir dropped her off at the front door.

'I know you won't listen to my advice, but if I were you, I would head straight to your room and keep the door locked,' he said as she climbed out.

Libby slammed the car door and watched as he drove towards the car park. She resented Amir issuing her orders. What right did he have to tell her what to do? She was at a wedding, surrounded by people. She would be safe as long as she stayed in the building, and besides, no one had any reason to hurt her, had they? All she had done was ask a few awkward questions. Amir was trying to scare her, steer her away from finding out the truth. Clearly Matthew's secret also implicated him.

She walked back into the hotel reception. She had no desire to join the evening do but she wasn't prepared to let what happened to Matthew go. He had nearly died tonight. If it hadn't been a mistake, then perhaps one of the kitchen staff or the waiters had seen someone acting suspiciously?

She found the manager in the cavernous kitchen. The room was a hive of activity as the food for the evening buffet was prepared. She recognised some of the staff from breakfast and realised that they were pulling double shifts for the wedding; they must be exhausted. The manager was remonstrating with a man with a large white moustache wearing chef whites. He noticed her and glowered, muttering expletives under his breath in French. The manager turned around and steered her out of the kitchen.

'I'm very sorry, madam, but we cannot allow guests in the kitchen. Health and safety.' The manager looked like he had the weight of the world on his shoulders but was still maintaining a calm unruffled persona.

'Of course, I just wanted to talk to the chef…'

'I strongly advise you don't right now. Jacques is a man of great culinary talent, but he has a chef's temper. Perhaps you could talk to me instead and I will pass on your message.'

'My boyfriend has been hospitalised and I would like to know what happened,' Libby said, surprised at the assertiveness in her voice.

'I have asked the same question myself and I can assure you that there were no nuts in that dessert. Jacques is very careful; he has allergies himself. He has given me his full assurance that the dish was not contaminated.'

'So how do you explain Matthew's allergic reaction?'

'There's only one explanation, really. The nuts were added to the dish after it left the kitchen.'

At last, someone who shared her suspicions.

'So you think one of the guests did it.'

'My dear, I have been in this game for so long that nothing surprises me anymore. Perhaps it was someone's idea of a joke. Or an attempt to claim compensation. You really can't put anything past people in these days of litigation. Now, unless I can help you further, I really do need to be getting along…'

'But what about the tyres in the car park? Was that just a joke as well?'

'Madam, I really don't have time for this.'

'I won't keep you long, I promise. I think they're connected.'

'I doubt that very much,' he said. 'We caught the culprit on CCTV and informed the police. I believe they arrested a woman this afternoon.'

'Was she called Brenda, by any chance?'

The hotel manager hesitated, reluctant to divulge the information but clearly deciding he would be more likely to get rid of her if he did. 'I believe so. Not a guest at our hotel. I can assure you that these things are not common occurrences. We take great pride in our functions, they always run smoothly, but we certainly seem to be having a run of bad luck this weekend.'

'And what about Natalya?'

'I have already told you. We have no reason to suspect that Ms Bisset has not simply left without checking out.'

'Well, has she been in touch?' If Natalya had gone home, then she would have surely called the hotel about her mobile phone by now.

'That's confidential information.'

'I could go to the police and let them deal with it.' Libby was aware of a slight threat in her voice.

The hotel manager blanched. 'I hardly think that is necessary, madam. I think we've taken up quite enough of the emergency services' time tonight, don't you? Any more flashing lights and we'll have the media on our doorstep wondering what's going on.'

Libby resisted the urge to tell him that she was the media. 'My boyfriend has been attacked and a guest has gone missing. Don't you think we need to do something?'

'And what exactly would you like me to do, madam?'

Libby stood her ground. She wasn't going to let this officious man intimidate her. 'I would like you to investigate. I'm not satisfied with your explanation about the gunshot this morning. You said yourself that it couldn't have been the gamekeeper. Do you keep guns on the premises?'

'Under lock and key.'

Libby stood her ground. 'And no one could have taken one?"

'None of the guests have access to the guns. Only the gamekeeper. Although...'

'Yes?'

'No, that's highly unlikely.'

'Tell me, please. So many things are happening, and I think I'm going mad.'

The manager hesitated. 'Well, we do run shooting parties from here. It's possible that one of the guests might have seen the combination to the gun cupboard if they'd been here before. But it's hardly likely, is it?'

'How often do you change the combination?'

Libby took the manager's silence that it wasn't often enough. Which meant anyone who had stayed at the hotel before could potentially have accessed the gun cabinet.

'Do you recognise any of the guests? Would you know if they had stayed here before?'

'My dear, I deal with hundreds of people every week. I wouldn't remember them all. But it would be in our system.'

'Could you take a look?'

The manager sighed. 'I am exceptionally busy tonight, Ms Steele. It will take a while and Marion, the head receptionist, is not on duty until tomorrow.'

'Please, it's an emergency. I really think something terrible has happened to Natalya and the same person could be responsible for what happened to Matthew. I need your help.'

The manager looked like he was going to refuse but then shrugged. 'Well, all right. But you will need to give me some time. There are 100 guests here today, and that's not including the evening guests. I also have a busy hotel to run. I will need a few hours.'

He ushered her towards the marquee. 'Why don't you re-join the party? I'll find you if I have some information.'

Libby let it go. The hotel manager had a business to run, and it was clear that she was getting in the way. It was interesting about the gun cupboard, but it didn't really help her. There was no evidence that Natalya had even been shot and if she had, wouldn't a killer use their own gun instead of leaving it to chance? And how would they hide the body? They would have to know the grounds very well. It was a huge risk with so many guests milling about. Had they really got away with it without anyone seeing?

Libby caught her reflection in the mirror – she looked red-cheeked and flustered, and her hair was all over the place. It was no wonder the hotel manager was speaking down to her. He probably thought she was as mad as poor Brenda. The only person who seemed to be taking her suspicions seriously was Peter. Could she trust him not to relay everything to Amir? She didn't have much of a choice. Maybe if they pooled their resources, they could work out who the killer was before they struck again.

Chapter Forty-Four

Thailand, 1997

As the air-conditioned limousine pulled out of Bangkok Airport, Matt felt his sense of excitement build. Bangkok was their first stop of their tour of Asia, and they were all beside themselves with excitement. Alex had bought guidebooks for everywhere they were visiting, even though their schedule didn't allow them any time for sightseeing. She had talked non-stop during the flight as Matt drank steadily and tried to quell his anxiety. Far from getting better, his nerves seemed to be getting worse the more famous they got. He was certain that one day this would all come crashing down and it would be all his fault; one day he would freeze on stage or let his nerves get the better of him. It hadn't happened yet, but there was always time.

Bangkok was a sea of colour. Advertising for familiar brands – Toyota, Esso, even McDonalds – sat comfortably next to the golden spires of brightly lit temples. They passed huge billboards promoting beauty products and signs written in English and Thai cursive script. As they got closer to the city centre, the traffic ground to a slow crawl and he watched colourful tuk-tuks and motorcycles carrying entire families weave their way through the cars. The pavements were filled with lit-up food carts and people crouched on plastic stools slurping bowls of noodles.

The car stopped at an opulent hotel with a security guard outside who waved them through. The hotel was central and top end, surrounded by massive shopping malls and skyscrapers that screamed money. There was a helipad on the roof and a private VIP entrance. They were taken to the penthouse suite which was elegantly decorated and had floor-to-ceiling windows with views over the city. The suite was ice cold from the air-conditioning and had every convenience they could ask for, including a private concierge who was on call twenty-four hours, and their own personal masseuse. The fridge was full of expensive vodka and champagne. Daniel directed the bellboy to place his bags in the biggest room without any consultation. A woman dressed in a fuchsia traditional silk dress handed them glasses of chilled champagne and gave a bow with her hands pressed together. Alex returned the gesture of welcome.

'This is amazing,' she said, sipping her champagne, and looking out of the floor-to-ceiling windows at the sprawling city below.

Craig was all business as he handed out their promo schedules. Between meet and greets, press interviews, private acoustic sessions for rich businessmen and the concerts they were headlining, there was hardly any time to explore the city, but they did have this one evening free.

'I thought you might need some sleep...' Craig suggested half-heartedly as Daniel tapped up the concierge for information about the nightlife in Bangkok. 'Please be careful. I need you all on good form tomorrow morning.'

No one was listening and an hour later, they ended up in Patpong, the notorious red-light district in Bangkok. The area was packed with bars and clubs with a street market running down the middle of one of the roads. There were crowds of people: young backpackers, older tourists peering into the doorways, and old single men out on the pull. Loud disco music spilled out of the bars. Even though it was night, it was still hot, and the smog mixed with the diesel fumes from the traffic and the smells rising from the sewers, made it difficult to breathe.

The driver, a quietly spoken man in his early fifties, dropped them off at the top of the street and pointed out a club that the concierge had recommended. They climbed out of the limousine and were immediately approached by a woman old enough to be Matt's mum asking them if they wanted to see a 'pussy show'. Another man approached them with a laminated menu of dance acts they could watch. Alex pulled a face as she read it.

'Good for ladies too,' the man insisted, trying to steer them towards the bar.

The man pursued them for a few minutes as they walked down the road, drinking in the atmosphere and browsing the tat on the market stalls, then left them to pounce on a group of backpackers that had just arrived and who were peeking in the bars to get a glimpse of the goods on offer. Bored-looking girls dressed in their underwear were dancing half-heartedly on revolving platforms or sitting on tall barstools trying to draw in the punters. A few girls were playing pool with old western men who looked like they had died and gone to heaven. Stunning ladyboys sashayed passed them in tall stiletto heels, handing out leaflets for a show. It was good to feel anonymous again, mixing in with the crowds of tourists.

'*Yaba*?' a man sidled up to them.

'You what?'

'*Yaba*, is good, yes? Get you high?' He made a gesture of smoking.

'No, we're good, thanks,' Matt said, quickly walking away but Simon stopped to chat to the guy. 'He cannot be serious.'

He waited with Alex, watching with disbelief as Simon followed the dealer down one of the dark alleyways that criss-crossed the street.

'Is he mental?' Alex said.

'Just leave him.'

'We can't leave him in the middle of Bangkok. Anything could happen!'

'Well, I'm not following him. We'll get mugged... or worse if we go down there. What's he playing at?'

Reluctantly, they joined Daniel and Amir who were standing at the corner of the alleyway looking as bewildered as Matt felt. A rat ran across their path as they peered down the dark *soi*. They could see a little boy playing in the gutter with a stick and a woman staring at them from an upstairs window.

'Where'd he go?'

Amir shrugged. 'Into one of those buildings, I guess. I didn't see which one.'

'Try his mobile.'

Daniel obeyed but shook his head after a couple of minutes. 'Voicemail. Come on, let's find a bar. He'll turn up sooner or later.'

They found a bar opposite the side street and ordered some drinks. The bored waitress flirted half-heartedly with them as she served their rum and cokes.

'This is so typical of Simon. He could be hours. What is *yaba* anyway?'

'Some sort of street drug, I think,' Alex said. 'Did he have much money on him?'

An hour later and there was still no sign of Simon. Matt tried to quell the fear that was rising inside him. Simon was always taking risks when it came to drugs; this was no different from the nights that he had left them in London, but there was something about disappearing in Bangkok that felt different. Among the fear, he felt a surge of anger. They were always looking out for Simon, like he was some sort of child.

Daniel suggested a club, but no one was in the mood, so eventually they rang the driver and arranged for him to pick them up.

'Who's going to tell Craig that we lost Simon?' Matt said, as they climbed back into the limousine, sinking into the leather seats. The air conditioning was a relief after the sultry heat of the city streets.

'Hopefully, we won't need to.'

'Fuck him,' Daniel concluded as they made their way through the city. Every time they stopped at a traffic light, beggars crowded around the vehicle, tapping on the blacked-out windows, their thin hands held out for money. There was so much poverty at street level it made Matt feel sick. They passed old women in rags sleeping under the bridges and barefoot children with wide eyes staring at them as they returned to the comfort of their opulent hotel. Why didn't anyone do something about it?

'You wan' some girls?' the driver asked.

Girls, drugs. They could have literally anything they wanted while people starved in the streets. Matt was suddenly sick of it all; he wanted to climb into his bed and wake up to an ordinary life. There was something repellent about having everything.

Simon was waiting for them in the hotel suite, bouncing with excitement and as high as a kite. 'I got a tuk-tuk back,' he explained. 'You need to try this stuff, man. It's fucking incredible.'

Matt felt like punching the self-satisfied grin off his face. 'We were worried about you. You can't just piss off like that.'

'Fuck off, I'm a grown man. I can do what I like.'

Matt squared up to him, his fist clenched as the anger that had been building up all evening threatened to release itself.

'Go on, do it. You haven't got the balls,' Simon taunted him.

Daniel dragged him away. 'It's not worth it, Matt. Let it go.'

He swallowed his anger. It threatened to overwhelm him at times, and he struggled to control it. Simon was so irresponsible; all he cared about was getting high. He didn't give a shit how it impacted the rest of them. Matt wondered how much more he could take. He felt like he was walking on a precipice and it was only a matter of time before he fell off.

Chapter Forty-Five

Tokyo, 1997

I f Bangkok had been an assault to the senses, then Tokyo was in another league altogether. The city was so busy, it was hard to comprehend how many people lived and worked there. There were vending machines on every street corner, selling snacks and drinks twenty-four-hours a day. The train stations, which were large enough to house several shopping centres, were like miniature cities themselves, the shops an endless source of fascination as they browsed the goods on offer, trying to work out what things were.

Amir headed off to restock his collection of anime, while Simon took up an invitation to test his nerves with the infamous blowfish which promised instant death if cooked incorrectly. Daniel wanted to buy a samurai sword to take home and enlisted the help of the concierge who promised to show him the finest craftsmen in the city. Alex and Matt headed off in different directions to go shopping. The city was full of the latest gadgets and high-end fashion and Matt spent a small fortune getting it all shipped back to the UK. As he walked back to the hotel, businessmen in identical suits streamed out of the subways, still commuting at 10pm, and girls dressed in cosplay outfits tried to entice him into neon-lit bars. Every corner of Tokyo offered something new and unexpected. It was a city you could lose yourself in. Matt wondered whether he could consider moving here. It would be fantastic to live in a place with so much energy, away from everything he had grown up with.

They were playing for three nights and tickets for the shows had sold out within minutes. They had a huge fan base in Japan and their hotel suite was filled with welcome gifts and flowers. It didn't matter where they were in the world, people loved them. Album sales had been going through the roof and the money was pouring in. Matt didn't even need to touch his capital; he could live off the interest alone.

Their opening night was a huge success. The stadium was packed, the fans respectful, and the atmosphere electric. They came off stage on a high to the sounds of the crowds screaming out their names. They were dripping with sweat as they signed autograph books and posed for pictures.

The afterparty was held in a penthouse apartment belonging to one of the richest men in Japan. There was plenty of saké, and girls, and lines of coke on the table. Someone brought out a karaoke machine and the Japanese businessmen took it in turns to sing the band's songs at them. In the early hours of the morning, a stretch limo arrived to take them back to their hotel. Matt was wired with adrenaline and coke; the last thing he wanted was to go to bed, but Amir and Alex were obviously ready to call it a night. Daniel refused to come back with them, calling them 'boring bastards' and promising faithfully he would arrive at the airport in plenty of time for their next flight.

Back in their suite, Matt poured them all vodka shots and opened another bottle of champagne. He looked out over the Tokyo skyline and felt like he owned the world. Three years ago, he had been sitting in the library, surrounded by books and worrying about his A levels. Why would anyone settle for an ordinary life when they could have all this?

It wasn't long before Simon slunk off to his room with a bottle of bourbon and his stash. Amir went to bed next, claiming he had a migraine coming on. They all knew he was planning to phone his boyfriend long-distance. Matt dimmed the lights and brought over the bottle of champagne to where Alex was curled up on the sofa, a contented smile on her face. He sat down next to her and stroked a hair from her cheek. Her skin was flushed with all the excitement from the evening, and she had never looked more beautiful.

'It's been the best night,' she said, pulling away from his hand.

'You were amazing,' he said.

'Matt?'

'What?'

'Stop looking at me like that.'

He turned away, embarrassed. There was an awkward silence between them as all his unspoken feelings rose to the surface.

'I do love you, Matt, but not like that.'

He swallowed hard. Why was she trying to ruin the perfect night by talking about their relationship? Surely it was better to say nothing and leave things as they were.

'You're like a brother to me.'

Her words felt like a knife through the heart. He had known, deep down, that Alex didn't feel the same way about him, but they had never discussed it. All these years, she had let him hope and now he felt like his whole world had caved in.

'Maybe we could give it a chance, see what happens.' He looked at her, hating himself for begging.

'You know what Craig says about relationships between band members.'

'Fuck Craig. This has nothing to do with him. This is about me and you.'

'It wouldn't work, Matt.'

'You don't know that.'

'I do.' She pulled herself up into a sitting position and placed her hand over his. 'You need to let it go. Find someone else.'

He grabbed her wrist. It was so skinny he felt that he could snap the tendons. 'I don't want anyone else. I love you.'

She tried to shake free of his grip. 'Matt, you're hurting me.'

'*You're* hurting *me*.'

'What do you want me to do?' she shouted. 'Pretend to have feelings for you that I don't? How would that be fair, on either of us?'

He wanted to pin her down, to force her to love him. He wanted to show her how much he cared about her, how much he needed her, but he had to let her go. She stood up and rubbed her wrist.

'I am sorry, Matt. I hope we can still be friends.'

Matt couldn't look at her. He heard her walk to her room and lock the door behind her. He only raised his head when he was sure she wasn't coming back. Hot angry tears ran down his face. He picked up the champagne bottle and threw it against the wall. It smashed with a satisfying shower of broken glass. He looked around at the hotel suite – the whole place was trashed. The maids would clean it up in the morning. His heart, on the other hand, was not going to be quite as easy to fix.

Chapter Forty-Six

Libby

L ibby slipped back into the marquee. It was hot and noisy inside the tent. The tables had been moved to one end to make way for the dance floor and a DJ had set up his equipment at the back. The tables had been redecorated for the night-do with balloons and little disco balls. There was space for the buffet at the side of the tent and the cake had already been cut into individual pieces for guests to help themselves. Libby guessed she had missed the cake-cutting ceremony while she was at the hospital. Many of the day guests had got changed, heels had been left under tables, and ties and jackets were discarded over the backs of seats. Most of the guests were drunk.

The DJ made an announcement, and everyone turned to watch Daniel lead Vicky to the centre of the floor for the first dance. They were both good dancers and had obviously rehearsed a routine to an instrumental version of one of the band's romantic ballads. Libby vaguely recognised it from listening to Absolute 90s Radio. All eyes were on the bride and groom as they swirled around the floor and as the song came to an end, they were joined by other couples. The guests cheered as Daniel pulled Vicky towards him and gave her a lingering kiss. Libby glanced over to where Vicky's kids were sitting with their grandparents. The boy, who was about eleven, looked like he was going to be sick at his mother's public display of affection while his younger sister was taking advantage of the distraction to steal sips of her grandmother's wine. Libby thought of Matthew stuck in his hospital bed. He had nearly died but the wedding was continuing as if nothing had happened.

The tempo changed and an S Club 7 song came on, prompting a surge of women of all ages onto the dance floor and the men to retreat. As the women shook their hair and their hips in time to the music, young kids ran around them, twirling and making themselves dizzy.

She looked around for Peter but before she could spot him, she was accosted by Daniel who had extricated himself from the well-wishers on the dance floor. There were beads of perspiration on his forehead from the dancing, his eyes were sparkling, and his cheeks were flushed. He really was very handsome – by far the best-looking member of the band – and it was no surprise that he had a reputation as a ladies' man.

'How's Matt?' He seemed genuinely concerned as he sat down next to her at a table and met her gaze. Daniel had the ability to make you feel like you were the only woman in the room.

'He's going to be fine. They're keeping him in overnight just in case.'

'Thank God. I swear, I told the kitchen to be careful about nuts. I made it very clear how bad Matt gets. Vicky's devastated. First, Natalya does a disappearing act and then this happens to Matt. She thinks we're cursed.'

Daniel looked upset but Libby reminded herself that he was a presenter; he was paid to put on an appearance. And he had known about Matthew's nut allergy. All the band members had. They had lived together, eaten together, toured together for three years. You didn't spend that much time in someone's company without gaining a solid understanding of their dietary requirements.

'Is Natalya still missing then?' she asked.

'No one has seen or heard from her since this morning.' Daniel ran his hand through his hair. 'I reckon there must have been an emergency back home, but she could have called. I guess she didn't want to disturb the wedding.'

'You don't think she's…'

Libby considered telling Daniel her suspicions, but she bit her tongue. He might think she was trying to ruin their big day. They had already created enough drama when Matthew collapsed. She thought she caught a glimpse of Peter among the dancers but when she looked again it was a different guy entirely. The disco lights were making it difficult to recognise anyone.

She turned around to question Daniel again, but he was

being dragged back to the dance floor by a group of small children. Libby resumed her search for Peter. She spotted Amir sitting at one of the tables talking to Simon. She crept closer, keeping hidden behind the other guests, but the loud music was obscuring much of the conversation, and she could only catch the odd word. It sounded like Amir was offering Simon a large sum of money to stop the publication of the book.

'How much are we talking?'

Amir wrote a figure down on a napkin. Simon snorted derisively. 'Are you having a laugh? Add a couple of zeros and we can have another conversation.'

Simon stood up and left. Amir wiped his face with the napkin, looking like a broken man. Could Amir have slipped nuts into Matthew's dinner? He was obviously desperate to keep their secret quiet. She was trying to think if Amir had walked past their table during the wedding breakfast, but it was all a blur. She hadn't been taking any notice of people milling about. But why would Amir want to hurt Matthew? It was Simon who was causing problems.

Maybe Simon was the culprit? She didn't like the man, that was true, but was he a murderer? She couldn't imagine why he would have a grievance against Matthew. And deliberately contaminating someone's food to trigger an allergic reaction didn't seem his style. He was obviously not someone who shied away from confrontation.

Maybe she was over-reacting? Jumping to conclusions? Maybe this was all just a series of coincidences? She certainly seemed to be the only one at the wedding worried about Natalya's disappearance and there was no proof that Matthew's allergic reaction had been anything other than carelessness on the part of the hotel. Of course the manager would defend the chef – he was probably frightened of being sued.

Libby finally found Peter at the bar nursing a beer.

'How's Matthew?' he asked, as she ordered a Coke from the barman. She needed to keep a clear head.

'He'll be OK.' Libby scrutinised his reaction. Did he know something about the nuts in Matthew's dessert? Was he disappointed that Matthew had survived the attack?

'That's good.' Peter seemed distracted, looking around the marquee. 'Have you seen Amir at all? I haven't seen him for ages.'

Did Peter know he had gone to the hospital?

'He was sitting talking to Simon a few minutes ago.' She nodded over to the table where the two men had been sitting, but it was empty.

Peter groaned. 'I told him he needed to leave it, at least for tonight, but he's obsessed. Thinks he can appeal to Simon's better nature.'

'I'm not sure he's got one. What are they so worried about anyway?'

Peter didn't answer. He stared into his pint of beer like it held all the answers. Libby felt a surge of frustration. 'You know, don't you? Why won't you tell me?'

'It's not my secret to tell.'

'But it could be important.'

'If Matthew hasn't told you, then he obviously doesn't want you to know.'

She had worked that one out for herself. Peter was so smug and irritating, passing judgement on her relationship. She thought they'd gone past this point scoring.

'You and Amir tell each other everything then?'

'Yep, no secrets between us.' He took a long slug of his drink.

'So you know he's just offered Simon money to keep quiet?'

Peter looked momentarily taken aback but then swiftly covered it. 'Yes, I know about that. Listen, sweetheart, you don't know anything about my relationship with Amir. It's unconditional, OK?'

'So if Amir had murdered someone, you would still love him? You'd stand by him?'

'He hasn't, but yes. Wouldn't you stand by Matthew?'

Libby thought about Matthew's act of vandalism, how she had kept quiet about that. That had been bad enough. Could she really stand by someone capable of murder? No, she couldn't. If she knew that Matthew was guilty of murder, then she would report him. It was as simple as that. And if that made her a bad person, a bad girlfriend, then so be it. Maybe Peter was right. Maybe their relationship wasn't that strong after all. It was certainly being tested this weekend.

The waiter put her Coke in front of her. She sipped the cold drink, grateful for the caffeine hit.

'I've always thought people with food allergies were fussy eaters, to be honest, but that was some reaction,' Peter said. 'I didn't realise it could be so bad.'

'A lot of people think like that.' She scrutinised his expression. Was he feeling guilty? Perhaps he had put the nuts into Matthew's dish, hoping to get him out of the way for a few hours, not realising the impact it would have. Had Amir told him to do it? 'I guess you have to see it with your own eyes.'

'You would have thought the hotel would know about this kind of stuff. I mean, isn't this covered in basic training?'

'I'm not entirely sure the hotel is at fault. I spoke to the manager and he swore blind that the dish didn't have any nuts in it.'

Peter ingested this information. 'So what are you saying?'

'I think someone did it deliberately.'

'But why?'

Exactly. Was Peter playing dumb? He was in love with Amir. Was he covering for him?

'The same reason someone would hurt Natalya.' She told him about the gun cabinet, how easy it would be for a former guest to steal a gun and return it before the gamekeeper did his rounds.

'You really think there's a serial killer on the loose?' Peter joked. 'Blimey!'

She glared at him. 'Do you think we should call the police?

'What, now? Ruin the wedding?'

Libby thought about it. She thought about the manager struggling to hold everything together, Daniel and Vicky enjoying their special day, all the guests who had travelled to the party, the family and friends who had been planning this for months. They couldn't ruin everything without any evidence to back up their suspicions.

'No, you're right. They're not going to take us seriously. I think we should do some more digging, see if someone lets something slip. Maybe we should talk to Simon?'

'Do you think he'll talk to you?'

'Well, there's only one way to find out.'

Chapter Forty-Seven

London, 1997

M att had sung about heartbreak often enough, but it was the first time he had ever experienced it. The next day Alex acted like nothing had happened, and none of the others seemed to pick up on the vibe between them. Daniel, predictably, was late for the flight and came back boasting about what the others had missed by going home early. Matt sat back in his seat, closed his eyes, and pretended to be asleep. He couldn't bear to look at Alex. How could she be so cruel? She said she loved him; so how could she stand by while he died inside? Had she no compassion? He had been cynical about heartbreak before – misery sold records. There had been as many hits written about sorrow as there were about love. Now, he finally appreciated Simon's lyrics. Everyone experienced loss at some point in their life and music provided some solace. A sense of shared experience, a connection.

Alex said she wanted to be friends. Was that even possible? The thought of life without her was unbearable, but could he ever be happy with just being her friend? Standing to one side as she met another guy, got married, had kids? No, he could never do that.

Maybe he should have been more forceful. Proved to her how much he loved her. He thought about that closed bedroom door – had she really wanted him to come knocking? He shouldn't have let her go without a fight. Seeing her every day, knowing that he could never have her, was going to be pure torture. He couldn't stand this for years on end, knowing that all his hopes and dreams of them having a life together were never going to come true. She had let him believe, for years, that something might happen between them. She wasn't the person he'd thought she was. He loathed and loved her in equal measure.

In the meantime, they were forced into each other's company. Smiling and laughing, giving their fans what they wanted to see from their idols. Everything felt so fake and futile. Their audience didn't want to know about rifts and rivalries. There were cracks forming in the band that weren't going to heal. They were all physically and mentally shattered as the intensity of their tour of Asia took its toll.

Matt was drinking too much, but he didn't want to stop; it blurred the pain and was the only way he could get any sleep. No one seemed to notice or care that he was getting through a bottle of vodka every night. Every morning, the cleaning staff at the hotels discretely cleared away the empty bottles and some assistant or other replenished them for the next day. He woke up needing a drink and when he went for too long without it, he noticed that his hands had started to shake. He worried it would start to affect his music, but he couldn't imagine going on stage sober. He told himself that it was all part of the rock 'n' roll lifestyle; everyone was doing it. He had years ahead of him to grow up and be sensible, to kick any addiction that he may or may not be developing. He was young, free, and loaded. Why shouldn't he have a bit of fun? He wasn't like Simon; he could control it.

Up to that point, Matt had held himself back to a certain degree when it came to girls but now that there was no point in waiting for Alex, he screwed anyone who would have him. He flaunted his conquests in Alex's face, making sure they stayed for breakfast, sitting on the kitchen stools wearing his T-shirt and lacy knickers. She looked at him in disgust and what might even have been pity.

Simon was increasingly out of control. The drugs were ravaging both his body and his mind. He looked ten years older than the rest of them. Natalya was desperate to get him into rehab, but he wouldn't listen to anyone, even when she threatened to leave him. Amir retreated further inside himself, locking himself away in his hotel room, only emerging to eat and yell at them to keep the noise down.

Towards the end of the tour, Alex's health started to suffer; her vocal cords had been pushed to their limit and she was in danger of dropping out altogether. They had to cancel a few gigs to let her recover and there was a nasty backlash in the media. Simon had been unsympathetic, blaming her for bad reviews and falls in sales figures. They had some vicious rows about it, each declaring the other impossible to work with.

By the time they arrived back in the UK, they were all sick of the sight of each other. Craig, sensing the atmosphere, gave them a month's holiday and Matt took the opportunity to visit some family in Scotland. Up in the Highlands, cut off from the rest of the world, he spent his days hiking, eating good food, and listening to classical music. He started to feel himself again and although he was still drinking every day, he cut it down to manageable levels. The fresh air and the soporific effect of the landscape made him feel alive again and when he returned to London, it was with refreshed vigour and a more peaceful outlook. The investments Amir had convinced him to make were doing well. He was even thinking of buying himself a shooting lodge; a bolt hole where he could get away from the others and spend time by himself.

Alex had been to Goa and returned looking more gorgeous than ever with sun-kissed skin and a new haircut. She had changed her trademark peroxide blonde to a chestnut brown and looked older and more mature. She had turned vegetarian and was espousing the benefits of detoxing. She had even agreed to let Craig start negotiations with a publisher for a book about clean eating.

Daniel was as full of himself as ever and had started a relationship with a supermodel. Their faces were all over the press as they stumbled out of nightclubs and were seen at exclusive parties. Even Amir seemed more relaxed after spending time with his boyfriend. Simon had spent the month in London working on a batch of new songs he wanted to develop. He couldn't wait for them to get into the studio but there was no time before the start of their American tour.

'Don't even think about taking drugs into the US,' Craig warned Simon as he handed out their itineraries.

Simon shrugged. 'I'm not stupid.' If Simon picked up a criminal conviction in the US, he might not be allowed back.

As Matt packed for Miami – the first city on the tour – he looked around their miserable cramped flat that they had never found time to upgrade and resolved to move out as soon as possible. He could afford to buy a nice place of his own outright. He could move to a better area, make new friends, start dating properly. Creating and playing music was his only real passion in life and being in a band with his best friends had been the ultimate high, but maybe it was time to think about the future and moving on. Maybe a clean break was best for everyone.

Chapter Forty-Eight

Libby

L ibby sipped her Coke and surveyed the dance floor but she couldn't spot Simon. Had he already left the party? It was 10pm. Surely only people with young children would be going to bed this early? Even Vicky's grandma, who had proudly told everyone she was eighty-one, was up and dancing with a circle of women who were teaching her how to floss. Libby scanned through Instagram on her phone. People had posted some pictures of the wedding already and Daniel had updated his status with a picture of himself and Vicky down by the lake with the word *blessed*. There was still nothing from Natalya and the fuss over her disappearance seemed to be already subsiding.

As far as she could tell, Simon didn't have any social media accounts. He had a profile on Wikipedia, but it mostly related to his time in the band. A few years back he had been involved in a high-profile court case about copyright and had apparently lost a lot of money. Libby wondered how much he would get from his tell-all memoirs. Was that the reason he was so desperate to publish the band's secrets?

Matthew had always spoken about Simon with respect. He had been an integral part of their group and instrumental to their success. He was responsible for writing their best-known single and most of their other hits. He had gone on to do the same with some other well-known artistes. She knew that he lived in Los Angeles and he didn't appear to be in a relationship.

Libby took her drink and hovered outside the men's toilets for twenty minutes, but Simon didn't emerge, and she started to attract some funny looks. She searched the whole of the marquee and went back inside the hotel to look around the reception. A couple of teenagers had claimed one of the high-back chairs and were ardently snogging. Everywhere she looked were party guests in various states of inebriation.

The hotel manager was sitting at reception, doing something on the computer. She wondered if he was looking through the database, as promised, and whether he had found anything. She thought about asking how things were going, but as soon as he spotted her, he stood up and disappeared through a door behind the desk revealing an office behind. She hadn't even noticed the door; it was so well concealed by the oak panelling.

She resumed her search and finally found Simon outside the front entrance, smoking a cigarette. He looked up as she approached, and she caught a look of exasperation run across his face.

'Are you here to have a go at me as well? I am Mr Popular tonight.' He took a drag of his cigarette and exhaled the smoke into her face.

'I'm not here to cause any trouble.'

'So what do you want?'

'I want to know what you've put in your book.'

'Why don't you ask Matt?'

'Because someone put him in hospital.'

He stared at her and then laughed. 'And you think that was me? Seriously, what else am I going to get the blame for tonight? Donald Trump? Global warming?'

A series of explosions made them both jump. They looked upwards to see the sky lit up in a riot of colour like the kaleidoscope Libby had played with as a kid.

'Fireworks,' she said, feeling her heart rate return to normal.

'What did you think it was?'

Simon was mocking her, but Libby wasn't going to be intimidated.

'Why did you come to the wedding, Simon? Was it just to wind everyone up?' Or was it something more sinister? Had Simon hurt Natalya? He had been in the woodland that morning; he'd had plenty of opportunity. And had he put nuts in Matthew's dessert?

'I thought Leo would be here. I haven't seen him for a while and, I dunno, it seemed like a good opportunity to reconnect.' He sounded sincere.

'But Leo didn't come to the wedding.'

'Had a gig apparently. Avoiding meeting up with his old man, more like. Can't say I blame him. I haven't been much of a father.'

'I need to know what's going on.' It was difficult to speak over the noise from the fireworks and she had to shout to make herself heard.

'And why should I tell you?'

'Maybe I can persuade Matthew to support your right to publish your memoirs.'

He dropped the cigarette on the ground, making no effort to stub it out. The smoke spiralled from the ground and Libby could smell the enticing scent of tobacco. She had given up smoking five years ago but still craved a cigarette now and then. 'Aye, maybe you can.'

She waited while he took out another cigarette and lit it, resisting the urge to tell him he would have more money if he stopped smoking. There was nothing worse than a reformed smoker. She could hear people outside on the lawn, gasping and cheering as the fireworks rose into the sky and exploded. A taxi made its way down the driveway and a giggling couple emerged from the hotel and climbed into it, oblivious of their presence. She thought about Matthew, alone in the hospital. Was he missing her?

'I'll tell you what they're all so worried about,' Simon said. 'But not here. There are too many people about. Meet me on the jetty in an hour.'

Libby hesitated. She wanted to know Matthew's secret, desperately, but she would have to be crazy to agree to Simon's suggestion. She didn't know the guy, and she certainly didn't trust him. Why would she agree to meet him in a deserted spot in the dark?

'Why don't you tell me inside?'

'Walls have ears. Meet me by the lakeside or don't. It makes no odds to me.'

He walked off abruptly. Libby shivered in the cool night air. She stood watching the last of the fireworks creating illusions in the sky, leaving behind a trail of smoke. Matthew had promised to tell her everything tomorrow, but could she trust him? It might be too late by then. What if the killer struck again? Only an idiot would follow a stranger into the darkness, a stranger she already suspected of murder, to find out a secret that she wasn't even sure she wanted to know. Simon could be dangerous. If he was responsible for Natalya's death, and had poisoned Matthew, then he might want to hurt her too. Was that his intention, to lure her away from the party and then dispose of her in the woodland? Is that what had happened to Natalya?

Libby sent a text to Matthew, hoping he was still awake. His reply came back almost instantaneously.

Don't trust him.

Was Matthew genuinely concerned, or was he trying to keep his secret a bit longer?

Don't worry, I'll be fine.

I mean it, Libby. Don't go.

Tell me what's going on and I won't.

Matthew didn't respond. Libby waited a few minutes before going back inside. If she were going to meet Simon by the lake, then she was changing out of these ridiculous heels. Matthew had explicitly told her not to trust Simon and Amir had said it wasn't safe for her at the party. Maybe she should heed their advice? She didn't know these people; she didn't know what any of them were capable of and she had her own responsibilities. What if something happened to her? Patrick would grow up without a mum. Was she putting herself in unnecessary danger? Matthew had promised to tell her the band's secret when they left the wedding; maybe she just had to be patient.

Chapter Forty-Nine

Libby

Libby returned to her hotel room, locking the door behind her. Momentarily she wondered whether to place one of the chairs under the handle for added protection but decided she was being ridiculous. She kicked off her heels and felt the soft carpet beneath her bare feet. The room felt lonely without Matthew. His possessions were neatly folded in a pile beside the bed. On the top was a black leather case which Matthew used to carry his spare EpiPen. She opened it. The pen was still there in its plastic tube. Had Matthew had it all along? She could have sworn that he had given it to her to carry that morning. Was all this in her head?

She walked over to the window and looked out over the marquee. She could see disco lights flashing red, blue, green, and yellow against the tarpaulin, and the silhouettes of guests walking around inside. She opened the window and pop music wafted through with the cool evening breeze. She could hear couples laughing together and the scent of cigarette smoke. Libby closed the window again and sat on the bed, Amir's warning going around her head. She could get changed into her pyjamas, find a film on the television, and stay cooped up here until morning. That would be the sensible thing to do.

Could she do that? Look after herself and forget about everyone else? It didn't seem right but what else could she do? In desperate need of advice, she took out her phone and rang Emma's number.

'What's up?' Emma asked straight away. Libby could hear the television in the background. The sounds of everyday life brought a lump to Libby's throat.

'Why would anything be up?' Her voice came out more defensive than she meant it to be.

'Aren't you at the wedding?'

Libby reprised what had happened, including Matthew and Amir's advice to stay where she was.

'Holy shit, are you OK?'

'Yeah, I'm fine.'

'Where are you now?' Emma had kicked into big-sister mode as Libby had known she would.

'I'm in my room. Don't worry, I'm safe.'

'Why don't you come home?'

Libby shivered at the thought of navigating the winding roads of the Yorkshire Dales in the middle of the night, driving Matthew's car. Besides, she'd been drinking and while she felt sober, she could well be over the limit. It simply wasn't worth the risk.

'I can't leave Matthew in the hospital.'

'You don't think he might have…?'

Libby had a feeling she knew what was coming next. 'He might have what, Emma? Spit it out.'

'You said he was hiding something. I'm just saying that maybe he might have put the nuts in the dessert himself. To put you off the scent.'

Libby thought about it. Matthew had been up and dressed when she got back from the hotel room this morning. Had he had enough time to sneak into the woodlands, kill Natalya and get back before she did? It was possible. But would he really have endangered his own life like that? He couldn't have known that she didn't have her EpiPen with her. Unless he had removed it himself. Had he played Russian roulette with his own life?

No, it couldn't possibly be Matthew. No one would play around with a nut allergy. It was far too dangerous. You couldn't possibly predict the severity of a reaction. Besides, Matthew wasn't a killer. It was ridiculous to even suspect him.

'No, I don't think that. Matthew would never hurt anyone.'

'Sorry, I'm just worried about you.'

'I'm fine. I'm safe.'

'Well, stay where you are then,' Emma ordered. 'And if anyone tries to get in, ring the police straight away.'

'I will, don't worry. It's just…'

'Just what?'

Libby knew what Emma's reaction would be if she told her what was on her mind, but she couldn't help herself.

'What if something else happens and I didn't say or do anything?'

'Libby, you don't have to save the world all of the time,' Emma snapped. 'This is none of your business. Don't get involved.'

'I can't leave it. Someone could get hurt.'

'I mean it, Libby. Call the police if you have to, but don't go looking for trouble.'

'I'm not.' Libby sounded sulky. She hated the way the way she reverted to the role of little sister when speaking to Emma. She should never have called her.

'Don't trust anyone, OK? You're a terrible judge of character.'

Emma didn't know how right she was. Patrick's father was a case in point. Libby had been flattered when Ryan had spent the evening with her at the party, plying her with drinks, before leading her into the bedroom. She'd thought he meant it when he told her she was beautiful and kissed her, laid her down on the bed and promised nothing would happen if she didn't want it to.

'Is it your first time?' he'd asked, unzipping her jeans. She didn't want to admit it, but he must have known, surely? Her head was clouded with alcohol but not so much that she didn't know what was happening. She could have stopped him, perhaps she should have stopped him, but she didn't. Libby had been too embarrassed to ask Ryan to use a condom. The whole thing had been over in a few minutes. It had hurt and she hadn't enjoyed it, but she'd thought it might be better the next time they did it. Only, after it was over, Ryan's whole attitude changed. He couldn't get away quick enough. He didn't speak to her again at the party and he ignored her the next day at school. He probably laughed about it with his mates the next day; gave her a score out of ten.

'I'm sorry. Please look after yourself, okay?' Emma's tone was softer now. 'Listen, do you want to speak to Patrick?'

'Is he still up?' It was half past ten – way past his bedtime.

'Not for much longer.'

Libby could hear him protesting.

'Yeah, put him on.'

There was a shuffle as the phone exchanged hands and then the voice that never failed to lift her spirits came over the airwaves.

'Hi Mum.'

'Hi sweetheart. How are you feeling? Aunty Em said you'd been sick.'

'I'm OK. Aunty Em made me popcorn.'

'Oh, that's nice of her.' Patrick was going to be in serious need of fruit and vegetables after spending the weekend with her sister. 'What are you up to now?'

'Watching *Toy Story*.'

'*Toy Story*? Again?' Poor Emma must have seen the franchise as many times as she had.

Patrick giggled. She imagined them snuggled under a blanket on Emma's sofa, sharing a bowl of popcorn.

'Yes, I'm Buzz. Aunty Em's Jessie and you can be Woody.'

'Why do I have to be Woody?'

'Cos you're brave. Like Woody.'

'What about Matthew?'

Patrick thought about this a minute. 'He can be Mr Potato Head, if you like.'

'Well, you be good and make sure you brush your teeth after all that popcorn.'

'Aunty Em said I could stay up til midnight.'

'No, I didn't!' she heard her sister shout. 'It's already well past your bedtime.'

'Are you coming back tomorrow?'

'Yes, I promise. And we'll do something nice together.'

'OK, bye,' he said in the abrupt manner of seven-year-olds who have suddenly found something more exciting to do.

She heard a shuffle and Emma's voice. 'Last of the great conversationalists.'

'Are you sure he's OK?'

'He's fine. Full of beans. I'll get him off to bed as soon as the movie finishes. Listen, don't do anything stupid, OK?'

'OK. I love you.'

'Love you too. Ring me in the morning and let me know you're safe.'

'Night.'

Libby switched off the call, feeling better, normal. She fell back on the plump pillows and switched on the television. She would do as her sister suggested and stay in the safety of her hotel room until the morning.

But her brain couldn't settle. There was nothing on the television that she wanted to watch, and she could hear noises from the party coming from the marquee outside.

She got up and paced the room, looking out of the window every few minutes. How could she sit up here when someone could be getting hurt? She checked her phone but there had been no more messages from Matthew. She was torn with indecision – stay here where it was safe or meet Simon and find out what was going on, once and for all.

She was a reporter; it was literally her job to find out the truth. She couldn't sit there while there might be a killer on the loose. Simon had made no stipulations that she should come alone. She would ask Peter to come with her. Out of all of them, he was the one she trusted the most.

Decision made, she pulled on her jeans and grabbed her boots from under the bed; there was really no point in sacrificing comfort for style any longer, and she wanted to be confident she could run if she needed to. She felt instantly better in these clothes, back to her old self again. She checked her phone – there was only 30% charge left. Not a lot, but she didn't have time to charge it and she wasn't intending to use it much anyway. She would go and find Peter, meet Simon down by the lake, and find out once and for all what Matthew had been hiding from her.

Chapter Fifty

EXTRACT FROM SIMON GREENE'S MEMOIR, *UNTOLD STORY*.

I was thirty, divorced, and broke when I finally got clean. I thought withdrawal was hard, but at least it was short-lived. The hardest part was when I had to leave the rehabilitation centre, with its counsellors, art therapy, and wellness suite, and go back to the life I left behind. I had to face up to what I'd done, everything I had destroyed in the course of my addiction. I hadn't spoken to my parents in years. I was estranged from my son. I owed money to everyone. I had ruined my career and gained a reputation for being difficult, unreliable, erratic. No one wanted to work with me.

I missed my family, my friends, my band, but I didn't want to go back to my life in the UK. Too much history, too many triggers. I had grown out of my all-encompassing need for fame and adulation and wanted a quieter existence. I moved to Los Angeles. The city was awash with addicts; it wasn't hard to find a group and build a support mechanism, to spend my Saturday evenings listening to other people's sob stories.

Eventually, I started writing again – at first, favours for the few friends I had left in the industry but after a while, I started to pick up some paid gigs. Writing for other singers and watching them perform my songs brought me a quiet sense of satisfaction that I hadn't expected. I started paying off my debts. I learnt to live with myself. I was far from perfect, but I could go through this life without hurting anyone else.

I was still drinking but I knocked most of the drugs on the head and adopted some of the clean-living habits I was surrounded by in California. I've even taken up jogging, for Christ's sake, although the sight of me red-faced and puffing down the boardwalk is not pretty. There are still nights when I lose myself, when I allow the music and the drink to carry me away into that turbulent world where time has no meaning, but they are few and far between now. I'm getting older. The world has changed. The reckless hedonism of the 90s has been replaced by mobile phones and social influencers. People download and stream music, and bands are so manufactured, you don't even need to be human to play in one.

You may have read about the lawsuit in the papers. I am legally obliged not to write about it. A vow of silence in return for them dropping the case against me. But you should know it crippled me financially. Natalya offered to pay for flights back to the UK so that I could see Leo, but I had missed so much of his life already. I told myself he was better off without me. The truth is I was a coward. My absence hurt him in ways I could never make up for. I couldn't look him in the face.

I realise now that the inevitable decline into a settled middle-

age, a thought that terrified me throughout my twenties and for most of my thirties, is actually quite comforting. There is a certain grace about passing the baton to a younger generation, watching new talent emerge and take your place, laughing at their youthful exuberance and arrogance, knowing that they are destined to make the same mistakes.

Leo is trying to make it in the industry. I watch his videos on YouTube and see so much of my younger self in him: that naïve optimism, that drive and ambition. Part of me hopes that he doesn't succeed. I can't bear to see him follow in my footsteps. A larger part of me wants him to be true to himself and his music, to be a better musician, and a better man, than I ever was.

When I was in the band, I didn't think I would live to see forty; now, I want to be one of those old timers drinking whisky at the bar, with a twinkle in my eye and stories to tell. Not that everyone appreciates my stories; no, there are those out there who will do just about anything to keep me quiet.

Chapter Fifty-One

Libby

Hoping no one would notice her casual attire, Libby re-joined the party. The fireworks had finished now, and the guests had come back inside. The DJ put on a popular tune and suddenly she was being pushed and shoved about as people made their way onto the dance floor. They formed a line and started dancing in unison, stumbling and giggling. One man took off his jacket and waistcoat, twirling them around his head in a mock striptease.

Simon was sitting at the far end of the bar. When he caught sight of her, he tapped his watch and nodded towards the door. She watched him leave and looked around for Peter. She checked her phone again. Still nothing from Matthew. It was utter madness to meet Simon alone, particularly after Matthew had explicitly told her she couldn't trust him, but she needed information and he was the only person willing to give it to her. She wondered whether she should just call the police. But would they even listen to her? At this time on a Saturday night, they'd probably assume she'd had a bit too much to drink and was letting her imagination run riot. No, she was on her own. It was time to find out what Matthew was hiding from her once and for all.

With one last sweep of the marquee, Libby followed Simon out of the door. She wondered if she needed to take a weapon with her. She cast around, looking for something that had been discarded by the gardener. A pair of shears or a trowel perhaps, but everything had been cleared away. Libby had been given a crash course in self-defence at university, but she had never had to test her skills and she wasn't sure how much she could remember. Could she defend herself if Simon attacked her? Still, there were plenty of people milling about outside. If she stayed in sight of the hotel, she should be safe. Simon wouldn't be stupid enough to hurt her in front of witnesses.

The cold night air was speckled with rain. A teenager was being sick in one of the bushes, cheered on by his friends, and people were huddled together in the walled garden, sharing cigarettes and secrets. Disco music floated on the wind as she left the conviviality of the party behind and walked towards the lake. She could feel her nerves jangling in her tummy and all her instincts were telling her to go back, but she had to find out what had happened to Natalya and Matthew.

'Libby, wait!'

She turned around to see Peter running towards her,

his jacket open, his shirt gaping at the stomach and his tie flapping around his neck. He was bright red and panting with the exertion. He stopped a minute to catch his breath.

'What do you think you're playing at?' he demanded. 'Going off by yourself in the middle of the night?'

'I'm going to meet Simon. I'm going to find out once and for all what you're all hiding.'

'Are you crazy?' Peter looked unduly angry. 'You have seen horror films, haven't you? You never go into the woods at night alone.'

Libby sighed. Now was not the time to tell him that no, she hadn't seen any horror films, but that didn't make her stupid.

'This isn't a film, and I'm not going into the woods. I'm meeting him at the jetty, in full view of everyone at the party. He won't hurt me.' She wasn't as certain about that last statement as she sounded.

'Look, you're right, let's call the police,' he said. 'We'll do it now.'

Peter pulled out his phone from his jacket pocket.

'They won't believe us.'

'Well, at the very least it might put the wind up our murderer. Stop them from hurting someone else.'

'It might be too late. Tell me what their secret is, and I won't go.'

Peter hesitated. 'I can't do that, I told you.'

'Then I'm going to meet Simon. Come with me.'

Peter shook his head. 'I promised Amir I wouldn't help you. I'm sorry.' He looked back over his shoulder and Libby followed his gaze to see a shadow standing by the window, watching them.

'Why would you make a promise like that? What's Amir hiding?'

'It's not what you think. He wasn't involved. Well, not to the same extent as the others.'

'Tell me. Tell me what they did. Is this about Alex? Is this the reason she killed herself?'

Peter hesitated and then stepped backwards. 'I can't tell you. I'm sorry. I'm not going to betray Amir.'

They were closing ranks against her. 'Fine.' She started to walk away from him.

'Libby, please don't go. You're being reckless.'

She ignored him and walked towards the jetty. She glanced back to see him watching her, his hands in his pockets. Would he ring the police? Or change his mind and come after her? She thought Peter was her friend, but she barely knew him. It was hardly surprising he would put his commitment to Amir over her need to find out the truth.

The jetty was deserted. Moonlight highlighted the ripples on the lake and the sky was full of silvery-grey clouds which drifted lazily past. She walked to the edge of the jetty, feeling the wooden slats adjust to her weight, and looked down into the inky black water below her. It looked sinister and full of secrets in the dark. A rowing boat tethered to the jetty bobbed up and down in the water. Had it been there this morning? She couldn't remember. Could it have been used to get rid of Natalya's body? It was big enough, but using it would have been a hell of a risk in broad daylight when the hotel was full of staff and wedding guests. The killer wasn't that audacious. Everything so far had been done so subtly that people hadn't even noticed.

Simon had left a good five minutes before her, so where was he? Libby shivered as she waited for him. She would stay here, in the light, where Peter could see her. She looked back at the hotel, but the bright lights meant that everyone was in silhouette and she couldn't tell if he was still standing there. Had he gone back to Amir and told him what she was doing?

Libby checked her phone. There were no more messages from Matthew and her battery was running dangerously low. A sound of rustling came from the woodland beside her. Libby tried to steady her breathing. It was probably just a fox or a cat, using the cloak of darkness to stalk its prey. She felt anger build inside her. Was Simon wasting her time? Was this all a joke to him? She would give him five more minutes and then she would go back to the party. Maybe Peter was right; she should leave it to the police to sort out. Simon clearly wasn't coming.

She was about to give up when there was another sound, louder this time and more insistent. A rustling that was too loud to come from a cat or a fox, then a shout from deep inside the woodland followed by silence. Libby felt her heart miss a beat as adrenaline flooded her veins. Had it been a shout or a scream? She was already doubting herself. Her feet felt rooted to the ground. Had she imagined it? Could it have been a bird or an animal in pain? It had sounded like a man's voice, but she couldn't be certain. Was it Simon? Was he in trouble? Or was someone else out there?

Then suddenly another sound, and there was no mistaking it this time. The scream of someone in agony. Libby turned to the hotel. Had it been loud enough to alert the guests? Would they come running or should she go for help? She forced some feeling in her legs and started to walk quickly towards the hotel, not daring to look behind her. She broke into a run. She had almost reached the lawn, her breath coming out in sharp rasps, burning her lungs, when she stopped. She slowed her pace down to a walk and took deep breaths. Her mind began to clear, and she could feel her brain kick into gear, dismissing her primeval urge of fight or flight.

She should go back to the party, raise the alarm, and get a search party out. That was what a sensible person would do. That's what her friends and family would tell her to do. That's what Peter would do. But could she really wait for the police to arrive when Simon could be in trouble right now? Those minutes standing around waiting for the emergency services could be critical. They could be the difference between life and death. She knew basic first aid; she could save someone's life.

Patrick had said she was brave. It was time to find out if he was right.

Chapter Fifty-Two

Las Vegas, 1998

With the success of the album and their tour of Asia, the label now stepped up a gear and there was talk of trying to crack America. It was every band's dream, but it was a tall order. Matt hardly dared believe that it would happen but gradually the plans came together. Thirty dates in just three months. Some of the venues were small, intimate bars but others were huge stadiums that had hosted big names like Queen and Bruce Springsteen. They were going to play in Los Angeles, Nashville, Memphis, New York, Philadelphia, San Francisco, Las Vegas – places Matt had dreamed about visiting since he was a little boy. The itinerary was insane, but they were never going to get an opportunity as good as this.

Craig encouraged them to hit the gym and eat healthily. They would need stamina for a tour of this scale. Matt quit smoking – again – and tried to include at least one vegetable in his daily diet. He had been starting to put on weight thanks to all the alcohol he was consuming most nights. His face was bloated and at least one of the teen mags had described him as 'cuddly' recently.

Everyone was in a frenzy in the lead-up to their departure, sorting out luggage and updating the calendar as performance dates were confirmed. It was a sell-out tour and new dates were being added all the time. At one point it looked like they were going to play in Los Angeles and New York on the same night until Amir pointed it out. There were a lot of phone calls, a lot of contracts to sign and a lot of dollars exchanging hands.

Finally, they were on their way, flying first class to Miami. As they stepped off the plane at MIA, into the hot sunshine and the bright light of the east coast of America, Matt felt like he had entered another dimension. Miami was filled with healthy, wealthy, and impossibly beautiful people, a long, long way from the rain-drenched streets and the fish and chip shops of home. They were given a whistle-stop tour of the city's highlights before being dropped off at their first venue for soundcheck.

As suspected, the tour was exhausting. They found themselves in a constant rotation of media interviews, meet-and-greets with record label executives, and performances. The attention from journalists, publicists, and fans was incessant. It was hard to get any time alone. They took full advantage of the freebies on offer and their riders got bigger and more ridiculous as they tested the boundaries of their new-found fame. Nothing was too much trouble for them.

Performance dates had to coincide with the availability

of venues which meant that the gigs weren't even in a logical order. One night they were on the east coast performing to thousands of fans in rain-drenched Boston; the next they were flying to Austin, Texas before heading back again to New York. They even had use of a private plane. Matt thought this was a lifestyle he could get used to. The hotels they stayed in were the height of luxury, with infinity pools, state-of-the-art gyms and well-stocked bars.

Sometimes they were supporting major acts and other times they were headlining. It didn't matter. Their popularity was increasing by the day and sales of their album were rocketing. Their hardcore devotees followed them around on tour, waiting for them to emerge from backstage, stretching out their arms to touch them, slipping phone numbers and silky knickers in their hands, exposing their breasts to be signed. Security had to be heightened at most of the venues as fans tried to sneak into their dressing room to steal memorabilia or leave them presents.

Daniel's number one fan, Brenda, had even followed them to America. They had to call security when she tried to break into their hotel suite at 3am. She was removed, in tears and declaring her undying love for him. Craig had advised Daniel to get a restraining order, but Matt suspected that he quite liked having a stalker.

Only the prettiest girls were allowed backstage, and Matt grew accustomed to always having someone on his knee, telling him how fit he was. The tour manager took no chances. The girls were frisked at the door, their cameras removed, and their IDs checked for age. The band had a reputation to maintain; they couldn't afford any more scandals. Now that Alex had made it crystal clear that she wasn't interested, Matt had no reason to hold back. He was always careful, always wore a condom, and never made any promises. The girls became interchangeable after a while and he called them all 'sweetheart' to avoid having to remember their names – a trick he had learned from Daniel.

Simon found the groupies amusing but he had Natalya and seemed to have no interest in playing around. She accompanied him on tour for the first three weeks but quickly got bored and went back to London where she could at least party with her friends. In her absence, Matt was surprised that Simon behaved himself. It certainly wasn't due to lack of offers, but it seemed he genuinely was a one-woman man.

'Why have hamburgers when you have steak at home?' he said smugly as he batted off the attentions of yet another fan. Getting married hadn't changed his drug habit however, and he was constantly tapping up the hotel staff to find a dealer.

They had four nights in Las Vegas at the end of their US tour. Between interviews and gigs there was enough time to let loose and enjoy what the city had to offer. They had a limousine to take them wherever they wanted to go, and they enjoyed cruising down The Strip, marvelling at the huge hotel complexes including the Luxor with its dominant sphinx sculpture, the fountains outside Caesar's Palace and the colourful turrets of Excalibur. They passed brightly lit wedding chapels where you could be married by Elvis impersonators and showgirls with huge feather headdresses and tiny bikinis advertising adult entertainment. The air-con in the car was a welcome relief from the desert heat which made the air shimmer.

'It's like Blackpool on acid,' Alex complained.

Afterwards, they took advantage of the complementary cocktails and sophisticated bars, watching the high rollers win and lose millions at the huge casinos. Daniel made the most of the strip clubs – returning late morning with dishevelled clothes and empty pockets, while Simon exercised his unique ability to find trouble wherever he went when he was arrested attempting to buy drugs from one of the croupiers.

It was never quiet. The gaming rooms were open all night and you could order huge steaks from room service at any time of the day. You didn't really need to leave the hotel. Everything – shopping, gambling, eating – was all under one roof. It was like being trapped in an opulent cocoon, an oasis of greed and gluttony, where anything could happen.

One night they got back to their hotel to find two gorgeous women waiting for them in the suite. They looked like sisters, maybe even twins, in their matching denim shorts and snakeskin boots. Daniel winked at Matt.

'A little birthday present for you,' he said. He went over to the fridge and took out a bottle of champagne, holding it up to check the label.

Alex snorted in disgust and went to her room. It wasn't long before Amir made his excuses while Simon took a seat in the living area and started to roll a joint, happy to watch the show, if not to participate. He had a bottle of bourbon in front of him and was clearly intending to drink himself into a stupor. He had no interest in the girls.

Matt sidled up to Daniel, keeping his voice low. 'Are you sure they're old enough?' Craig had warned them of the dangers of sleeping with underage girls. Apparently, plenty of pop stars had fallen foul to blackmail that way. The girls looked over the age of consent, but it was sometimes hard to tell.

'Relax, mate. I arranged it with the concierge. These are good girls, clean, pro-fess-ion-al.' Daniel handed out glasses of champagne and sat down between the two women who introduced themselves as Candy and Sandy.

Matt shrugged. At least you knew where you stood with escorts: they didn't hang around in the morning asking for your number and they didn't come with expectations that you might actually like or fancy them. They were just providing a service. And the girls were gorgeous. He couldn't deny that. He was, however, starting to get sick of meaningless one-night stands; he wanted something real.

The women said they were nineteen and both students, working to pay their way through college. They said they were big fans of their music. Matt put on their album and the girls started dancing provocatively to it, taking it in turns to give him and Daniel a lap dance. Candy was a giggler and kept whispering in her sister's ear. They were both quite sweet really, like normal girls. Matt started to relax. They drank more champagne and the girls tried to flirt with Simon, who rebuffed their advances kindly. He seemed more amused by them than anything else.

Matt slipped his fingers under the hem of Candy's tiny

shorts, feeling the warmth of her inner thigh. Her skin was soft and pliable, and he could feel the lace of her knickers underneath the shorts. He felt himself get hard.

Another girl. Another night. How many women had he slept with now? He had lost count. He couldn't remember them all if he tried. How many men had Candy slept with? Did it even matter? Sex was meaningless. Matt had stopped associating it with love a long time ago.

He stood up and offered Candy his hand, leading her towards his bedroom. It wasn't long before she was bent over giving him an expert blow job. Matt tried to get in the mood, but he was thinking about Alex in the next room and wondering whether she could hear them through the thin walls. He promised himself this was the last time he would have casual sex. From now on, he wanted the full works, a relationship. No more mindless fucking.

He could hear Daniel and Sandy in the next room. Giggles and moans, the sound of the headboard banging repeatedly against the adjoining wall. And then silence. A long silence.

'Fuck!' Daniel's voice rang through the apartment, loud and urgent. 'Oh, fucking hell.'

Matt threw Candy off him and ran, still naked, into the living room.

'Put some clothes on for God's sake,' Alex scolded, already at Daniel's door. She was dressed in Winnie the Pooh pyjamas and looked about twelve. 'Dan, let us in.'

The door opened and an ashen-faced Daniel beckoned her in. Matt grabbed a hotel robe from the back of his door and followed them through to Daniel's bedroom.

Candy was right behind him and screamed when she saw her sister lying on the bed. The naked girl's eyes were open and staring right at them. A tray containing lines of coke and a rolled-up note was on the bedside table next to them along with a bottle of bourbon and two shot glasses.

'What the fuck's going on?'

'She's dead,' Daniel was shaking uncontrollably. Matt found him another robe. Everything seemed to be happening in slow-motion, like he was watching a film or something. His brain was struggling to catch up with what he was witnessing.

Alex crouched beside Sandy and reached for her pulse. 'What happened?'

'We were fooling about. You know, just a bit of fun. I didn't mean to do it.'

'Do what Daniel?'

'Oh God, I killed her. I didn't mean to. She said she liked it rough.'

Hysterical screaming filled the air as the woman's sister pushed through them. Matt had almost forgotten about Candy.

'You monster!' she shouted, spitting at Daniel. She pushed Alex out of the way and stroked her sister's hair away from her face. Sandy's lips were swollen and there were red marks around her neck.

'Does anyone know CPR?' Matt asked, trying to remember the first aid lessons at school.

'I've already tried.'

'So, what do we do?' Matt asked.

304

'We've got to ring an ambulance,' Alex said, reaching for her mobile. 'What's the number?'

'No,' Amir calmly took the device from her hand. 'No ambulance. No police.'

'Are you kidding me?'

Candy was clinging to her sister's body, her long blonde hair obscuring her face. Matt nodded to the door and they left her in private while they formulated a plan.

'Ring the concierge; he'll know what to do.' Daniel suggested.

But this wasn't the sort of mess they could ask housekeeping to sort out. Matt moved to the window. They were sixteen storeys up. If they threw the body from their hotel suite, could they make it look like an accident? He felt bile fill his mouth at the very thought. Besides, the window was locked – the temperature of the room strictly controlled by the air conditioning.

'He'll call the police,' Amir said. 'And look at the state of Simon – do you really think they won't find anything on him? You'll both go to jail. If you're lucky. You do know they have the death sentence here?'

'It was an accident. It was consensual.'

Amir looked at Daniel like he'd lost his mind. 'She consented to be *killed*? You really think you're going to get away with that as a defence?'

'No, it was… it's supposed to enhance the experience.' Daniel explained.

'You strangled her,' Amir said coldly.

'I didn't mean to kill her. I've done it before. It's always been fine.'

Matt thought back to the accusations in the tabloid newspaper, Daniel's protestations. The purple bruises around the girl's neck. How could Daniel have been so stupid?

'We should ring Craig,' Matt suggested.

'I don't think even Craig can get us out of this one,' Amir said. He looked around at his band members. 'No, we've got to sort this out ourselves.'

Chapter Fifty-Three

Las Vegas, 1998

A mir opened the door to Daniel's bedroom, averting his eyes from the body on the bed.

'Do you have someone we can call?' Amir asked Candy gently.

The girl sobbed and looked away. Then, after a few minutes, she stood up and walked into Matt's room. She came back dressed and handed Amir a piece of the hotel notepaper. On the top was a number written in pencil. The coquettish girl Matt had gone to bed with had disappeared. Her face was streaked with tears, but her eyes were hard and cold. She despised them all. He couldn't blame her. He wanted to ask her if she was OK, but it was a stupid question.

'Thank you.'

Simon was slumped in one of the chairs, passed out and oblivious to the chaos around him. Amir went through his jacket and found his mobile phone and dialled the number. He left the room, speaking softly into the handset. Ten minutes later he came back.

'They're coming over.'

'Who? Who did you speak to?' Matt asked.

'Her pimp. We've agreed to keep things quiet. But it's going to cost us. He wants half a million.'

Alex looked horrified. 'What the hell are you talking about? You can't just pay him off. This is a girl's life. Matt, back me up. You can't believe this is a good idea.'

Matt looked at her. Hesitated. Alex was right but if he stood by her, it would mean the end of everything. He couldn't do it. Not for some girl that he didn't even know.

'Half a million what? Dollars?'

Alex looked at him in disgust as he tried to calculate how much that was.

'We don't have that kind of money.'

He looked over to where Simon was passed out on the sofa. He was going to be absolutely no use whatsoever. Was he even aware of what was going on?

'No. No way. You can't do this,' Alex protested. 'We need to call the police.'

'She was a prostitute.' Daniel said, as if that absolved him of everything.

'She was a human being. Someone's daughter. Candy's sister. Have you lost your fucking minds?'

'No, but we stand to lose a lot more than that if we don't handle this,' Amir said.

They walked back into the living room. Daniel rolled a joint from Simon's stash and passed around the bottle of bourbon. Matt felt the alcohol soothe his nerves. They were in shit. Deep shit. Alex was right. They should do the decent thing, ring the police. Maybe they would understand? It wasn't likely. More likely they would see them for what they were: a group of spoilt, rich kids who thought they were above the law. They would put them in prison and throw away the key. Daniel may deserve it, but what about the rest of them? It would be the end of everything. The end of the band. The end of their careers. Daniel could spend the rest of his life in jail. Or worse.

'How much cash have we got?' Amir asked, looking through his wallet.

'Not nearly enough.' Daniel said dejectedly.

'What the fuck were you thinking?' Matt said.

'I didn't do this on purpose! Look, I can get my hand on a few thousand, but this is serious money. We can't afford this.'

'We can if we all put in,' Amir said quietly. 'Alex?'

'No way. I'm not getting involved with this.'

'You already are.'

'I think we should ring the police.'

'It's too late for that. Are you in or out?'

Alex sat with her arms folded, looking furious, but eventually shrugged in reluctant agreement.

'Matt?'

He nodded mutely. They really didn't have much choice. He wondered if they would all do the same for him but didn't really want to know the answer. The money didn't matter; there was plenty more where that came from if they salvaged their reputations. He took another gulp of bourbon.

Finally, there was a knock at the door. Amir went to answer it. Three men walked into the room. The tallest spoke with a Texan drawl. The other two thin men wearing tight jeans and leather jackets didn't speak at all. Matt caught sight of a holster underneath one of their jackets.

'Where's the girl?' The pimp said. Amir nodded over to the bedroom. Candy followed him and they could hear them arguing.

The expression on the faces of the two men at the door were inscrutable. Was this all in a day's work to them? The pimp emerged from the bedroom and started to discuss money with Amir. Bartering over a girl's life. Matt felt an overwhelming urge to be sick but managed to hold it together. From what Matt could gather, Amir was agreeing to pay a sum in cash now and the rest by bank transfer by the end of the week. The pimp was giving him instructions on how the payments should be made.

'You need to leave now,' the man instructed. 'Come back in three hours.'

Matt grabbed some clothes and left with the others. They had to half carry Simon out of the room. The hotel was covered by CCTV. How would the men get a body out without being caught? What would they do with her afterwards? Dump her in the desert? Did this sort of thing happen a lot? Did they have some sort of arrangement with the hotel?

He tried to tell himself that it didn't matter. She was a prostitute – risk came with the territory. She had died quickly, painlessly. In fact, maybe she wasn't dead at all. Maybe this was another one of those notorious scams designed to fleece rich tourists from their hard-earned dollars. Maybe she was walking out of their hotel suite now as right as rain, laughing about how gullible these rich kids could be. Maybe it had all been a big set-up from the start.

He could tell himself fairy tales all night long, but it didn't make them real. Daniel had killed a girl and now they were all helping him cover it up. They were in deep trouble and he wasn't sure whether they were making everything a thousand times worse. Would it be better to face the consequences and tell the truth or spend a lifetime living with what they had done? He tried not to think about the girl's family; would they ever know what happened to their daughter?

It was 4am but the city was still throbbing. Matt was sweating but he couldn't tell if that was fear or the humidity. He couldn't look at Daniel, let alone speak to him. He wanted to be alone, but he was too scared to walk the streets on his own. The city, which had initially felt like a big playground, seemed sinister now, toxic. He longed for home. The uncomplicated pubs and clubs that they frequented on a Saturday night. Football and a roast dinner on Sunday. He wanted his mum.

They found a hotel bar still serving drinks and ordered shots of bourbon. In a few hours' time their limo was due to pick them up for a day of promotion and they would have to perform their duties like nothing had happened. They would have to smile and laugh and tell journalists how much they loved America like they hadn't killed a woman and paid to cover it up. They would have to perform on stage like they were the best of friends when the very sight of Daniel made Matt want to vomit. He was sick of pretending. Money and fame didn't bring you happiness; it brought a bigger set of problems. Matt downed his drink and gestured to the barman to pour him another.

Chapter Fifty-Four

Libby

Libby walked into the woodland, using the light from her mobile phone to guide her. The trees seemed to swallow her and when she looked over her shoulder, she could no longer see the lights of the hotel or work out which way the lake was. It was noisy among the trees; she could hear birds above her and small animals rustling in the undergrowth. An owl shrieked in the distance.

It was pitch black, the only light coming from her phone and glimpses of the moon through the canopy. The trees in the woodland seemed to have closed ranks and its dark depths could hide a hundred strangers. She felt like a character in a fairy tale, lost in the forest. Only, she had much worse than wolves to worry about.

The ground was uneven and full of tree roots that twisted her ankle and prodded into the soles of her feet. She could hear the squelch of mud as it sucked at her ankles and she was glad she had changed into her boots. It was difficult to make out the path in the darkness and she had to hope she was going in the right direction. Branches scratched at her face as she felt her way through the trees, calling Simon's name. Was someone out there, watching her? What if she couldn't find her way out again? She tried to reassure herself. She was in the hotel grounds, not the outback, and Peter knew where she was going. He would call the police if she didn't come back soon.

'Simon?' she shouted, her voice ringing through the woodland. She heard twigs snapping behind her and tried to tell herself it was only an animal. Her heart was beating fast, like the wings of a bird trapped in a cage.

'Over here!' It was a weak, feeble voice. Libby hesitated. Was this a trap?

She took a deep breath and followed the sound of Simon's voice, emerging into a glade. Overhead the moon was bright, and she could make out a figure at the far side of the clearing, slumped against a tree stump. Simon's face looked ashen and his eyes were half-closed. He was moaning softly. She could see a dark pool of liquid in his lap. Libby ran over to him. He looked like he was losing consciousness.

'Simon? Stay with me.'

Libby examined him quickly. He was clutching his stomach, his hand covered in blood. Prising his hand away gently, she saw a stab wound through his white shirt. She felt a little faint at the sight and smell of blood and had to steady herself. She looked around. There was no sign of his attacker, but they couldn't have got far.

'Who did this to you?'

'Get help, please.' Simon's eyelids were flickering, and he looked like he was about to pass out. Libby whipped off her jacket and pressed it into the wound to try to stem the blood; Simon was too heavy for her to lift and he didn't look like he was capable of walking by himself. She would have to leave him to get assistance. She looked around her, trying to remember the way she had come. Libby checked her mobile phone battery. Only 3% left and no reception. Fuck.

She heard a movement behind her and held her breath. Was someone watching them? She swung her head around and thought she could make out a shadow shifting in the darkness. Her heart was racing. If it was Peter, if he had followed her, then he could stay with Simon and she could run back to the hotel for help. But what if it wasn't Peter? What if the person that had stabbed Simon was out there watching her right now?

'Who's there?' she shouted, sounding braver than she felt. Her hands were covered in Simon's blood and his face looked drained of all colour.

There was silence but she could sense that the figure was still there. What were they waiting for?

'Please, I need your help.'

The dark figure moved. She couldn't make out their features in the darkness. Simon snapped awake, his eyes widening as he viewed the stranger, and he made a sound she couldn't distinguish. Libby felt around for a branch or something to defend herself.

The figure emerged from the shadows and into the

clearing. She held her breath as his features came into focus. Her mind must be playing tricks on her. It wasn't possible. It couldn't be him.

'Libby?'

Matthew stepped into the light.

Chapter Fifty-Five

Matthew

Money can buy you out of trouble, but you can't pay off guilt.

Matt told himself lie after lie to justify what they did that night in Las Vegas. He told himself he wasn't to blame. That he'd only gone along with the others. That he'd had no choice in the matter. The girl had chosen to enter a risky business. She knew what she was getting into. If it hadn't been Daniel, someone else would have killed her. He pushed his guilt to the furthest recess of his brain and told himself that there was nothing he could do to change the situation. He just had to live with it.

He dreamt about Sandy sometimes. Her eyes staring up at him, taunting him. He dreamt that she rose from the bed, wrapped her hands around his throat and squeezed and squeezed. He tried to prise her cold dead fingers from his neck but she was too strong for him. He would wake, gasping for breath, dripping in sweat, and it would take him several hours to feel normal again.

Alex announced her departure from the band as soon as they got back from the tour. She didn't discuss it with any of them beforehand and it knocked Craig and Simon for six. They begged her to reconsider until she stopped taking their calls. Matt was relieved. There was some talk of getting another lead singer, of carrying on without her, but Amir was quick to follow Alex, and Matt saw his way out. He had lost any enthusiasm he once had for the music industry and he didn't want anything to do with his former friends.

Shortly before her death, Alex came to see him. He hadn't spoken to her since the band split up. He told himself he was giving her space, but the reality was he was too afraid to speak to her, to talk about what they'd done. She looked terrible: she had lost a lot of weight and her skin was grey, her eyes ringed red with exhaustion.

'I want to go to the police and tell them what we did,' she announced.

He poured her a glass of wine. 'You can't.'

'Yes, I can. You can't stop me.'

Matt's brain flew into a blind panic, but why was she even here if she was so determined to go through with it? Clearly, on some level, she wanted him to stop her.

'Think of the consequences. Daniel will go to prison. We all helped to cover it up so we'd probably go too. That's five lives you're ruining... for what? Some sort of misplaced sense of justice?'

She shook her head. 'Every time the phone rings, every

time there's a knock on the door, I think it's going to be the police. It's better that we tell them ourselves.'

'It's been six months. If there was going to be an investigation, they'd have contacted us by now.'

There was no question that if the girl had been found, if the death had been reported, that the police would have come knocking at their door. The girl died in their hotel room; Amir had used Simon's phone to call her pimp. The evidence against them would have been damning. The men had clearly done a good job at hiding the body. Matt's main fear was that her pimp might track them down and ask for more money. Or Candy. Had they been stupid letting her walk out like that? Should they have found a way to silence her too?

'But what about the girl's family? They'll never know what happened to her,' Alex said.

'You have to keep quiet. For all our sakes. This isn't just about you.'

Alex stood up, leaving the untouched wine on the table. 'I can't live with this, Matt.'

He should have run after her, he should have gone with her to the police, he should never have let her go like that. Instead, he rang Daniel and told him what happened.

'I'll talk to her,' he promised.

Matt never knew if Daniel spoke to Alex. The next day, news of her suicide was blazoned across every tabloid. He stared in disbelief at the headline and the photograph of Alex on the front page of the *News of the World*, as if by staring at it hard enough he could change the words, reorder them so that the love of his life had not been found dead in her Chelsea apartment, had not taken an overdose, had not abandoned him. He scrutinised the photograph; it was a publicity shot from a few years ago and Alex looked too polished, too posed. It was not the girl he remembered. Not the girl he had loved.

After Alex's suicide, Matt felt like his only anchor in this world had disappeared. He was the only member of the band who attended her funeral. The paparazzi stayed a respectful distance away from the mourners, but he could see them by the railings with their long lenses. Predictably, his anguished face was plastered all over the newspapers the next day. He couldn't stand the outpouring from the fans, the sympathetic glances of his family, the constant intrusion by the press. He had to get away.

He sold his flat and went travelling around South America. He lived simply and carried all his possessions around in a backpack. He stayed in hostels and basic guesthouses, grew his hair and beard and became quite unrecognisable from the pop star that had graced the gossip columns of every tabloid. He saw the Atacama Desert in Chile, the Iguazu Falls in Argentina, llamas in Peru, and penguins in Patagonia. He spent the millennium night in a small bar in Bolivia and raised a glass to Alex, his friends, and the life he had left behind.

Seeing other cultures and places proved to be the balm he needed. There was death and suffering all over the world, but also happiness and love. Hope. There was no point in dwelling on the past; he had to make the most of the time he had left. There were things he couldn't change, no matter how much he wished he could, but he could become a better person as a result of his mistakes.

He finally felt ready to go back to the UK. He moved away from London, bought a house in Leeds, and started to take charge of his financial affairs. He got a few offers from other bands, but he was sick of making music. For a long time, he couldn't even listen to it. Music had been his whole life but after Alex's death he couldn't bear anything that reminded him of her. Even now, if their songs come on the radio, he has to switch it off. Just the opening beats of one of their hits is enough to send his heart racing and his whole body into a state of anxiety. Her voice over the airwaves brings back too many emotions, too many memories.

He found, instead, that managing money made him happy. There was a simplicity to buying and selling property, organising rentals and playing the stock market, that appealed to him. There was risk but there was also reward. He was fair in his business dealings and people respected him for it. From time to time, he syphoned off some of his profits to philanthropic concerns and that also made him happy. He cut off all ties with Daniel, Simon, and Amir and started forging new friendships, new relationships. Matthew had always been into fashion but now he started to invest in statement pieces and supporting young designers. He lost a lot of money that way, but he had enough to lose.

He started thinking about having children, leaving a legacy. When he met Libby, he thought she might be the one. She wasn't part of the celebrity world and she didn't give a toss about money. She was honest and sincere, refreshingly normal. And Patrick was cool. Matthew loved him and felt that he could be a good dad to him. They could be a proper family.

Libby had never asked about Alex. Not until that weekend. Now, everything was starting to unravel. Being around the other band members again, he could feel himself slipping into old habits, old attitudes. He could feel the years falling away, revealing the same messed-up kid underneath his adult exterior. He should never have come to the wedding, and he certainly should never have dragged Libby into this mess. They were going to destroy everything he had built up, and it was already too late for him to stop it.

Chapter Fifty-Six

EXTRACT FROM SIMON GREENE'S MEMOIR, *UNTOLD STORY*.

In all honesty, my recollections of that night in Las Vegas are pretty hazy. I was completely out of it for most of the evening. I remember the girls, but I couldn't tell you which one was Matt's, and which one went with Daniel. I remember screaming and hysterics and being dragged out of the room and into a bar, but the rest is cloudy. Of course they told me about it the next day but each of them had a different version of events and it was hard to know who to trust. Not that it mattered – the deed was done.

If I had been sober, would I have gone along with it? Probably. Amir – the bastard – made sure I was implicated by using my mobile phone to call the pimp and I paid my share of the money. All I cared about was saving the band. Clinging on to the sinking ship. Of course we should have done the decent thing, but what difference would it have made? The girl would still be dead, and we would have lost everything.

In the end, of course, it meant nothing. There are some things you can't walk away from. Every action, every decision, has its consequence. I don't know how the others justified it to themselves, but I know it destroyed Alex. She couldn't live with what we'd done.

Ultimately, it will destroy us all if we continue to keep quiet.

If this memoir gets published, if the others don't find a way to silence me, then I hope this confession will bring some closure. To us, and the family of that poor girl in Las Vegas. We deserve to suffer for our sins. All of us. It doesn't matter who killed the girl. It doesn't matter whose idea it was to pay for it to be covered up. We all have blood on our hands.

Chapter Fifty-Seven

Libby

'It's not what you think.' Matthew held up his hands like a guilty schoolboy.

Libby took a step backwards, her mind trying to catch up with the scene in front of her. The moon slid behind a cloud, casting Matthew's face in shadow. 'What the hell are you doing here?'

Matthew remained where he was, about ten feet away from her. From what Libby could tell he was unarmed, but that didn't mean he wasn't responsible for stabbing Simon. He could easily have discarded the knife in the woodland.

'Was it you? Did you do this to him?' Simon's eyes were closed now, and his breathing laboured. He wasn't going to make it unless they got help fast.

'What? No! Of course not. I thought you might be...'

'Might be what?'

'In trouble. When I got your text, I panicked. All I wanted to do was keep you safe.'

Libby's heart was racing. None of this made sense. Had Matthew faked his allergy attack? Surely that was impossible. She had seen it with her own eyes and the doctors had confirmed it; Matthew could have died. He couldn't have been pretending.

He stepped towards her gingerly. 'I didn't hurt him, OK?'

'Why aren't you in the hospital?'

'I was so worried when I got your message that I discharged myself. I came here as quickly as I could. I saw you go into the woodland and followed you.'

His story was plausible, but she still didn't believe it.

'Why didn't you ring the police?'

He bit his lip. 'I didn't know what to tell them. Help, my girlfriend's going into the wood with a stranger?'

The missing EpiPen, the nuts in Matthew's dinner, the cold cup of coffee this morning. It had been Matthew all along. She had been such an idiot. Why had he even brought her to the wedding? As some sort of alibi?

'It was you. You killed Natalya and then put nuts in your own dinner when I got suspicious. And now, Simon. You're a monster.'

He flinched at the word. 'No, that's not true.'

'Natalya told me not to trust you. She told me you killed Alex.'

'Me? No, I would never hurt Alex. I loved her.'

'Who's next, Matthew? Me?'

'Of course not. What do you take me for? Libby, all I

wanted to do was save you.' Matthew looked sincere but she didn't trust him now.

'Why would you do this? Over a bloody book?'

'Libby, I swear to you I didn't hurt Simon. Tell her,' he said, but Simon was slipping out of consciousness and unable to speak.

'We don't have time for this; we need to get him some help or he's going to die.'

Matthew crouched down beside her. He looked visibly shaken by the sight of Simon's injury but was he faking it?

'Here,' she said, placing his hand on the jacket. 'Hold this and keep pressure on the wound.'

Matthew did as he was told, and she released her hold. 'I'm going to go back to the hotel and get help.'

'Just listen to me... for a minute,' Matthew pleaded. 'I didn't hurt Natalya. Or Simon. Or Alex. And I would never hurt you. I love you, Libby.'

'So tell me the truth.'

'It's a long story.'

'Give me the short version.'

Matthew hesitated and then told her about what happened in Las Vegas. About a woman Daniel killed. About a cover-up and how it had split the band. How Alex couldn't live with the guilt and had killed herself six months later. How sorry he was. How he wished he could turn back the clock and do everything differently. Tears were running down his face and he was gulping for breath as he spoke. He looked like a little kid.

'Simon would have ruined everything. Everything we had built up over the years. Our reputations.'

'Is that why you argued with Daniel? Did he want to come clean?'

'No! Quite the opposite in fact. I told Daniel that we should go to the press, pre-empt the book and the bad publicity, but he wouldn't listen to me. He always thinks he knows best. You have to remember that he has more to lose than any of us. We were only accomplices. He was the killer. And there's no evidence, no evidence at all, despite what Simon says. We don't even know her real name. It could have all been a set-up. When we got back to the hotel, it was spotlessly clean, like it had never happened.'

Libby tried to imagine what the girl's family must have gone through. Losing their daughter. Never knowing what happened to her. Her pimp casually disposing of her body and pocketing the money to keep quiet. No doubt replacing her the next day with another naïve student trying to make ends meet. The whole thing made her sick. Matthew seemed genuinely remorseful, but he had kept quiet about it all these years. There was only one way to find out if he really meant it about coming clean.

'I'm going to go back to the party, to get some help, and then I'm going to call the police,' she said steadily. 'If you're still here when they come for you, then I'll know that I can trust you.'

He looked torn. 'They'll think I did it. They'll think I killed Simon.'

He was right; they were both covered in Simon's blood and Matthew had a motive to kill him.

'Just tell them the truth. Tell them everything.'

'They're going to ask a lot of questions.'

'Isn't it about time you answered them? Face up to what you all did. You're not innocent, Matthew, no matter what you try to tell yourself.'

'I didn't hurt anyone, Libby. I promise.'

Would Matthew make a run for it as soon as she was out of sight? Or would he be true to his word and try his best to save Simon? It was a risk she had to take.

Darkness engulfed Libby as soon as she stepped out of the clearing. She tried to get her bearings, but nothing looked familiar. She needed help. Fast.

She pulled out her phone, her hands still slippery with blood, but it had run out of battery. Damn it. She started to run, praying she was going the right way.

A sound came from behind her. Was Matthew following her? Could she fight him off if he attacked? He was tall and strong, and he might still have the knife. She wouldn't stand a chance.

Branches tore her face. She tripped over a tree root, nearly fell, and had to steady herself. She looked behind her, but she couldn't see more than a metre. Her heart was pounding, and tears were streaming down her face, blurring her vision.

A flash of white through the trees. Was it him? She didn't stop to find out. If she could just get back to the wedding, she'd be safe.

At last, the trees started to thin, and she sprinted towards the light. Oh, thank you, God. Only it wasn't the bright lights of the hotel that had drawn her here, it was the shimmering silver of moonlight on the lake. Shit. She'd been running in completely the wrong direction.

The gamekeeper's hut must be close by. There might be a phone in there or a walkie-talkie device. She was sure she had seen the gamekeeper with one earlier. A padlock hung loose from the lock but when she pulled the handle, the door wouldn't open. It had been latched from inside. Libby pushed her way through the undergrowth at the side of the hut and spied a dirty, cobwebbed window just above eye level. It couldn't have been opened for years.

There was a flickering light inside. Was someone there?

'Hello? Hello?' she said, louder this time. No response. She rapped at the window and thought she heard movement.

Libby made her way back to the door and tried again, willing someone to answer. There was someone in there; she was sure of it. But she didn't have time to waste. Simon could be dying. There was no choice – she'd have to take the longer path.

She had only taken two steps away from the hut when she heard a shuffle, the noise of a latch being lifted, and the door was pushed open.

Chapter Fifty-Eight

Libby

'Daniel?'

Vicky was standing in the entrance to the hut, her beautiful wedding dress splattered with blood and caked in mud. Her matted hair hung loose around her face and make-up was streaked down her face. She looked distraught, her appearance a far cry from the perfectly polished bride she had presented to the world a few hours ago. Was she hurt too?

'Vicky? What are you doing here?'

The bride ignored her question, looking past Libby into the woodland behind. 'Have you seen Daniel?'

'No, I—' Why would Daniel be here? Or Vicky for that matter? The last time she'd seen them they had been with their guests at the firework display. Why were they in the woodland? Had they also followed Simon? Had they seen

Matthew stab him? But there was no time for explanations. 'Listen, Simon's been hurt. We need to get help.'

Vicky stared at her, then stepped back into the hut and started to close the door behind her. Libby pushed against it and followed her inside.

'Didn't you hear me? We need to get help.'

The interior was dimly lit by a small candle burning on top of a crate. It didn't look like anyone lived here; it was just a place to store tools and supplies. It smelt of engine oil and soil. A pair of dirty wellington boots stood upright by the door and a muddy spade was propped up against the corner of the room. There was no sign of a phone or a walkie-talkie and it didn't even look to have any electricity.

Vicky was crouched in the corner, her bare arms wrapped around her chest, gently rocking herself. She was moaning softly. Libby kneeled down in front of her and noticed how cold she was. Something was very wrong.

'Are you hurt?'

Vicky shook her head.

'You're freezing. Come back to the hotel with me,' Libby suggested.

'No. I'm waiting for Daniel. He told me to meet him here if we got split up.'

Libby bit her lip. Should she leave her here and run for help? Vicky didn't look like she was in the right state to be left alone but every minute she wasted with Vicky was a minute closer to death for Simon.

'Do you have a mobile phone?'

Vicky pointed to her phone on the workman's bench. Libby turned on the screen. There was plenty of battery but no mobile reception. Damn it. Next to the phone was the ornamental knife that had been used to cut their cake earlier. Only now it looked to be coated in a thin substance that looked like... blood. It was blood. Why would Vicky have the cake knife if she hadn't...?

She turned to look at Vicky who was staring right back at her. She had got it all wrong. It was Vicky. Vicky was the killer.

'Wait, you don't understand—'

Libby backed towards the door, willing herself to stay calm. Her fingers scrabbled for the latch as Vicky lunged at her. She ducked but lost her advantage as she fell to the floor and Vicky took her place. She stood with her back to the door, blocking the exit and holding the knife out in front of her with a shaking hand.

'Stay where you are. We'll wait for Daniel. He'll know what to do.'

Libby swallowed hard. Her mouth was dry, and she wasn't sure she could scream if she had to. Not that anyone would hear her. Had Peter called the police? Even if he had, would they find her in time? She had to buy herself some time, to find a way of getting past Vicky without getting hurt.

'It was you. You stabbed Simon?' Libby was surprised that her voice sounded calm. Adrenaline was pumping through her body, but her mind was clear as it weighed up the escape options.

Vicky looked down at the knife, as if noticing it for the first time. 'There was so much blood. I never thought there would be so much blood, my dress is ruined.'

Vicky seemed completely deranged. She had just stabbed someone, and she was worried about her dress? The fact that she was confessing didn't bode well for Libby's chances of escaping, but it seemed like a good idea to keep her talking. There was no way Vicky was strong enough to stab Simon alone. Someone must have helped her then left her to pick up the pieces. But who? Matthew?

'Then we heard Matthew coming so we ran. We got split up, but he'll come back for me, I'm sure of it. We're soulmates.'

Daniel then. That made more sense.

'Why would you want to kill Simon?'

'That awful book. It's all lies. Vicious lies. Daniel wouldn't do something like that. Simon just wanted to make money. We tried to persuade him not to publish but he said he wanted to make amends. For what? They hadn't done anything wrong. Daniel's entire career is based on his reputation. What do you think Simon's book would do to that? He would have ruined everything.'

'You planned all this?'

'Of course not. All I wanted was a perfect wedding. The perfect husband. I told Daniel it was a mistake to invite them, but he thought he could persuade them to get back together again. One last reunion tour. It would have been the making of them. He even paid for Simon's flight to come over. He really thought they still had a bond. But they betrayed him.'

'What about Amir? He knew about the book.'

'He was never going to say anything, was he? Matthew on the other hand…'

'Matthew told Daniel he wanted to go to the media. He would have confessed.'

'Exactly. He's kept quiet all these years and then he caves under a little bit of pressure.

'You put nuts in his dessert.' Libby had got it all wrong. She should have believed Matthew. She had never suspected Vicky and Daniel. 'He nearly died.'

'It wasn't hard. The plates were marked, you see. I waylaid the waiter as he came out of the kitchen, acted like a Bridezilla making a fuss about the dessert, and slipped the nuts into the dish when he wasn't looking. Simple.'

'And what about the EpiPen?'

'I stole that when we were in the toilets. Remember, I said my dress had no pockets? I lied.'

While Vicky was talking, Libby scanned the hut for a weapon. There was a spade propped up in the corner. She had never hit anyone in her life, but then again, her life had never been in this much danger before. Vicky and Daniel had killed or tried to kill three people. Libby was in no doubt she would be their next victim if she didn't fight back.

She edged towards the corner of the room, taking it slowly so that Vicky wouldn't notice. Fortunately, she was too busy justifying her actions to see what Libby was trying to reach.

'What about Natalya? Did you kill her as well?'

'Natalya was supposed to be my friend. We were just going to talk to her. Warn her off and then we saw her talking to you. I can't believe she betrayed us like that. Talking to a journalist about what happened in Las Vegas.'

'Natalya didn't tell me anything about Las Vegas.'

Vicky looked momentarily confused. 'She didn't? What was she saying to you then?'

'She was warning me about Matthew. Saying he wasn't the person I thought he was.'

Vicky bit her lip. This was clearly new information.

'Did Daniel shoot Natalya?'

Vicky shook her head. 'I did. We came here, you know, on a shooting party last year. That's why we chose it for our reception. It was a good job Daniel remembered the combination to the gun cabinet. He took the gun to threaten Simon, but when we saw Natalya talking to you by the lake, I just saw red. We followed her into the woodland, and I shot her. If only she had left the past alone, none of this would have happened.'

'But I saw you at breakfast. There's no way you had chance to hide Natalya's body.'

'Daniel did it. He weighed her down and threw her in the lake. Then I cleared her room to make it look like she'd left. I told you, we're a team. We're perfect for each other. Everybody says so. I'd do anything for him, anything.'

'You won't get away with this, even if you kill me. They'll know it was you.'

'Oh, we've worked that one out for ourselves, but Daniel's resourceful. He has a plan. He'll be here soon.'

Libby would bet her life on the fact that Daniel wouldn't be turning up. He was probably already in their car, putting as many miles as possible between him and the scene of the crime, leaving Vicky to take all the blame.

'I don't think Daniel's coming, Vicky.'

'What? No, don't say that. He'll never leave me. Til death do us part. That's what we promised. He can't have left me. He just can't. Not after everything I've done for him.'

'What about your kids?'

'They'll be fine with their dad. They love him more than me anyway, the ungrateful little shits.'

She was unbelievable. Libby could never imagine for one minute putting Matthew before her own son.

'Daniel's a murderer. He killed that girl in Las Vegas.'

'You don't know that.'

'Did Daniel hurt Alex as well?'

'He did her a favour really, put her out of her misery.'

She was completely deluded. Libby was willing to bet that Matthew had no idea that Daniel had been involved in Alex's death.

'Vicky, you still have a chance to put things right. Come back with me now and we can still save Simon.'

'No, you don't understand. I could never betray Daniel like that. Simon's ruined everything. This was supposed to be the happiest day of my life, but it's the worst!'

Tears spilled down Vicky's face as she sank to the floor, oblivious to everything but her own self-pity. Libby felt a wave of disgust as she wailed like a spoiled child. She wrapped her hand around the handle of the spade, feeling the relief of the cold metal against her skin. It was heavy. Could she swing it hard enough to knock Vicky out?

Libby took a deep breath. It was now or never. She had to get back to the hotel, she had to get help for Simon, and she had to stop Daniel escaping. Libby made a run for the door, wielding the spade, but Vicky was too quick for her, rugby tackling her to the ground before she had chance to use it. Libby felt a gush of pain as her cheekbone hit the concrete floor and groaned. She was close to passing out with the pain.

Straddling her, Vicky prised the spade from Libby's hand and threw it against the crate which toppled, knocking over the candle in the process. Libby watched in horror as the flames started to lick across the floor, fuelled by spilt oil and dry leaves. Acrid smoke started to fill the hut. She could hardly breathe with Vicky's weight pressing down on her.

'Please Vicky, let me go. I have a son.'

'If I let you go, you'll call the police.'

'I won't, I promise,' Libby lied, hoping Peter had already done so.

Vicky still had the knife. It would be easy for her to stab her in the back and leave her here to die. Libby closed her eyes and prayed it would be quick. She thought of Patrick and Emma. They had already agreed that she would be his legal guardian if anything happened to her. Would he grow up and forget about her?

Suddenly Vicky stood up, releasing the pressure on her back. Libby gulped for air and tried to get up as Vicky ran from the hut, slamming the door behind her. For a second she thought she was safe. Then she heard the sound of the padlock being locked from the outside.

Chapter Fifty-Nine

Libby

Libby hammered at the door, shouting to Vicky to help her but there was no reply. She tried in vain to push the door open, to break the lock, but there was no give in it. The room was filling with smoke, irritating her eyes and throat. She knew she didn't have long to go before she would be overwhelmed by the toxic fumes. She looked around the hut for something to quell the fire. Surely there must be a water source or a coat that could she throw over the flames. It hadn't reached the gas cannisters yet, but she knew that if they caught alight, she wouldn't stand a chance.

She grabbed the crate and placed it under the window. With the extra height she could reach the latch but to no avail. Libby screamed with frustration. She was going to die in here. The spade. She threw it against the window and with a satisfying smash, the glass shattered, sending fragments everywhere. As the fresh air came through the space, she realised her mistake. The wind fuelled the flames, spreading them around the hut. She had only a matter of minutes before they engulfed it. She climbed on the crate and tried to prise herself out of the window, broken glass tearing at her hands as she did. It was too high for her; she wasn't going to make it.

She screamed as loud as she could out of the window. Would someone be looking for her now? Would Peter have called the police? Even if he had, they wouldn't know where to look. She reached into her pocket for her mobile phone, willing it to have somehow recovered some battery life but it stubbornly refused to switch on. She looked around for Vicky's phone, but she must have taken it with her. Libby could feel the heat from the fire start to cook her jeans – she didn't have long.

Libby gulped down every last breath of air as the heat and the fire built up behind her. She prayed it would be quick. She wished she could tell Patrick how much she loved him, how she had never wanted to leave him. She wished she had never met Matthew, never been invited to this stupid wedding, never gone down to the woodland to meet Simon.

Suddenly she was doused in cold water. Blinking, she tried to make out what was happening as another bucket of water was thrown at the window and suddenly hands were grabbing her and pulling her, telling her to *'be careful, we've got you, you're OK'*. Libby dropped to the ground and was immediately wrapped in a blanket. The whole area was shrouded in thick grey smoke but she could make out the hotel manager organising a group of men – staff and guests from the wedding by the looks of it – to fill up buckets from the lake and form a line.

'It's OK. You're safe now.'

Someone lifted her and carried her back to the hotel. The motion made her feel sick and she closed her eyes, barely caring now whether she lived or died. She opened them again to see the reassuring blue lights of police vehicles as they crossed the lawn and into the dining room. She was placed on one of the chairs as a paramedic looked her over, asking her some basic questions, and checking her skin for burns.

'You've been incredibly lucky,' he concluded.

A cup of sickly tea was thrust into her hands, and she gulped at the hot liquid as if her life depended on it. Libby didn't feel lucky, but at least she was safe. Her hands were shaking too hard to hold the cup.

'Simon, he's in the woodland. He's hurt...' she finally managed to say.

'It's OK, they're out there looking for them now,' Peter replied. He was hovering over her, a concerned expression on his face, and she realised he was the one who had carried her into the hotel. 'They'll find him.'

'Matthew's out there too.'

'Matthew? I thought he was in hospital?'

'He discharged himself. I thought he was the killer.'

'Matthew? But Vicky...'

'I was wrong. Has she been arrested?'

Peter glanced behind his shoulder. 'The police are going to want to talk to you but yeah. She came out of the woodland like Lady Macbeth, covered in blood and looking for Daniel. He's completely disappeared.'

'You saved my life. Thank you.'

'Don't be daft. I should never have let you go into the woods alone. As soon as I got back, Amir and I called the police. I'm only glad we got there in time.'

The tea went some way to reviving Libby's senses. She looked around the room to see several police officers in high visibility jackets questioning the guests. They were keeping everyone in the hotel until they had been photographed and their details obtained. She could see people drunkenly protesting that they wanted to go home or to bed, and kids getting crotchety. This must be a nightmare to handle with just a handful of officers. A woman in her late forties and looking as if she would rather be at home in bed was striding towards them, pushing through the guests impatiently.

'DS Helen Charman,' she said abruptly. 'I'd like to ask you a few questions if you're feeling up to it.'

The detective looked at her top which was covered in soot and Simon's blood.

'And we're going to need to take your clothes, I'm afraid.'

An officer accompanied Libby to her room and supervised as she changed her clothes and handed them over. They were placed carefully in evidence bags and sealed. She was desperate for a shower, but the detective wanted to speak to her first.

DS Charman was waiting for her in the library which had been turned into a makeshift interview room. It was lined with floor-to-ceiling bookcases and under any other circumstances, Libby would have loved to have a nosy at the shelves. A fire had been lit and she tried not to flinch at the flames and the crackle of the burning wood. She would never look at fire in the same way again.

'Are you OK in here?' the detective asked. Libby nodded.

Her mind was still reeling from the events of the night and she could barely think. She was tired and filthy, her mind shattered, and all she wanted to do was sleep but she knew the detective would need every detail about what had happened in the woodland.

Two green leather armchairs were sitting opposite each other beside the fireplace and DS Charman took one, indicating that she should take the other. Libby was shivering uncontrollably but she wasn't sure if that was from the temperature or from the shock. She pulled the blanket around her shoulders; it still smelt of smoke from the hut fire, but the warmth was starting to creep back into her bones.

'Are you sure you're feeling OK?' the detective said. 'Would you like someone with you?'

'Do I need a lawyer?'

DS Charman leant forward, her eyes sharp and intelligent. 'Do you think you need a lawyer?' she asked carefully.

'No, I've done nothing wrong.'

'You can call one if you wish, but this is just a witness statement to find out what happened down in the woods tonight. Are you happy to go ahead?'

Libby nodded. 'I'm fine.' She wasn't. She wouldn't be fine for a long time, but she wanted to get this over with. Her fingernails were black with soot and she tightened her fist to hide them. DS Charman seemed to notice every movement.

'OK, then. Just to let you know, I am recording this interview.' She pointed to the body-worn camera on her chest. 'I believe you're Matthew Barnes's girlfriend?'

'That's right.'

'And you were with Mr Barnes in the woods just now?'

'Yes, and Simon Greene. He was badly hurt; I think he'd been stabbed.' She told her everything that had happened in the woods, trying to keep her voice steady. Libby felt herself tripping over words, worried that her report was inconsistent, that the detective would think she was making things up. It all seemed so unbelievable.

'Do you know why Mr and Mrs Acroyd would want to hurt Simon and Natalya?'

She hesitated, remembering Peter's words: *It's not my secret to tell.* Telling DS Charman about what happened in Las Vegas could mean Matthew going to prison. It would also implicate Simon, Daniel, and Amir. But she had a responsibility to tell the truth, didn't she? 'There were some allegations, about something in their past.'

'What type of allegations?'

'He'd written a book about them. They were trying to stop him publishing it.'

'What kind of book?'

'A memoir, I think. I haven't seen it. Simon had accused them... well... he'd accused them of killing someone. A long time ago. When they were in the band.'

The detective nodded, wrote it all down in her notebook and asked her more questions about Simon's allegations. Libby told her everything she knew.

'You say he had proof?'

'That's what he said at dinner.' She suddenly felt overwhelmingly tired. It must be past midnight. Would they let her go to bed soon? She wondered if she would feel safe enough to sleep. 'Have you found Daniel yet?'

'Not yet. But don't worry, he won't get far.'

She read through her notes and asked her to sign the statement.

'I will also need your mobile phone, if you don't mind.'

Libby hesitated. Her phone was the only way Emma could get in touch if anything happened to Patrick.

'You'll get it back in the morning,' DS Charman reassured her. 'We need to see if there are any pictures that might help our enquiries.'

Reluctantly Libby handed over the mobile phone and passcode to unlock it.

'Thank you, Ms Steele. I think that's all I need for now. I suggest you get some rest. You've had quite an ordeal.'

Libby was too tired to cry, too tired to think. Her brain couldn't take any more; she needed some sleep. She could see other guests staring at her as she walked through the hotel and up the red-carpeted stairs to their room. She thought about ringing Emma from the phone in her room, but she was too tired to talk, and she needed time to process everything that had happened. She lay on the bed, telling herself she would get undressed in a few minutes, and fell fast asleep.

Chapter Sixty

Libby

Sunday morning

It was gone ten o'clock when Libby finally woke. Instinctively, she reached out for Matthew before the full horror of the previous night's events came back to her. It all felt surreal – like waking from a terrible nightmare. She crawled to the window and looked outside. There was still plenty of police activity going on and she noticed a team of divers at the lakeside, no doubt trying to recover Natalya's body. She took a long shower, trying to rid her hair of the smell of smoke and calm her thoughts which were still trying to put the events of the day before together like a complicated jigsaw puzzle. There were going to be a lot more questions – from the police, from Emma, from

Matthew's family – and she wasn't sure she had any of the answers.

Matthew hadn't come back to the hotel room and his clothes were still neatly folded by the bedside. Had he been arrested? Would they – could they – charge him over what happened in Las Vegas? Daniel may have been the killer, but Matthew had been complicit in the cover-up. He had carried this terrible secret with him for more than twenty years, and she had never suspected a thing. He had told her he loved her, that he wanted to spend the rest of his life with her, but he hadn't trusted her enough to tell her the truth. How could she not have seen him for what he was?

She knew that their relationship was over. She couldn't stay with someone who willingly covered up a death like that. And she would have to give evidence against him, and his friends. No relationship could survive that. What would she tell Patrick? He worshipped Matthew and was too young to understand any of this. It would break his heart.

Peter was sitting in the reception area drinking a cup of coffee when she eventually went downstairs. He stood up when he saw her and gave her an awkward hug. He looked – and smelt – like he hadn't slept all night. She wasn't the only one who had lost everything this weekend.

'They've arrested Amir.'

'I'm sorry.'

'It was you, wasn't it? You told them about what happened in Las Vegas.'

Libby hesitated. Peter must hate her. She knew how much he loved Amir and she had destroyed everything they had. 'I had to. It was the right thing to do.'

Peter slumped back into his seat and ran his fingers through his hair. 'God, what a mess. Has Matthew been arrested too?'

'I haven't seen him, but I'm assuming so.'

'This will destroy Amir. His job, his reputation. What if he goes to prison? Oh God, what am I going to tell his parents?'

'What about that poor girl's parents?'

'I know. I know they need to face up to what they did. But this will kill him.'

Libby bit her lip. Had she done the right thing? She had been so sure last night when she was speaking to the detective, but it wasn't only Matthew who would suffer through her actions.

'What happened with Simon? Did they save him?'

Peter shook his head. 'They came out of the woodland with his body not long after you were interviewed.'

Libby's heart stood still. Was Simon's death her fault? Had she wasted time listening to Vicky when she should have been saving Simon? Would he have been hurt at all if she hadn't been so desperate for answers?

'It wasn't your fault,' Peter said, as if reading her thoughts. 'Do you want some coffee? You look like you might need it.'

The coffee smelt divine, and she realised how hungry she was. 'Are they serving breakfast?'

'You read my mind.'

With plates piled with food they settled at a table. The breakfast area was deserted. They spotted a few guests, getting ready to depart, saying muted goodbyes, but most people were quiet, still shell-shocked from the events last night.

'What happened to Daniel?'

Peter showed her a news story on his phone. 'Arrested at a private airport just outside Preston. Trying to get to France apparently.'

'Leaving Vicky to take all the blame.'

'Well, she was hardly Miss Innocent in all this. Those two were made for each other.'

Libby took a huge bite of her bacon and egg sandwich and instantly regretted it as her stomach lurched. The events of the night before were catching up with her. She pushed her plate to one side and looked out of the window to the garden which was littered with empty bottles and fag ends from the night before. Crime scene tape had been wrapped around the path leading to the lake and was fluttering in the breeze. A uniformed police officer stood guard as crime scene investigators in protective gear gathered their evidence.

'Do you think they'll have to go to America to face trial?'

Peter shook his head. 'Amir always said that extradition was unlikely. There's no evidence that anything happened, no matter what Simon said to the contrary. It's the trial by media Amir was worried about. He might not go to prison but his career's up the spout when this gets out.'

Libby tried to look sympathetic. Amir was right; the press would show no mercy when this all came out, but didn't they deserve some retribution?

'So, are you heading back to Leeds now?'

'Yeah, I'll get the train back.'

'I can give you a lift to the station if you want.'

'That would be fantastic, thank you.'

'Well, I've not got much else to do while they decide whether to charge Amir.'

Two hours later, Libby arrived back in the familiar surroundings of Leeds train station. Journalists had already got wind of the story, and she and Peter had only just managed to avoid being caught on camera as they left the hotel. Aiden had rung her several times, but she didn't know what to say to him. She wasn't sure whether she was ready to write about her experiences yet, even if she were allowed to.

The police had returned her mobile phone and, on the train, she had scrolled through photographs of herself and Matthew, wondering whether to delete them. Her favourite was from their trip to Paris, their arms interlocked with the Eiffel Tower in the background. They had been giggling as they tried to get the selfie stick at the right angle. They looked so happy. Would she have stood by him if he had told her the truth from the start? No. Some things were unforgiveable. The hurt the band members had caused through their own selfish actions was immeasurable. In the end she kept the pictures. She didn't want to erase the past. Matthew was the first man she had truly loved, and it was going to take a long time to come to terms with the fact that he wasn't the man she'd thought he was.

As she exited the ticket barriers she was engulfed in a

huge hug. Emma was squeezing her so tightly she thought her ribs were going to break.

'Thank God you're OK.' Emma said, brushing her hair back and wincing when she saw her face. Libby knew the bruising was quite dramatic.

'I'm fine. It looks worse than it feels.'

'Only you could go to someone's wedding and nearly get murdered.'

Emma took her bag and led her to the car park. Patrick placed his little hand in Libby's, and she felt overwhelmed with love. Whatever happened, she had Patrick. He was the only man she needed in her life right now.

Chapter Sixty-One

Libby

Six months later

Libby took a deep breath before pushing her way through the crowds of people gathered outside the courthouse. She shielded her face as cameras flashed at her and she heard reporters shouting her name. At one side, being held back by security, were Daniel's fans, holding banners and chanting for justice. She wondered if Brenda was among them. She narrowly avoided an egg being thrown at her.

The events at Harrington Hall had reignited the public's interest in the band and now that Daniel was not just famous, but notorious, all of his die-hard fans had come out of the woodwork to demonstrate their loyalty to the former pop star. In the aftermath of Daniel's arrest, and subsequent trial, Libby had been bombarded by messages from them, accusing her of lying about what happened at Harrington Hall, refusing to believe that their idol was capable of such things. It would appear that people who had never been near the hotel knew more about what happened that night than she did. It was as much a trial by public opinion as it was by jury.

She had already been called to give evidence on the strength of her statement, so she was familiar with the building. Today, it was Amir's turn to take the stand. Peter had asked her to come for moral support.

It was quieter inside. She held out her bag for security and passed through the metal detectors before heading up the stairs. Peter was waiting for her at the top.

'You got through the angry mob OK?' he said as she greeted him.

It was the first time she had seen him since the wedding. The last few months had taken their toll and he looked pale and tired.

'Just about.'

Amir and Matthew had both denied Simon's allegations about the murder in Las Vegas. And with no body, no evidence, and no name, the authorities in Las Vegas had been unable to verify Simon's account. It seemed unlikely that they would be taking the case any further, so Matthew and Amir had escaped extradition for now. They couldn't escape the scandal, however. The media had already had a field day with the gory details that had been revealed through the court case, and Simon's book would be published straight after the trial, if Daniel was found guilty.

It was inevitable he would, given the wealth of forensic evidence he and Vicky had left behind.

Daniel was getting off lightly. He had been charged with conspiring to murder Natalya and Simon and the attempted murder of Matthew. There had been insufficient evidence to charge him with Alex's death. Vicky was not so lucky. Daniel may have been the instigator, but it was she who had pulled the trigger – literally, in Natalya's case. She had been charged with murdering Natalya and Simon, and the attempted murder of Matthew and Libby. She was currently under psychiatric care, and it was unclear whether she would be fit for trial any time soon.

'How have you been?'

'Terrible. You?'

The truth was Libby was doing OK. She had been given a permanent position at the paper and had even been offered a book deal to write about her experiences. She wasn't planning on taking it – she'd had enough notoriety to last a lifetime. Patrick seemed to have taken Matthew's departure from his life in his stride, mourning the loss of the big TV more than her boyfriend. In the first few weeks after the wedding, Matthew had called her persistently, trying to win her back, but she had been resolute. He hadn't called now for a couple of weeks, and she thought he might have finally got the message. She needed a clean break and to move on with her life, for Patrick's sake as much as hers.

Libby and Peter joined the rest of the family and friends in the public gallery. She could feel Daniel's parents watching her. They must have gone through hell and back over this.

'All rise.'

Libby stood up as the judge came in and took her seat. Amir was called and took his oath. Peter reached for her hand as he watched his boyfriend explain what had happened at Harrington Hall. The journalists on the press bench were scribbling away and typing into their phones.

The court adjourned for lunch. Amir would face cross-examination in the afternoon and his lawyer wanted to meet with him, so Peter and Libby went for a drink in one of the bars at The Headrow.

'This will ruin him,' Peter said, miserably. 'Even if they believe him, no-one will want to work with him again after this.'

'Has he thought about what he might do?'

'Charity work for the time being, but we can't afford that forever. He may need to retrain. What about Matthew?'

Libby shrugged. 'He'll carry on, I guess, once all the fuss has died down.'

'You're not getting back together?'

'No. It's over.'

'I'm sorry.'

'Don't be. We didn't have what you two have.' It was true. There was a part of her that still loved Matthew, but things could never go back to the way they were.

Libby looked around the bar. They were surrounded by people drinking and enjoying themselves, seemingly without a care in the world. There was a group of women on a hen weekend, dressed in matching outfits, and some office workers at the bar making the most of an early finish. Students grasped pints of lager and talked ardently about the state of the nation while a couple of middle-aged women giggled over gin and tonics. Would they look over at their table, see Libby and Peter, and guess they had come from court? She guessed not. After all, who knows what really goes on behind people's façades? What secrets they're hiding behind their smiles and laughter?

'Well, come and visit me when you're next in York. We'll drown our sorrows. And who knows? Hopefully, we can have a night out with no murders.'

She clinked her glass against his. 'I'll drink to that.'

THE END

Acknowledgments

Thank you to my agent Camilla Shestopal for championing this book and reading many, many drafts. My editor Kathryn Cheshire for her continued support and excellent advice and all the team at One More Chapter for promoting my books and helping them to find readers.

Early readers – Amanda Kirkland, Phil Parker, Eleanor Whiteley, Sophie Barker, Gemma Allen, Mandy Huggins, Mum & Dad.

James Bate for sharing his experiences of being in a band in the 90s and Katherine Bayliss for sharing her knowledge of London.

Jenifer Loweth for helping me to get to grips with modern-day court reporting.

Zoe Bennett for sharing her experiences of having a peanut allergy.

Teresa Bramhall, Stephaney Linley and Sue Atkinson for supplying descriptions of their gardens in early spring.

Sophie Hannah for her sage advice and mentorship through the Dream Author programme.

Jericho Writers and Debi Alper for their continued support. And a big shout out to the members of the Murder Alibi Club who I met on the excellent self-editing course run by Jericho Writers and who are a constant source of inspiration and entertainment.

Lyndon Smith from Consulting Cops and Lisa Cutts for their advice on police procedure and Jo Mallard for her expert eye on forensics. All mistakes are my own.

And last, but not least, thank you to everyone who read *The Trip* and left a review or got in touch. I hope you enjoyed *The Wedding Murders* just as much.

Enjoyed *The Wedding Murders*? Make sure to pick up Sarah Linley's previous book!

It should have been paradise. But it turned into hell...

It was supposed to be the perfect trip. Four friends, fresh out of university, backpacking around Thailand. But among the sun, sea and sand, something went horribly wrong...

In the years since, Holly has tried hard to push memories of that terrible summer from her mind. Now a schoolteacher, she believes her life is finally coming together when she meets Tom and his adorable five-year-old son, Jack.

But then, Holly starts receiving anonymous messages, showing photos which she was sure she destroyed years ago. Someone clearly knows the truth about what really happened. The only question is, how far will they go to get revenge?